WHITE HERON

A RUN AND HIDE THRILLER

JJ MARSH

PREWETT
BIELMANN

White Heron

Published by Prewett Bielmann Ltd.
All enquiries to admin@jjmarshauthor.com

First printing, 2021
eBook Edition:
ISBN 978-3-906256-03-0

Paperback:
ISBN 978-3-906256-04-7

For Chris and Maxine Benallick, my adoptive godparents

My name is Ann Sheldon. A tourist? Yes, but having hopes to become a local. I'm a poet. I hunt peace and quiet and inspiration. Ha, ha! Very little money in poetry. No, not rich and not American. I come from a small village in Britain nobody knows. Oh, the wedding ring? My husband is dead several years. Thank you, that's very kind. I like very much to stay here, but I don't know how long. The plan is to survive the rainy season and take profit from the summer, but we'll see. So beautiful this island, you're lucky. I must return to my poems. Nice talking to you, have a good day.

Just fluent enough to be understood with sufficient mistakes to mark her as a *gringa*. It takes practice to do something you do well badly. Ann practised and did very badly indeed. Patronising looks, amused smiles and gentle corrections were proof that her strategy was convincing. The weather worked in her favour, keeping people mostly indoors, so that her occasional encounters were generally limited to a nod and a smile from beneath her umbrella.

Speaking the language poorly was only one of her achievements. In all her other skills, she aimed for excellence. Security took priority and she devoted several hours a day to ensuring her shack was as safe as she could make it. Not quite an underground panic room but there were ways of protecting herself, even in a wooden hut on a Brazilian beach.

The old woman who negotiated the six-month rental had made no secret of her bewilderment. "But there's nothing there," huffed Dona Emilia. "Just rain and mosquitoes and water buffaloes until the rainy season is over. The restaurants are closed, there is no market and even if you bring food from Soure, how do you want to cook? There's no electricity, no Wi-Fi, none of the things you people want. It's not a good place for a single lady, I'm telling you."

Ann stood her ground and due to the woman's own downselling of the place, managed to rent the house for a pittance. What she saved on accommodation, she spent on purchasing a generator. As the old lady had said, certain things she did want. Whether it was a good place for a single lady or not, Ann could think of worse. She spent two weeks fixing the place to her own specifications. For a driftwood shack with a corrugated tin roof on a remote beach, it was the equivalent of MI5.

Nothing here, Dona Emilia? Ann had never heard anything further from the truth. Cranes and blue herons clattered out of the jungle, often heralded by their plangent call, the sound of a grieving widow. Cormorants and vultures scanned the shoreline for fish corpses and snatched the odd unwary crab. Buffaloes lumbered in and out of the mangrove swamps, giving her no more regard than a snort. When the rains ceased for a moment, Ann wandered along the edge of the jungle, spotting hummingbirds, a group of foraging capybara and squirrel monkeys shrieking from the trees. She retreated to the safety of her hut. The monkeys were warning each other of a predator; perhaps an alligator or a leopard. She didn't stay to find out which. Above her head, a hawk was trying to escape a pair of kiskadees dive-bombing it from above, releasing their two-syllable curses. This little corner of the world teemed with bird, animal and insect life. The only thing missing was humans. And that was exactly what made it perfect.

People were naturally curious about this foreigner coming to dwell amongst them in the most inhospitable months of the year, but after discovering her name and marital status, they generally left her alone. She limited herself to the minimum of pleasantries and discouraged small talk. Her nearest neighbours, around a kilometre up the beach, were a young couple who seemed to do nothing but argue. They showed no interest in her, for which she was grateful. The days passed peacefully enough as she tended her tomato plant on the veranda, sewed up tears in her clothes and made soup once a week. One evening, when the sun began to set, she buried broken bottles in the sand, jagged side up, all around the property except the path leading to the steps.

Depending on the severity of the nightmares, she woke early and performed her exercises. Weights and skipping, usually, or a beach run if the weather allowed. Twice she walked into Soure for provisions, which was a twenty-kilometre round trip. 20K was not unreasonable for her level of fitness, but half of it with a full backpack in torrential rain took its toll. She skipped the beach run the next day. She ate what the locals ate, not just out of a desire to blend in, but because she had no choice. Manioc flour, rice and cassava, black or red beans made up the bulk of her diet, complemented by plantains, papaya, tomatoes and açai. Fish was an occasional treat to begin with until she grew more confident about approaching the river fishermen returning with their hauls of crab, prawns and catfish. Buoyed by her success in negotiation, she tried her hand with the sea-going boats. Some days, she could score anchovy, tuna and *cação*; others, she was lucky to get enough scraps to flavour a stew.

The last few days she'd come back empty handed and her tinned or dried supplies were running dangerously low. Rain or no rain, she would have to buy something to eat. When the wet season ended, there would be a market, a bakery and even a restaurant at the other end of the beach. Fewer than two kilometres away. But when would the rains ever end?

One morning after a particularly horrible night of broken sleep, Ann was drinking coffee at the table, watching waves curl towards the shore while attempting to psychoanalyse last night's dreams. It wasn't difficult. In the most vivid, she'd been trying to carry an armful of live crabs over a narrow bridge. Whenever she dropped one, it fell into the water and vanished. People were watching for her from both riverbanks and every crab she lost meant more trouble. Her dream self yearned to release all the spiky, wriggling crustaceans into the river and dive in after them. Subtle, her subconscious was not.

Someone was walking along the beach in a sou'wester and a wide-brimmed hat to keep off the rain. Whoever it was carried a checked bag, the kind people use to take their clothes to the laundrette. The nearest laundrette must be three hours' journey away. When the figure took a right onto the wooden slats that passed for a path to her house, adrenalin shot through Ann's system. She slipped behind the front door, her hand resting on the machete, listening to her visitor draw closer. Footsteps thumped up the steps and the rap of knuckles on wood made her mouth dry and her pulse throb. Rehearsals were over. It was show time.

"*Olá?*" yelled a woman's voice over the constant drumming of the rain on the roof.

Ann opened the door to see the female half of the argumentative couple scowling over her shoulder at the rain. Her face cleared when she saw Ann.

"Oh, you are here. I thought the weather was too shitty to be out jogging, even for a crazy person like you. I'm Fátima and I've brought you something. Is that coffee I can smell? I'll leave my coat and hat out here or they will soak your floor. Come on then, I like mine thick enough to stand up a spoon."

Concentrating hard on comprehending the woman's fast, slangy Portuguese, Ann was too surprised to refuse her entry. "Hello, my name is Ann Sheldon. I come from a small village ..."

"Yeah, I know. I heard all about it from Patricio. You know he's overcharging you for the tuna, right? Don't let him get away with that. Next time, yell at him and call him a thieving son of a ... *ai, ai, ai*! What are you doing with that great big knife?"

Ann had forgotten she was still carrying the machete. "I was going to ... chop something. Doesn't matter." She closed the door and placed the knife behind the curtain. "Is black coffee OK? I don't have any milk."

"Black with plenty of sugar. What did you do to your arm?"

Ann looked at the cluster of angry red bumps on her elbow. "Mosquitoes. The candles don't seem to work."

Fátima's eyes followed her sightline and she picked up what was left of the citronella stub. She sniffed it and shook her head as if unimpressed. She wore a pink jersey with faded jeans, wet from the knees down. Her thick hair, plaited to one side of her head, was the same muddy putty colour as the river when it tumbled into the sea. Her age was difficult to pin down, but she could be no more than a couple of years younger than Ann. Twenty-nine, perhaps? With sharp eyes and a ready frown, her expression cleared when she saw the coffee cup on the table.

She even lifted the corners of her wide mouth into a brief smile.

"Candles are a waste of time and money. Get yourself some *jambú* plant, they hate that. Or better still, a net. Nuno, that ugly little gnome, usually has a couple to sell in among his fishing gear. Tell him I sent you and you can also tell him that if he tries to charge you any more than 20 reais I will kick his dirty arse. This coffee's not bad. Don't you have any aguardente? Or whisky, brandy, anything to give it something extra?"

"Umm, yes, I think I do have some whisky somewhere." Ann rummaged through her dry goods cupboard and found a half bottle of Tullamore Dew she'd bought on impulse at Duty Free. She tipped a slug into Fátima's cup.

With an approving nod, her guest grasped the cup with both hands and took a sip. "Now that's what I call a good morning coffee. After this, I can face the walk home. Don't you want to know what I brought you?" Fátima threw a glance at the bag.

"Oh, yes. That's very nice of you."

"Wait till you see what it is. Are you squeamish?"

Ann didn't recognise the Portuguese word. "Am I ...?"

"You know, delicate." She mimed covering her eyes and fainting.

"No, I'm not." Her voice sounded convincing but she eyed the bag with some trepidation.

Fátima leaned over and hauled out two dead chickens by the feet. "Fresh. Killed them myself before bringing them over here, because you don't look like the type who can wring a chicken's neck. That idiot brought half a dozen live ones home from Soure, then tells me he's off to Belém for a week. What am I going to do with six bloody chickens, I asked him? Keep them till you're ready for a chicken stew, he said. Keep them where? In my bedroom? His brother must be using the family brain cell this week. Anyway, I cooked two, exchanged a pair for a bag of potatoes and thought maybe you could use a couple. You eat so much fish, you'll start growing scales."

The dead birds lay on the table, scrawny and bedraggled and completely unappetising. Ann remembered her manners. "What a kind thought. I must give you something in exchange, as a good neighbour. I haven't been to the store for a while, but ..."

"I don't want any food. Next time you see a bottle of whisky, think of me. What happened to your husband?" Her gaze rested on Ann's left hand.

"He died."

"Yeah, I heard that. How did he die?"

She told the truth, for a change. "He had an accident at work. What does your boyfriend do? Or is he your husband?"

The woman snorted, threw back the rest of her coffee and got to her feet. "As if I'd marry anything that stupid! I'd rather marry one of these." She prodded the limp poultry. "He works for the ferry company. At least until they realise what a workshy bone-headed lump he is. Before I go, I have another question for you."

Ann's heart sank. "What's that?"

"I want to know why you're so scared. Don't look surprised, I've seen you. Sticking broken glass around this hut, the bolts on the door, that crazy big knife, you're as jumpy as a squirrel monkey. Is someone after you? Tell me, what are you frightened of?"

Five minutes this woman had been in Ann's house and she instantly hit the target. *This is why you should never talk to people.*

Ann unclenched her jaw with an effort, but lied with more ease. "Everything. I travelled here from Rio de Janeiro and learned to be security conscious. I was robbed three times."

"This place is nothing like Rio! For a start, Rio de Janeiro has some decent men. You don't need to be scared of us. Unless you're afraid someone is following you?"

Her eyes narrowed and Ann faked a laugh.

"Who'd be following a poet?"

"If that's what you are. Anyway, I'm going now. Enjoy the chickens. Hey, the *padaria* opens tomorrow morning. Finally the village comes back to life. The rains have lasted for ever this year in this shitty place. As for you, poet lady, leaving Rio for this godforsaken backwater? You need your head examined. *Tchau*."

She muttered to herself while hauling on her raincoat and hat, then with a wave, or perhaps a wag of her finger, she splashed off down the path towards the beach. Ann watched her go and turned to face the chickens. Where the hell did she start?

Three hours later, she finished cleaning the house. It wasn't just the feathers and mess she'd made while preparing her chicken stew, but erasing all evidence of her visitor seemed almost more important. She didn't want anyone in this house. Next time anyone came to the door, Ann would talk to them on the veranda. As it was, Fátima's knowledge of her circumstances showed that the *gringa* was a subject of local gossip. Now everyone would know the foreigner carried a big knife, drank whisky and had a bad reaction to mosquito bites.

She stirred the pot, half resentful and half grateful to her intrusive neighbour. This would be the richest meal she'd enjoyed for months, despite the limited amount of flesh on the fowl. She sighed. Even when selecting her destination, she knew there was a greater chance of remaining anonymous and out of sight in a big city. Greater chances too of someone catching up with her. The list of pros and cons was extensive, but overall, a remote fishing village in North Eastern Brazil came out top. As for nosy neighbours, she reiterated her promise. *Just keep yourself to yourself.* She tested the meat, bit into a potato and pronounced it done. This would last her a couple days and then she could make a stock with the bones. Look at her, making the most of the local produce. Next she'd be shimmying up palm trees to lop down a coconut for breakfast.

She ate a bowl of stew while watching the curtains of rain glisten and billow in the moonlight. Maybe Fátima was right. She did need her head examined.

2

A few days after her unexpected visitor and her gift of chickens, Ann opened her eyes at first light to see three things had changed. Firstly, she'd slept through till morning. No flailing around in the wee hours trying to swat a mosquito or snatching up the machete after hearing a creak on the porch. Secondly, it had stopped raining. The constant thunder on the corrugated tin roof was part of the tonal background, like the waves rushing up the shore. Its sudden absence was eerie. Thirdly, and most uplifting of all, a golden light filled the hut. Sunshine. She had almost forgotten what it looked like.

Ann lay perfectly still, tuning into her environment, her eyes performing an inventory of the sleeping area and what she could see of the rest of the hut. Satisfied nothing was amiss, other than new mosquito bites on her neck and shoulder, she untangled herself from the covers and made her first coffee of the day. She shoved the heavy wooden bar securing the door into its open position and stepped out into a new world. It was a different beach. No longer mustard yellow, the sand gleamed white, causing her to squint at its brightness. The brown river water mingling with the sea seemed to have accepted its subordinate role and the ocean showed off, flashing its sapphires, diamonds and aquamarines in a display of splendid might. Even the palms along the edge of the jungle were still, as if watching the show.

Tempting as it was to run into the water and frolic in the waves, Ann took no risks. The ocean could be dangerous. She showered as usual in her tiny bathroom. The tank on the roof collected rainwater, which was available in abundance. After washing away the night, she sat on the porch to drink more coffee and eat a breakfast of fresh açaí with some cassava pancakes, mesmerised by the movements of the sea. This morning, the jungle was exploding into life. Birdsong rang out at volumes which would make the neighbours complain, if she had any. Maybe they were always that loud, she just hadn't heard them over the rain.

She rinsed her crockery and checked the cupboard for provisions. She could put it off no longer; it was time to go to the market. The last three days she'd said the same thing, but one look outside at the torrential weather had dissuaded her. Thankfully, Fátima's chickens had kept her going. She slipped on her trainers, shoved a cagoule in her rucksack and made sure the hut was secure, then set out along the beach in the direction of Praia do Pesqueiro. Two water buffalo lumbered out of the jungle, each laden with a basket, followed by an older man with a long switch. The animals turned to walk in the same direction as her and the man gave her a curious look.

"*Bom dia!*" he called.

She wished him the same and he placed his hands together in prayer, lifting them to the sun with his eyes closed. She laughed in agreement and watched as he and his beasts trudged over the sand to the village. He had a weather-beaten face, reminding her of a walnut. If she saw him at the market and whatever was in those baskets was edible and affordable, she'd buy something to support the old fella. As she passed the first restaurant, Adega Lusitania, she saw Fátima perched on the steps, smoking and shouting into her phone. The woman looked up with a cheery wave while continuing her litany of furious grievances into the mouthpiece. Ann waved back but kept walking. Friendly, but keeping her distance.

Beachside restaurants or food shacks grew more plentiful as she approached the village. Most were still boarded up, but a few enterprising vendors were open for business. The heat took her by surprise, even this early in the morning, and she berated herself for leaving without sunscreen or a hat. A dog was barking outside the bakery. Dogs were always barking somewhere.

The village was transformed. Whenever she'd come here to buy fish, the roads were empty, with only the occasional house-wife stepping over puddles on her way to haggle with the fish-ermen. Now children ran up and down between the buildings and people greeted one another as if they'd been separated for months. Perhaps they had. Bicycles whizzed past and occasion-ally someone called out a warning to pedestrians as there was nothing resembling a pavement. The rough dirt road was a free-for-all. In one of the cafés, a football match was on TV, watched by half a dozen men, drinking *cafezinhos* and brandy.

The market was quite a bit smaller than she'd expected, just a dozen or so stalls but with plentiful produce. Fruit and vegetable vendors retracted their awnings, allowing the natural illumination of the day to spotlight their wares. A large woman in what looked like a ticket booth was bellowing to all and sundry, extolling the virtues of her manioc and cassava flour. The sign above her head read Tia Maria, a name which made Ann smile. In the shade of the church wall sat *peixeiras* in their widows' weeds behind tables laden with crabs, prawns and an array of fresh and saltwater fish, probably caught less than a couple of hours ago.

Towards the end of the market, she spotted a man selling

fishing tackle. He was squat with a face that at best could be described as 'lived-in'. This had to be Nuno. Ann approached with the intention of enquiring about mosquito nets but something in her peripheral vision set off alarm bells in her head. She ducked behind a palm tree and studied the scene. Her instinct honed in on the anomaly as if she was scanning covert footage. A man leaning against the wall of the bakery-cum-café had a particular air that marked him out as a stranger. Of course it was ridiculous to call him a stranger when none of these people were familiar to her. Still, he stood out. He wore jeans, like everyone else, but his were clean. His striped shirt looked expensive and on his feet were cowboy boots made of snakeskin. With recently trimmed hair and a clean-shaven face, he seemed alien to this small society just emerging from forced confinement. But it wasn't just his looks that drew her attention. The reactions of the villagers marked him as different. People steered away from passing too close, tracing a wide arc to avoid his orbit, keeping their eyes to the ground. He ignored everyone, smoking his cigarette as if he was advertising the brand.

Ann's breathing calmed. He wasn't a recent arrival, a foreign hit man waiting for her to emerge from behind the tree so he could put a bullet in her spine. He was known and possibly feared by these people. That still didn't mean she was in the clear. The people who wanted her dead often used local muscle to do their dirty work and it certainly seemed he was waiting for someone. A ruckus erupted at the end of the road and the group of youngsters Ann had seen hanging out at the beach made their way through the market. They were laughing, calling greetings to traders and all but swaggering in the direction of the bakery. The surfers. Defying the rain but respectful of the sea, these dudes had been out there at least once a week, cresting, cruising and disappearing into the swell.

When they spotted the guy in the sharp shirt, their

demeanour changed and their boisterous chatter withered into silence. He pressed himself away from the wall and strolled in the direction of the bakery entrance, his expression as animated as one of Fátima's chickens. The surfers fell into step behind him, their previous high spirits subdued. Before the man could walk through the ironwork arch onto the café terrace, a woman flew out of the bakery door and stood in his path with her hands on her hips. Ann was too far away to hear the exchange, but the little woman's body language spoke volumes. Shaking her head and gesturing to the street, she refused him and his cohort entry. Other patrons stared open-mouthed as the bakery owner raised her voice and roared an insult even Ann recognised. The guy shrugged, turned around and said something to the surfers. They laughed dutifully and followed him along to the river jetty.

Her instinct was to ask someone the reason behind the drama and she stopped herself. *None of your business. Buy your mosquito net and your groceries and get out of here.*

It took ten minutes haggling with the wizened little fisherman before she invoked Fátima's name, paid him 20R$ and promised him an extra two if would deliver it later that evening. He agreed and made her a present of a handful of prawns. Ann made a plan. Buy the basics first, followed by fresh items, then treat herself to a coffee and a sandwich at Padaria São João. Not that she was interested in local gossip, but it would be nice to eat and drink something she hadn't made herself. Her backpack was getting pretty heavy by the time she stopped for her coffee break, weighed down by black beans and rice, vegetables and palm fruits, along with a bottle of cachaça.

She sat on the terrace, under an umbrella, with a nod and smile to other customers. Her casual appreciation of the surroundings was anything but. Each coffee or beer-drinker was subject to intense scrutiny and judged on mannerisms, dress and their curiosity in her. As far as she could see, no one posed an immediate threat but she still started a little when a cheerful voice at her shoulder asked what she would like to drink. She turned to see a young man around sixteen years old smiling at her. Like the guy she'd seen earlier, this teenager also stood out from the rest of the villagers, but for very different reasons. Pale and freckly with a shock of red hair, he seemed incongruous amongst the other uniformly dark and olive-skinned inhabitants. He was still grinning at her, his wide mouth and blue eyes exuding friendliness. It was only then she realised he had addressed her in English.

"We have tea, beer, orange juice, red wine, guaraná and the best coffee you will find on the whole Ilha do Marajó. My name is Nelson. How do you do?"

His voice was loud and confident, and the fact he was speaking in a foreign language drew the interest of several people on the terrace. So much for not attracting attention to herself.

She answered him, also in English, but dropped her voice to a conversational tone. "Pleased to meet you, Nelson. My name is Ann. You speak English very well."

"Thank you! I study hard. I was very happy when I hear an English is come to the village. Now I can practise with you, no?"

She laughed, his enthusiasm difficult to resist. "And you can help me with my Portuguese." It was on the tip of her tongue to ask him where he came from but she couldn't be so rude. "Are you learning English at school?"

"Nelson!" The small angry woman from earlier stood in the doorway of the café, her hands once again on her hips. In rapid-fire Portuguese she asked him what she was paying him for, why she had to watch him like a hawk and how she was to serve any customers when he didn't bring in any orders.

Ann decided to help him out. "*Queria uma meia do leite e uma tosta de queijo.*"

The loud and furious rebuke from his employer did not seem to dent Nelson's positive attitude. He called over his shoulder in Portuguese. "All right, Viviane, I'm coming. I was speaking to this lady in English. How many of your other employees can do that? You're lucky to have me, you know, I'm an asset in the tourist season. Anyway, the English wants a milky coffee and a toasted cheese sandwich." He smiled down at Ann and switched languages. "Who wants to be a waiter, eh? Oh well, it is what it is. Hey, here comes my family! See you later, alligator." With that he bounced off to greet an older woman, four teenage girls and a toddler. Not one of them looked like him but their affection for one another was obvious. He settled them at a table, laughing with his mother and amusing the little boy by pulling faces.

The confident way he worked the tables made Ann smile. The kid was good at his job and obviously popular with the clientele. He delivered her toasted sandwich and coffee, stopped to make an observation on the weather and thanked her with an elegance rarely seen in one so young when she added his tip to the bill. It was time for her to leave the relatively bustling village and return to her hut. She'd had more interaction with her fellow human beings in the last twenty-four hours than she had in the last three months. The funny thing was, she'd missed it.

3

The noise of the village faded as she turned off the track onto the sand and began making her hot, sweaty way back to the hut. Although her mind was occupied with how she was going to fit her purchases into her tiny cool box, she was always surveying her environment. The beach was a lot busier than she'd ever seen it and this was only the first day after the rains had stopped. When the hot weather came to stay, the area was going to be far more crowded than she would like. Most people on the strand trained their focus on the ocean, appreciating its beauty in the midday sun.

Ann didn't ignore it but paid more attention to the views on her right, the beachside shacks and bars against the verdant background of jungle. In her experience, an ambush rarely came out of the water. The knowledge she was being watched was more than a sixth sense, it was the result of years of training. Instead of turning her gaze over her shoulder, she released her backpack to the ground and made some adjustments to the straps. Head bowed to her task, she took advantage of the sunglasses hiding her eyes and without lifting her head, she scanned the huts she had just passed. She located her observers immediately.

The surf dudes and the man who had earlier caught her attention were sitting outside a weather-beaten timber structure on rough driftwood benches, drinking beer from bottles. The building announced itself unambiguously with a large yellow and green sign saying, 'BAR'. All six males were staring in her direction, some of them making a point of turning to look over their shoulders. One of them picked up his phone and aimed it at her. She ignored their attentions completely, replaced the backpack and continued down the beach as if she hadn't seen them. Not entirely consciously, she pressed two fingers to her clavicle, registering the increase in her pulse rate. She forced herself to keep walking and not to check if any of them had risen to follow her. That was exactly what they wanted, to make her nervous. Only once she had passed Fátima's shack did she turn as if she'd heard someone calling her name. One swift glance at the beach told her that no one was following, at least not directly. Her footprints were the only ones to come this far.

Now the danger, or perhaps the perception of it, had passed, exhaustion overcame her. The backpack seemed to weigh twice what it had when she first heaved it onto her shoulders. Sweat trickled down her back, moistened her lip and ran into her eyes, the saline making her blink. She trudged on another kilometre, gladdened by the welcome sight of her own hut, its shady veranda, the closed curtains and …footprints going up the path. Instantly on high alert, she kept her head focused forward, but swivelled her eyes to the right, trying to assess if anything had changed. She walked a good fifty paces past her own building and stopped beneath a cluster of palm trees. Hidden from view, she eased her burden to the ground and dug in the side pocket to find her binoculars. If she were to walk away from the trees, she would be clearly visible from her hut, so she opted instead to climb between the trunks of the two lowest palms. Trees at the edge of the jungle tended to grow at a diagonal instead of vertical, stretching their fronds out towards the sea and up towards the sun. This enabled Ann to creep along one trunk while concealing her presence behind the other. She found a point where she could sit almost comfortably and observe any movement in or around her house.

Years of boring stakeouts had taught her the art of stillness. She held her binoculars to her face but did not raise them to her eyes, to avoid the chance of sunlight reflecting on the lenses. Only when there was something to see would she use them for magnification. With one more sweep around her to be sure no one was lurking behind, she dedicated her attention to the wooden structure she called home. Everything seemed normal. Shutters closed, door locked, nothing visible beneath the stilts or under the porch steps and no sign of any visitor. But those footprints did not belong to Ann, as she always stuck to the wooden slats for that precise purpose. As in every aspect of her life, she wanted to leave neither trace nor trail. She waited, checking behind and below her at regular intervals while constantly watching the house. From that distance, she had no idea if the person who made those steps had come and gone, or was still on the property

A shadow crossed over her, a bird in flight. A white heron glided over the beach, its brilliance making a mockery of the white sand, and came to rest on the roof of her shack. It released its tragic call, part bark, part shriek, like a sob that cannot be suppressed.

The veranda had a criss-cross pattern of wooden slats so that you could see if anyone were lying in wait at the top of the steps as you approached. At this distance, it would be no better than guesswork. Ann decided to take the risk and lifted the binoculars to her eyes. She started from the left, adjusting the focus until her tomato plant came sharply into view. Keeping her hand steady, she surveyed every inch of the platform, coming to a halt by the front door. Right where Fátima had hung up her bright yellow sou'wester a few days ago lay a black lump resembling a rubbish bag. She zoomed in and focused on the object which had certainly not been there when she left. She could discern no movement from within, so discounted the possibility Fátima had brought her some live chickens. The only other item she was expecting was Nuno's mosquito net, but she doubted he would leave it on the porch without collecting his tip. It was too small and flat to be a human being, but she was well aware of the dangers which might lurk within something no bigger than a blanket.

She looked down at her backpack, fully exposed to the heat now the shade had been completely eliminated by the midday sun. With one more 360° check of the beach, jungle and little hut, she clambered down, heaved up her provisions and made her way towards the path. It would have been possible to approach the building from the rear, seeing as she knew exactly the pattern in which she had planted the broken glass, but she chose the direct route. The binoculars were safely stowed in the side pocket and her four-inch flick knife nestled in her right hand. It would be no match for her machete if someone was lying in wait, but at least she was not completely defenceless. The steps creaked as she made her ascent, her eyes flicking from the object wrapped in black plastic, to the windows, to the front door and back to her unexpected surprise. With a clatter and sudden rush of wings, the heron took off from the roof, sending Ann's heart into her mouth.

Nothing else moved, the only sound being the rush and hiss of the waves, the continual cacophony from the jungle and her own steady breathing. She shrugged off her pack and placed it gently on the boards. With her right foot, she reached out and prodded the black plastic, meeting an inert resistance. She crouched and using both hands, pulled it away from the front door. It was lighter than she expected and moved easily in her direction, causing her to tumble onto her backside. In a second she was on her feet, clutching her knife, ready to defend herself, but no assailant emerged.

She took out her keys and began the process of opening the three separate locks which secured her front door. The place was empty. She knew that the moment she stepped over the threshold. Nevertheless, she performed a thorough check of everywhere someone could hide and made sure none of her markers had been disturbed. They were all exactly as she had left them. Returning to the veranda, she brought in her back-pack and stowed the items she had purchased that morning. She took off her sweaty T-shirt and threw it into the corner which served as the laundry basket. With a fresh top and long draught of iced water, she was ready to tackle the package.

Until she was sure what it was, she had no intention of bringing it into the hut. She squatted beside it and used the flick knife to slice open the black plastic. Inside were neat folds of grey netting. Good as his word, Nuno had delivered. She unfolded the unwieldy mass and spent almost an hour working out how the thing fitted together and the best way of securing it to the roof. Finally, after dismantling it all over again when she realised it was inside out and putting it back together, she managed to arrange it over her cot with a peg to hold the edges together. She parted the side flaps and slipped onto her bed, looking up at the semi-transparent tent which covered her. It was stupid, obviously, but the flimsy fabric lent her bed an extra layer of protection, making her feel cocooned and safe in her little nest. She spread her arms and legs out in a starfish shape whispering, "Try getting me now, you bloodsucking little bastards."

Twelve hours later, after a shrimp and vegetable paella washed down with one shot too many of cachaça, she lay in exactly the same spot, curled into a ball and sobbing uncontrollably. This time, instead of taunting mosquitoes, she whispered a different kind of mantra. "I'm sorry. I'm sorry. I'm so sorry."

The crying jag left her puffy and filled with self-loathing, like so many mornings after the night before. Ann battled her way out of the mosquito net and went to wash her face. To her surprise, she couldn't find a single mosquito bite. Yesterday, she'd cursed the unwieldy mass of fabric and the man who sold it to her. Now, she could have kissed him. Unbroken sleep, unbitten skin, it was worth every one of the 20 reais she'd paid. On top of that, the sun was shining again. She made up her mind to walk into the village early, find Nuno and give him the tip she had promised. Then she'd come back here and keep away from society for a few days. She needed to focus and social contact was a distraction she could do without. Her desire to walk into town and find an Internet café had increased to an insufferable degree. She wanted to know. She wanted to know so badly it was like an itch, driving her crazy.

She made coffee, chopped up some papaya and pineapple and sat on the veranda to give herself a good talking-to. The only way of remaining hidden was to cut all contact. The second she logged on to any site they were watching, a little red light somewhere would start blinking and then it was only a matter of time. During the rains, she'd been doing pretty well. Daily meditations and focusing inward reassured her she could keep the outside world at bay. She had everything she needed to survive. As long as she kept her eyes on the future and never looked back, everything would work out just fine. The intrusion of the neighbour, the visit to the village, the surfers and their slick associate had somehow penetrated the walls of her mental defences. What she needed was time alone, in silence with no other companion than her breath to recover her equilibrium. Decision made, she showered, dressed and prepared to walk into the village and return before the day grew too hot.

Nuno wasn't hard to find. He was in the middle of a small group surrounding a flatbed truck parked in front of the church. He seemed surprised to see Ann and even more surprised when she insisted on giving him two reais for delivery. His face scrunched into a grin when she told him how pleased she was with her net and he nodded with satisfaction. Then he returned his attention to the truck, where it seemed some kind of argument was taking place. She spotted the kid from the café, Nelson, right in the thick of things and despite her intention to go straight home, she watched for a moment or two, curious as to the fuss.

"Dona Ann! Do you want to come?" Nelson called. "Zé is driving his truck into Soure and can carry six of us, if we give money for gasoline. I'm going. I take orders for everyone if they give me a tip. Why don't you come? You only know Soure in the rain. It's a nice city, come!" He yelled something at a man beside Ann who turned and offered his arm to help her into the truck.

She tried to refuse politely but in a few quick moves, found herself standing beside Nelson and a dirty grey dog, looking down at the small crowd. The debate over who should go and who should stay raged on for another few minutes until three men helped an elderly lady up to sit beside Ann. She was hemmed in by the old lady on her right and a young man who smelt of smoke on her left. Opposite, Nelson was telling jokes, bad ones judging by the groans of the two guys beside him. His left hand stroked the dog, which leant against his leg. Ann noticed it was wearing a bandana printed with the American flag around its neck, so the mutt was clearly a pet and not as she'd assumed, one of the many village strays.

With a lurch, the truck took off and she had to grab the arm of the old lady to stop her sliding off the bench. The journey was noisy, due to the unhealthy sound of the engine and conversation became impossible as the vehicle bumped along the potholed track towards the town. Even though she'd had no plan to go into Soure for another two weeks, it was a good opportunity to buy some whisky. She was duty bound to thank Fátima for her present of poultry. Maybe she could find something to read and pick up one or two items they didn't sell at the village market. The bone-jolting trip took all of fifteen minutes down dirt roads, with the wind blowing through her hair like natural air conditioning. Her cautious self muttered darkly about spontaneity being her enemy, but she couldn't suppress her excitement about the excursion. Nelson was grinning at her, his wild red hair like a beacon as they left the jungle behind and passed single-storey buildings, separated by scrubland. It was unlike any other city Ann had ever seen.

The driver parked outside the hospital, apparently for the convenience of the elderly lady who had an appointment that day. With much fuss and plenty of debate, the woman got off the truck and one man escorted her into the hospital grounds. Zé told everyone to return by midday, when the shops closed for lunch, or he would leave them behind. Ann believed him. From a tarpaulin rolled up against the cab, Nelson dragged out a shopping trolley, the kind normally used by old women in the Clapham Co-op. He jumped down and called to the dog. "*Vamos*, Branca. Have a nice day, Dona Ann!"

He jogged off in the direction of the supermarket, the dog at his heels. Her fellow passengers scattered to the four winds and she was left standing on the red dirt road, wondering what to do next. Instinctively, she turned in the direction of the Paracauari river. From there, she could get her bearings and decide what she could achieve in the next three hours.

She turned a corner and spotted a low white building with young men lounging outside in plastic chairs. In bright blue paint on the whitewash were the words Cyber Cafe. Ann stopped to stare at the building for a moment, then forced herself to walk on. *You are here to buy whisky for your neighbour and a few luxuries for yourself. That does not include surfing the web. Just keep moving.*

The city of Soure was laid out in a grid format which made it very difficult to get lost. She took a right, a left and another right to find a supermarket, where she bought half a bottle of Scotch, *jambú* plants, milk, canned meatballs and a slab of salted cod. The latter would stink to high heaven but was always useful in emergencies. She wandered down to the ferry station and found a *papeteria* selling stationery, newspapers and books. Ann bought an outdated English copy of Time, a couple of gossip magazines in Portuguese and an exercise book to serve as a diary. The ferry departed and Ann watched it go, looking across the water to the opposite bank and Salvaterra, curious as to how that town might compare. All the while, she was ignoring a little voice saying, *just the news sites, mask your ID, visit some irrelevant links, cover your tracks, you've got time to kill.*

Fifteen minutes later, she was sitting in front of a computer, having paid for an hour's access. She chose a spot near the rear of the humid little building so she could keep her back to the wall. Not only did she dislike people reading over her shoulder, but it was also vital to know who might be coming in or out of the café. She started with the BBC, digging into UK crime stories. Plenty of news but no developments that affected her. The loading speed was not the best and she practised patience, flicking past fluff about celebrities and football managers until she spotted a sidebar piece on government questions about police methodology. It was vague and mentioned no names, but the question of undercover ethics had been raised in the House of Commons, related to a recent court case. Frustratingly, the case itself was under a media blackout to protect the defendants.

The only way to access the detail would be to log in to the

website of the Metropolitan Police. For obvious reasons, that was not going to happen. She tried other media outlets, searching in a generic sense for police raid, drugs bust, gang infiltration and undercover operations, and found several references to a series of arrests in South London mostly dated four months ago. The articles quoted 'a police spokesman' and gave no indication of the personnel involved. Twenty minutes of her allotted time remained. She glanced out of the open doorway at the young men smoking and watching the road. Their interest in her as a foreigner and a woman had lasted less than a minute, which suited her perfectly.

Her fingers hovered over the keyboard. She was browsing incognito, but particular searches would raise a flag and it was a risk not worth taking. Not Facebook, not The Yorkshire Post, not any of the notice boards. There was one place where she might pick up a clue. She navigated to Dewsbury Veterinary Practice and checked for online appointments. The surgery was open as usual. She entered a poorly spelled enquiry via LiveChat, asking if the practice could examine an injured owl. Fifteen minutes to go and she had to leave or miss Zé's truck and walk home. She opened another window and checked the parish records of Dewsbury's church, scanning recent obituaries. A message flashed. A reply from the vet's. *Yes, you can bring in an injured owl either today or on Thursday as those are the only days Dr Lane, our bird specialist, is on the premises. Would you like to book an appointment?*

Ann typed back. *Cheers. Will check and call u later.*

It wasn't much, but enough for her to read between the lines.

On the return journey, everyone seemed in high spirits. The old lady tucked her arm into Ann's to keep herself steady and rolled down a sock to show off her fresh dressing. Nelson's trolley bulged with all kinds of unrecognisable objects and even the dog was gnawing on something that looked like a piece of shoe leather. A few minutes before they arrived at the village, Zé pulled over and yelled something out the window at Nelson.

"*Bom idea!*" Nelson gave him the thumbs-up. "Dona Ann, Zé asks if you want to get off here. There is a path through the jungle to your end of the beach, you know it?"

Ann didn't but was eager to learn. It bothered her slightly that everyone knew where she lived, but it was too late to do anything about that now. She fumbled in her pocket and gave Nelson two reais. "That's very kind of him. Here's some money for the gasoline."

"Too much! We give him one real each. Is plenty!" He tried to hand back one of the coins.

Ann shook her head and picked up a backpack. "You keep the change. Thank you for taking me." She wished everyone a good day in Portuguese and jumped down onto the track. Zé tooted his horn and Ann waved as the truck drove off, dust puffing out from under its wheels.

The path through the foliage was not easy to find. She walked up and down twice, seeing no visible break in the greenery. Perhaps it had become overgrown during the rains when few people were likely to take the short cut. She wished she had known about it before her first foray into town. It would have lopped at least four kilometres off the trek. On her third pass along where the truck had stopped, she saw a small post driven into the earth. The top of it was painted blue, the one colour that stood out in this landscape. She looked closer, pushing aside some droopy leaves the size of umbrellas and saw there was enough space for a person to move between the trees. As for what might be waiting to drop from the canopy or lurking in the undergrowth, she dreaded to think.

The start was easy. Brushing aside leaves, she placed each foot with care, avoiding lizards and dodging huge spider webs.

The sound of monkeys and birds was a constant background noise in her life. Now, it seemed she was right in the middle of the orchestra, hot, sweaty and nervous.

Each pace forward took a lot of thought and she wondered if her sluggish progress was worth it. Tiptoeing through the dense foliage might easily take as long as striding from the beach. Sunlight dappled the ground ahead and Ann looked twice, three times before she could believe her eyes.

A jaguar was drinking from the river, its body low and tense, lapping fresh water until satisfied. In a slick, confident move, it padded into the jungle, with a flick of its tail. Ann stayed still for several minutes, less out of fear and more in admiration.

She'd read somewhere that the best thing to do when moving through territory where dangerous animals or insects might be present was to make a lot of noise, scaring away snakes and spiders. So she joined the percussion section, clapping her hands and singing 'These Boots Are Made For Walking' until she saw glimpses of white sand and flashes of sea through the greenery. This must be the path where she'd seen the buffalo driver coming out somewhere between her hut and Fátima's. With some relief, she tramped out of the forest and onto the sand, pausing to see if anyone was in the vicinity. Between some palm trees to her right, she could see her own shack, made more distinctive by the white heron once more perched on its roof. To her left, the distant buildings of the village, some people in the sea and a short distance away, Fátima's place.

Her stomach rumbled and she checked her watch. Lunchtime. She hesitated. Her plan had been to wait for the cover of darkness and leave the whisky on Fátima's porch, thereby avoiding any further conversation. But she was in the neighbourhood, the house was closed and apparently no one was home, so she struck out across the sand and through driftwood, shells and knots of fishing net, intent on completing her errand. As she got closer, she slipped the shoulder straps of her backpack off and swung it round to locate the bottle. A flash of light drew her attention. It came from further down the beach, past her shack towards where the sand ran out. It was exactly the kind of flash she had tried to avoid when using binoculars. Hers was the last building down this end of the beach. Nobody had any business down there. She squinted in the direction of the light but could see nothing more than sand, palm trees and at the very end, more jungle.

The heat was beginning to feel uncomfortable. Ann pulled out the whisky in its brown paper bag, tiptoed up the steps to Fátima's porch and left it beside the front door. With equal stealth, she went back the way she'd come and took a wide detour round the back of her own building and out the other side. The whole time she kept the end of the beach in her peripheral vision, alert for any inexplicable flashes of light. Eventually, thirsty and uneasy, she unlocked her own front door. Once inside and convinced nothing had been disturbed, she dug out her own binoculars, scanning the sweep from left to right. To an inexperienced eye, the scene looked completely normal. That flash could have been anything. All the same, she checked that end of the beach frequently as she sat on the porch eating her last portion of cold paella.

4

For the next five days, Ann spoke to no one and saw other people only from a distance. She spent her days working on herself, meditating, focusing on the present, doing physical exercise and reading. Her blonde roots were starting to show, so she mixed a pack of henna with milk and lime juice, slathered it over her head, tied the supermarket bag over the top and left it on overnight. The next morning, she stank to high heaven, but when the gunk washed out, her hair was restored to a rich coppery red. She ran just after sunrise, while the air was cool and the beach empty. Whenever her thoughts strayed to the Old Bailey in London or Dewsbury Veterinary Practice in Yorkshire, she brought herself firmly back on track. The here-and-now was all that mattered. With a struggle, she could control her waking thoughts. Nights were a different matter.

Katie made regular appearances in her dreams, sometimes as a child, sometimes as a teenager, but without fail, she was angry. Twice Ann woke gasping from a nightmare in which she was trying to attract attention and call for help but the people she was addressing were too far away or thought she was waving goodbye. It was wasteful, she knew, but after such night terrors, she switched on the lamp, using more of her precious generator fuel than was necessary. Candles were too risky when trying to go back to sleep. No matter how far she ran in the dawn light before the village stirred and the jungle burst into noisy life, no matter how exhausted her body when crawling under the mosquito net, her mind made sure she never slept through till morning. One brief contact with UK news and the nightmares returned with a vengeance. It wore her out.

She got into the habit of taking a siesta after lunch. Firstly, because the heat threw a torpor over the afternoon and secondly, she was invariably tired from another broken night. It was a vicious circle. If she slept in the afternoon, she'd have difficulty at night, leading to her dozing off the following afternoon. The mysterious flash she'd seen the day she returned from Soure had not recurred. On one of her jogs, she went as far as the tree line and strolled along the edge of the jungle, searching for any sign of human activity. Nothing more than the jungle creatures going about their business.

On the sixth day, Ann woke feeling more grounded than she had in a fortnight. A sense of calm suffused her and she poured her coffee feeling relaxed and positive towards the world. On the veranda, she gazed out at the sea and smiled. It was possible to just be. No point in worrying how long that might last. Just be. The longer she could insulate herself from the outside world, the better she felt. That said, it was market day and she had to stock up on fruit and vegetables. She would go early, almost as soon as the first stallholders had set up. That way, she could make her purchases and be home in her own shack before the place grew clogged with shoppers keen to catch up on the gossip and tourists cluttering up the roads with their jeeps, motorbikes and surfboards. Part of her was almost nostalgic for the empty ghost village of the rainy season.

When she drew closer, she could see she wasn't the first

early bird. The night fishermen were unloading their catch and already a group of around twenty were examining their haul. Ann wasn't brave enough to elbow her way to the front and decided to see what was left once she'd finished the rest of her shopping. The market was bigger than it had been at her previous visit and it took longer to examine the array of items on sale. Herbs, toiletries, palm fruits, live chickens, young goats, running shoes, spices, more vegetables than she knew the names for and all the bounty of the buffalo. Steaks, mince, cheese, milk, everything the horned beasts could provide. A dog was barking behind the church. As much a part of the background noise as the sea, barking dogs were ubiquitous. She ticked everything off her list and decided to stop for a coffee before tackling the fishermen's leftovers.

Last time she'd been to the bakery, she sat outside, relishing the sunshine. But today she was already hot, swollen and sticky, plus her backpack should be kept as cool as possible. Unlike the rest of the patrons, she sat inside. Viviane was wrestling with the huge Cimbali coffee machine. She frowned in Ann's direction and pointed to the cups, eyebrows raised. Ann nodded eagerly and mouthed the word '*agua*', fanning herself with her hand. It worked. A young girl brought a tray with a black coffee and a glass of water to her table.

"*Obrigada*," said Ann, taking a large swig of the water. The girl placed her order on the table and left the bill under the sugar shaker. Her face didn't crack a smile.

"Isn't Nelson working today?" she asked the girl in Portuguese.

"He didn't come in this morning. God knows why not. He knows it's market day and we're rushed off our feet. You wait till I see him. He's going to be sorry."

The bakery was certainly busy and more people crowded around the counter while Ann ingested her shot of caffeine. Not much opportunity for idle chatter as Nelson was AWOL.

She recalled his enthusiasm for practising his English, but Ann suspected he was drawn to a fellow outsider. Somewhere in his genetic code, there must have been a hiccup to create a light-skinned redhead in a family of typically Latino Brazilians. He was the odd one out, not that it seemed to bother him. She admired his ability to be philosophical about his lot. She should take a leaf out of his book. *It is what it is.*

An argument erupted on the terrace and Viviane marched out to settle the issue. How a woman so slight and diminutive commanded such respect was anyone's guess, but there was no doubting her authority. It helped that she could shout louder and curse more colourfully than any of the fishermen. The dispute was resolved and like a primary school teacher, Viviane insisted the two men shake hands. Drama over, the patrons returned their attention to their coffees, *natas* or sandwiches.

Ann paid her bill and with a wave to Viviane, she headed towards the fishing boats, planning on making a *moqueca*, or Afro-Brazilian fish stew that afternoon. The dog she had heard on entering the village was still barking somewhere behind the church. Just as she understood the squirrel monkeys' alarm call, Ann sensed this bark was something other than a demand for food. This was a distress signal.

Against her better judgement, she walked around the building and down the slope to the river. This was the bit the tourists didn't see, with rusting hulls of long-retired fishing boats protruding from the muddy river. When the water receded to summer levels, it would likely reveal all kinds of junk either washed downstream or dumped by careless day-trippers. She saw the dog standing on a rock close to the confluence where two tributaries joined the main coffee-coloured flow to roil and swirl out into the open sea.

The distance between her and the animal was mostly water, mud and some slippery-looking planks. If the dog was stuck, she'd never be able to rescue it without help. It was hard to see how it had managed to get out there in the first place. Ann left her backpack in the shade of the church, scrambled her way closer and whistled to attract the creature's attention. Its head snapped up to look at her, taking its focus from the water for a moment. It hopped off the rock and with sure-footed leaps, splashed its way in Ann's direction, its barks more urgent. As it got closer, Ann recognised the bandana which served as a collar. The Stars and Stripes. This must be Branca, Nelson's mongrel mutt. The creature came close enough to sniff Ann's hand and bounded back towards the river.

She followed, far more slowly, keeping her eyes on which-ever plank or stone she could step on next. The dog had stopped its rhythmic siren call, its attention switching between her and something in the water. When she got close enough to see what it was, she stopped in her tracks, refusing to believe what her eyes showed her. Tangled in the detritus of the river-bank was the body of a young man, partly covered in mud. He lay on his side, face submerged and hands behind his back as if he had just performed a dive. Even with so few identifying features, Ann knew who it was. Only one teenager in this village had a shock of ginger hair.

She stared at the body being buffeted by the hurrying waters, trying to comprehend what had happened. Drowned, right at the end of the rainy season? It made no sense. Surely everyone in Praia do Pesqueiro could swim and had the greatest respect for both river and sea? Youngsters like Nelson surfed and dived and rode water buffalo through flood waters as easily as they could walk. Her eyes scanned the body with a professional eye. There was something odd about the angle of his arms. She shuffled onto the rock with the dog, which was now silently observing her.

A sliver of white showed around the uppermost wrist and she recognised the ridged surface instantly. She glanced down at his ankles and saw the same plastic restraint binding his legs together. The strongest swimmer in the world would have no chance if unable to move his arms and legs. Nelson hadn't slipped or fallen into this fast-flowing current. Someone had tied him up and thrown him in. Worse, whoever killed this boy had made no attempt to make it look like an accident.

Ann's breath came in short, shaky bursts and panic constricted her chest. The scene was horribly familiar. Only a certain kind of man could perform such a cruel murder without a flicker of conscience. Nelson was one of the few people she had been seen with in public. Now he was dead, executed by a professional. Her worst fears had come to pass. She thought she'd escaped them, running 5,000 miles away to the Brazilian jungle. Obviously, she hadn't run far enough.

5

All thoughts of fish stew abandoned, Ann's only aim was to leave the village and get as far away as she could from the place. Leaving the dog sitting on the rock, she splashed and stumbled her way up the riverbank, evaluating all routes to the nearest airport. She yanked her backpack onto her shoulders and crept along the building, watching the street ahead for a potential ambush. She was about to step into the throng when someone came around the corner and bumped right into her.

She leapt away, reaching into her jeans for her flick knife, releasing the blade. In the shadow of the church, all she registered was a male shape.

The man spoke in apologetic tones. He hadn't seen her; the sun was in his eyes. So sorry. Did she want to pray? He was just about to unlock the church if she could wait a moment. Her eyes adjusted and took in the cassock and dog collar. She folded her weapon one-handed.

"Father, help me, please. There's a body in the water. I heard the dog and came to see what was wrong. Someone drowned."

The man crossed himself and Ann copied the gesture. "*Meu Deus*! Where?" he asked.

"Down there. By the dog. I'm sorry, Father, I have to go."

He gave no answer, already lifting his cassock to pick his way towards the river. She took her chance and ran, dodging the shuffling market-goers, sauntering tourists and giggling schoolkids, convinced every pair of eyes was on her back.

The jog along the beach seemed to have stretched to at least double its usual distance and the more effort she put into her pace, the more the sand resisted her. She wasn't even sure she should return to the hut. If Nelson's death was a warning, surely the smartest course of action was to take flight and not look over her shoulder. Flocks of sea birds screamed like teenage girls at a rock gig, aggravating Ann's panic. Exasperated by the slow pace and heat of the beach, she swung right, picking her way between the flotsam and jetsam at the tide line and onto firmer ground nearer the edge of the jungle. The cooler air calmed her thoughts and helped her get a grip on her shock. Of all the times she'd been confronted with sudden, violent death, this one had shaken her badly. Not just the unexpectedness of murder in this remote backwater, but the past crashing with such force into her new present.

She passed behind Fátima's house. A motorcycle with sidecar was parked at the rear, suggesting the boyfriend must be home, although there were no raised voices as yet. Her own rented property looked innocent and calm, framed by the sea, sky and palm trees. She approached with more than customary caution, every fibre of her being on a hair trigger, and weaved a path through her self-laid booby traps until she was at her front door. The dusting of flour on the door handle was untouched and a cotton thread still stretched across the top step. She dropped her backpack in order to be ready to run, unlocked the door and stepped inside, attuning herself to the silence. The machete was in its hiding place behind the curtain and the weight of its handle reassured her. The curtain marking the sleeping area was still tied up, as she had left it, and her mosquito net draped over her bed like a bridal veil. She performed her usual checks, took a bottle of water from the cold box and downed half of it in several swallows.

Her temperature settled and so did her thoughts. Rationality returned. She sat at the table, facing the open door and examined the facts. Nelson had been murdered. Horrifying in itself but not necessarily connected to her. Perhaps the kid had upset the wrong person and made himself an enemy. For some reason, the guy with the snakeskin boots floated into her mind. On the other hand, if it was the act of her pursuers, and it certainly had all the trademarks, what was the logic in killing Nelson? To frighten her? In which case, she'd be likely to run. Again. They would have to be pretty damn sure they wouldn't lose her. Not this time.

Her escape routes were limited. Limited, but possible. Walk to Soure airport and catch the next flight out to wherever; a ferry to Belém and a train south; or a ride on a fishing boat up the Amazon into the wilderness. They could be waiting at the first two but how could they be sure she didn't just fade into the jungle?

Nelson. Tied and thrown into the ferocious waters to be swept out to sea. If he'd not become tangled in the detritus behind the church, his body might never have been found. Now that it was, the villagers would have to involve the police. The very word made her leap to her feet and scrabble under the bed for her suitcase. She could not, would not talk to the police. The chances were negligible that she'd be recognised since her transformation, but there was still a chance. Of course it looked bad because she had found the body, told the priest and done a midnight flit. The alternative was far worse. Time to go.

Suitcase open on the bed, she started rolling her clothes

into tight little sausages and packed one after another in horizontal lines. The front door slammed shut, making her gasp in fright until she heard a rumble of thunder. The curtains blew inwards and one look at the menacing sky told her a storm was brewing. Whether that was good or bad news for her plans she could not decide. She bolted the door, just in case. She was prepared for exactly this kind of eventuality and travelled light, ensuring she could pack the essentials and disappear in under an hour. Rain began pattering on the roof, a familiar sound she told herself she wouldn't miss. Her case was over half full when someone knocked at the door.

Ann froze and in the next instant she heard Fátima's voice, calling "*Olá*, Ann?"

Of course. Fátima had heard the news from the village and knew of Ann's involvement. She had come to hear the story from the horse's mouth. With a groan of impatience, Ann untied the curtain separating the living area from her bedroom to hide her preparations and opened the front door. Obviously Fátima was in such a hurry she had not stopped to put on her souwester. Instead, she wore a denim jacket over a brightly patterned purple dress and Havaiana flip-flops.

"You saw the body!" she said, without preamble.

"Hello, Fátima." Ann kept a hand on the door, allowing only a narrow gap through which they could talk. "News travels fast."

Fátima's eyes widened. "I just came from the village. Everybody's going crazy. How did *you* find the body?" Her tone implied finding dead bodies was beneath Ann's level of competence.

"The dog was barking behind the church. I went to see what was wrong. The body was face down, but I recognised his hair. I'm pretty sure it was ..."

"Nelson Leal. Yeah, I know. They've just fished him out. You going to let me in? I'm not standing out here in this weather and I bought you some whisky, for the shock, you know?" She pushed the door with the palm of her hand and Ann had no choice but to take a pace backwards.

"Thank you, Fátima, but I'm not in shock. I don't need any whisky and I've got a lot to do. Sorry to be antisocial, but ..."

"I understand. You want to be alone." With that, she sat down at the table and pulled a half bottle of whisky from her handbag. It was the one Ann had purchased in Soure. "I was the same when I found somebody drowned. A fisherman who fell off his boat trying to get back to port before the storm. He couldn't swim. You'd be surprised how many of them can't. Have a shot of whisky with me and tell me what happened. Neighbours should look out for each other, that's why I'm here. Do you want to get some glasses? Never mind, sit down, I'll find them."

Ann rubbed at her forehead. "No, you sit down. We can have one glass and then I must get on. I'm busy today." She found two mismatched tumblers and set them on the table, sitting opposite her unwanted guest and attempted to deflect her attention. "When did you find a dead fisherman?"

"Years ago. He wasn't from around here." Her tone was dismissive as she filled both tumblers with Scotch. "This is different. Nelson's death wasn't an accident, you know." She held Ann's gaze. "Someone murdered him. In cold blood."

The jolt those words delivered made acting unnecessary. "Murdered? Oh my God!"

Fátima pushed a glass of whisky towards her. "Drink. You need it. Yes, the police have taken the body to do a post-mortem, but it's quite obvious someone killed him. They tied his hands and feet together then threw him in the river. What a horrible way to die." She took a swig of the honey-coloured liquid, shaking her head. "He was only seventeen. His whole life ahead of him."

"Poor kid," said Ann, her sympathy heartfelt. "Who the

hell would want to kill a teenage boy? I only saw him a couple of times but he seemed very popular in the village. I can't imagine he had any enemies." She sipped at the Scotch, welcoming the trail it blazed down her gullet.

"Enemies? Of course not! He's a funny-looking kid, there's no denying that, but he grew up in this village. Everybody knows him and his family. He's one of us. His mother is devastated. They had to sedate her, you know, she was screaming. The police took the whole Leal family into Soure. Bastards." The sound of the rain on the roof increased from a light shower to a full-on battering. Fátima raised her eyes to the corrugated tin above her head. "What a day! What a terrible day." It was unclear if she was referring to the storm or the teenage murder victim.

"Who are bastards?" asked Ann.

"The cops! All bastards, every last one of them. They pretend to care about us, fake concern and tell us they will try to solve the crime. Yeah, right. Only if there is any money in it for them. Well, there's no money in the Leal family and there will be even less now that Nelson is dead. Six kids to feed on a fisherman's wage? Bad luck follows that family around, I'm telling you." She poured herself another drink.

Ann placed her hand over her own glass. "Not for me. As I said, I have a lot to do today. Did the police mention any suspects?"

Fátima lifted her shoulders and pulled down the corners of her mouth. "Mention to who? Nobody speaks to the police, except maybe the priest. He said you told him the body was there, but then you disappeared. Why did you run off? It doesn't look good."

Ann swirled the whisky around her glass. "It doesn't look good, you're right, but that only occurred to me when I got home. I was shaken and upset and I wanted to be on my own. I told the priest I found the body and walked home. Actually, it was the dog who found the ..." She broke off, looking through the window over Fátima's shoulder. A motorcycle was coming along the beach, close to the shoreline. It stopped at the end of her path and the rider dismounted.

"Is that your boyfriend?" Ann asked.

Fátima whipped around, squinting through the rain. "Shit! It's the cops. I should have thought of that." She scrambled to her feet and looked wildly around the hut. "Of course they want to talk to you. I have to get out of here. Where's the back door?"

"I haven't got a back door. I mean, there was another exit but I blocked it up. Sorry."

Fátima looked cornered. "You blocked it up? What the hell is wrong with you? I have to get out! I'll jump out of the window."

"Not the window! Remember I planted broken bottles all around the house. It's my alarm system. Anyway, it's too late. He's coming up the path."

With a vicious curse, Fátima pressed herself against the wall behind the door. She glared at Ann and pointed an angry finger. "Don't let him in!"

"I can't refuse to admit the police. Look, go into my bedroom. Open the window onto the veranda and go out that way. I'll make a lot of noise and cover you."

Three heavy knocks came at the front door and Fátima slipped behind the curtain. Ann waited a moment and then opened the door just a crack. The motorcyclist wore water-proofs and carried a helmet. In his right hand, he held up his ID.

"*Inspetor Maduro. A senhora é Ann Sheldon?*"

She stared at him, frozen in place.

He tried again. "*Polícia Civil de Soure. Você fala português?*"

She found her voice. "Yes, I'm Ann Sheldon and I speak Portuguese. Please come in. I'll make some coffee.

Have a seat." She stood back to let him enter, slammed the door and began clattering around with a saucepan. A draught at the back of the neck told her the window was open and she addressed the officer with a louder than necessary voice.

"I'm sorry you had to come out here in this weather. I should have stayed to give a statement but I'm afraid I was in shock. Do please sit down. Is black coffee OK for you because I don't have any milk?" She glanced over her shoulder to hear his response and saw a shadow move down the porch steps. Too late she remembered she was supposed to speak the language badly.

The officer placed his helmet on the floor and eased himself into the chair Fátima had recently vacated. His eyes took in the whisky bottle and the two full glasses.

"For the shock," she said. "I poured myself a glass and then forgot about it and poured myself another. Would you like one?"

He brushed his hair off his forehead and assessed her. "Thank you. I like whisky and I like black coffee. Do you mind if I ask you some questions?"

She placed two cups of coffee on the table and was about to hand him Fátima's glass until she saw the lipstick. She switched it for hers. A loud bang came from the sleeping area and Ann jumped.

"Oh, I must have left my bedroom window open. Just one second while I close it." She ducked behind the curtain, wrestled the window shut and returned to sit opposite the police officer. He was younger than she'd first thought, with deep-set eyes and long eyelashes. His expression was neither hostile nor friendly but he watched her with an intensity that made her nervous.

"You said you had some questions?" Ann said, reaching for her Scotch.

He blinked at her and then turned to look around the room. "You here long?"

"Around three months, I think."

"Funny sort of place to choose." His gaze returned to her and he sipped his whisky.

She was about to launch into her poet-seeking-inspiration speech but he spoke again before she could open her mouth.

"My name is Inspector Gil Maduro and I work with the Soure police force. The priest of Praia do Pesqueiro called us this morning to report a dead body in the river behind the church. He says you discovered it."

"That's right. A dog was barking ..."

"That wasn't a question. Did you know the deceased?"

Ann's breathing was shallow. This man's lizard-like eyes boring into her instigated a feeling of panic she could barely control. She had to answer his questions and get him out of there as fast as possible. "I knew his name. He served me coffee at the bakery and he was one of the passengers on the truck into Soure last week. He is ... distinctive and attracted my attention because he speaks English. That's all I know."

"You asked for him at the bakery this morning, no? Why did you go looking behind the church? What were you expecting to find?" His voice was calm and his gaze steady.

Ann realised she was fidgeting, tugging at her earlobe, rotating her coffee cup and pulling at the neck of her T-shirt. She forced herself to sit still and breathe deeply.

"He's a friendly face. Sorry, he was a friendly face. I asked the waitress if he was working this morning and she told me he hadn't turned up. The dog was barking and I wanted to see if it was in trouble. It looked stuck on that rock. I wasn't expecting to find anything, Inspector Maduro."

He reached his right hand inside his jacket and withdrew a notepad. He wrote what looked like a full page of notes based on her brief reply. She stared at his thick dark hair as he rested his forehead on his left hand. He looked up and met her eyes, giving her such a start, she glanced away. Something about the intelligence behind that expression frightened her senseless.

"More coffee?"

He shook his head, replaced his notebook and got to his feet. With another searching scan of the room, he threw back the tumbler of whisky, his eyes on the curtain screening her bedroom. "Are you going somewhere?" he asked, his hands resting on the back of the chair.

"Going somewhere?" Ann echoed, her heart thudding.

He bent to pick up his motorcycle helmet and faced her, unsmiling. "The suitcase. I got the impression you might be planning to leave. In the current circumstances, I recommend you stay. We may have further questions. Thank you for the coffee and the Scotch. I will leave you now. Have a good evening." He opened the door, put on his helmet and descended the steps.

She watched him, his head bent against the rain. He mounted his bike and drove back in the direction he had come. Her knees sagged and she leant on the door jamb, wondering what the hell to do next. Three flashes of lightning lit the sky and the sounds of thunder moved further down the coast. She returned indoors, threw away her whisky, cleared all evidence of not one but two visitors and double-checked all the locks. Then she crawled under her mosquito net and closed her eyes.

Sounds of scrabbling on the roof woke her around four o'clock. Presumably the heron had returned. She wondered about going out there with a saucepan and a wooden spoon to chase it away, but it had probably lived here longer than her. Sun streamed through the curtains as if the storm had been part of a dream. The coffee cups and tumblers drying on the draining board were proof the last few hours had been only too real. She needed to breathe fresh air, avoid people and focus her mind.

The temperature on the beach was perfect. Sand still damp, brilliant blue skies and the remnants of a breeze blew in from the ocean. Ann strolled through the surf in the opposite direction to the village. She took the opportunity of a calm moment to address her own illogical thinking. Nelson's unnatural death was a tragedy, but to associate it with her past smacked of paranoia. Tracking her here and killing a local teen? Not even a plausible movie script. Whoever killed Nelson, it couldn't possibly be them. That raised another question. Who had reason to murder the boy? *Not your job*, she told herself. *Leave that to the professionals.*

The interview with the cop preyed on her mind. He'd been polite, yet intense, as if his questions masked a different line of enquiry. She dismissed the thought. He was curious, nothing more. Assessing the situation with a realistic perspective, the likelihood of local police blowing her cover was remote. Small-town cops had practically no interaction with the world of international law enforcement. If they sniffed around again, all she need do was stick to her role of eccentric *gringa*, a harmless British drop-out whose Portuguese was limited. The key was to be helpful and yet helpless. Then they would lose interest.

Surf pounded the shore, each wave a threat. Its relentless power took her mind back to the foaming river, battering the banks, sucking everything into its path and ejecting it out to the ocean. *Oh, Nelson, you must have been terrified*. She scrunched her eyes shut and tried not to imagine. The evening sky streaked with flaming orange and reds made Ann think of a tequila sunrise, reminding her of the bottle still in her cool box and the limes in her backpack. Tonight of all nights, she deserved a *caipirinha*.

Her hut was in darkness and unchanged as she approached the wooden structure on its skinny stilts. She had just placed a foot on the bottom porch steps when something moved beneath the house. With a gasp of fright, Ann reversed several paces, squinting in the dusk. The white shape crept out, swaying in an undulating motion.

"Branca! What are you doing here?"

The dog's tail wagged faster, her haunches rippling from side to side like a samba dancer. Ann crouched, smiling with relief. The animal's instincts had guided her safely. Branca rolled over, lifting one paw to pull Ann's hand to her stomach. She scratched the dog's belly, comforted by the warm body and simple interaction with another living being.

"I guess you'd better come in. I'm not sure what I can feed you, but we'll figure something out. Do you want to stay here tonight and be my guard dog? Then tomorrow I'll take you home. Good girl. You must miss him. I do and I only met him twice. Come on, then, indoors."

Ann found a chipped vase of green glass in one of the kitchen cupboards and used that for her cocktail pitcher. She'd regret drinking more than one *caipirinha* in the morning, but it was one way to guarantee no nightmares. As for the hangover, she'd worry about that tomorrow. She shared her rice and beans in chicken stock with the dog, poured herself a drink and sat at the table, looking out at the moonlit sea. The reassuring hum of the generator and regular ebb and flow of the ocean were interspersed by light snores from the scrawny dog on the rug. The calm induced by the peace and the alcohol made it difficult to recall the blind panic of that morning. Now, rational and only slightly fuzzy from the rough fermented sugarcane, it dawned on her that she'd become complacent. Since losing her pursuers, she'd become comfortable and lazy. Nelson's death woke her up with all the force of a slap in the face.

Nelson. Ann conjured up his face, doing impressions of all the Brazilian soap stars, laughing with his mouth wide open at his own jokes and rolling his eyes when Viviane yelled at him for slacking. He wasn't the best waiter in the world or the most typical kid in the village. He talked to people like her with more enthusiasm than suspicion. When she took his dog back tomorrow, she would try to tease some information from his family or his friends. Someone must know who had cause to hurt Nelson. The thought of someone in Praia do Pesqueiro planning and following through with a murder seemed farcical. But his body lying somewhere on a slab was chilling proof.

Branca sat up with a start, took in her surroundings and yawned, scratching an ear with a hind leg. The evening was warm and humid, mosquito heaven. Ann fetched two more cubes from the ice box and refreshed her drink, her mind running on parallel tracks. It wasn't that she distrusted the local police, exactly, just that murders were rare on this island. Not only that, but 'town' people were regarded with a wary eye by most people from the fishing villages and tourist spots along the coast. Whereas Ann, although far from one of them, was accepted as part of the community. Even with her clumsy language skills, she was better placed to gain confidences and keep secrets.

At the same time, she had to whip herself into shape. Her fitness, her caution, her discipline had all grown lax and that was something she could ill afford. In the morning, she would run and work out. Next week, she'd hitch a lift to town, visit a different Internet café and do some checking, post a rumour on one of the message boards, scour the UK newspapers for any developments and keep herself in the loop. While there was still chatter, she was safe. It was only if it went quiet she needed to worry. The trick was to stay alert. Always stay alert.

She drained the last dregs from her glass, a slice of lime bouncing off her lips. She found an old towel for the dog to sleep on, made sure the windows were closed, the door secured and the machete within reach beside the mattress. Then she cleaned her teeth and stared at herself in the mirror. There was something else beneath the panic she'd felt that morning. A sadness. Earlier that day, she planned to run from this place and never look back. It occurred to her that she really didn't want to leave. She was happy here. Or at least she had been until ten o'clock that morning.

6

D ulce and Ricardo Leal were in the throes of grief and shock, comforted by family members and neighbours. Their reaction to seeing Branca was not that of a doting family welcoming home a beloved pet, but a trigger for more tears and wailing. In the confusion of people and emotions in the small house, Ann struggled to know what to say. Several times she expressed her sorrow for their loss although she doubted anyone heard her. The dog she had come to return slunk through the forest of legs and out the back door. Someone made Ann coffee and another offered her a stool, so she sat, drank and observed.

Dulce, understandably, was a wreck. Her voice raw, her face swollen, she was constantly searching the surrounding faces, reaching for someone's hand and releasing it, restlessly moving from one comfortless embrace to another. She seemed incapable of a coherent sentence, simply calling out a name and asking for her husband, who was never more than two paces away. A girl a couple of years younger than Nelson moved around the room with a tray, collecting empty cups and distributing fresh ones. Her face was pinched and miserable, responding to the constant stream of condolences with a brief nod and a painful attempt at smile. The resemblance between the girl and her parents was unmistakable. Dulce's wide set eyes and Ricardo's high forehead stamped her as a member of the Leal family. Likewise her other siblings, three younger sisters and a small boy, around two years old, who was dragging a plastic hammer around the room. They were a good-looking bunch.

It occurred to Ann that Nelson's colouring may not have been a genetic throwback, but a result of different paternity. Taking on another man's child was quite a task, especially in a small, gossipy village like this. It spoke for Ricardo's character not against. She wondered who she could ask and immediately chastised herself. *None of your business.* She finished her coffee, shook hands with Dulce and Ricardo, and once again expressed her sympathies. Dulce was shaking her head, her hands covering her eyes, so Ricardo escorted Ann to the door. He thanked her politely, his voice hoarse and devoid of emotion. There was nothing more to say. She walked up the road and released a deep sigh, struggling to imagine the family's pain.

A voice called her name. She turned to see Ricardo lighting a cigarette and blowing smoke from the corner of his mouth. He said something she didn't catch and she retraced her steps. He repeated himself, with a nod in the direction of the church.

"*Um oração por a sua alma.*" A prayer for his soul.

Ann assured him with all sincerity that she would pray for Nelson. Ricardo had already forgotten her presence, absorbed in smoking and staring at the dust around his feet.

Returning to the church wouldn't have been Ann's first thought, but after Ricardo's request, she knew it was the right thing to do. The main drag towards the beach was emptier than the previous day although the terrace outside the bakery was already full by eleven o'clock. For a second, she found herself scanning the tables for Nelson's ginger hair, then picked up her pace in the direction of Igregia São João.

Unlike most of the buildings in the village, the church was typically ornate Portuguese architecture with whitewashed walls, two columns either side of the heavy wooden door and windows set high above head height, each framed with little green shutters. On the roof were two small towers, presumably for bells although Ann couldn't recall hearing them. She opened the door and entered the cool, hushed atmosphere. As it was her first visit to the place, she had no idea if the scattering of worshippers among the pews was a normal number or a reaction to the loss of a local lad.

She faced the altar and crossed herself, bowing her head in respect. Below the pulpit stood a glass case containing fake candles. Less of a risk than the real thing and more of an earner for the church, she assumed, then suppressed her cynicism. One said a prayer, inserted a coin and a battery-operated candle would light up in honour of the person's soul. It seemed somehow indecorous to approach the altar wearing a backpack. When she got to the front pew, she slipped the straps from her shoulders and placed it underneath the wooden bench. She said her prayer for Nelson, inserted the coin and watch the glow illuminate the red glass. She gazed at it for several minutes until the sound of approaching footsteps brought her back to the present. She crossed herself again and turned to retrieve her backpack, coming face-to-face with the dead-eyed man in his snakeskin cowboy boots.

She nodded, trying not to show how his appearance disconcerted her and moved out of his way. He did not return her nod, instead half turning to stare at her as she shouldered her backpack and walked up the aisle towards the street. It wasn't her imagination. For whatever reason, that guy was trying to freak her out. Maybe he did that with everyone in an attempt to intimidate the easily influenced. If she'd come across his type in her line of work, she would have taken him on, confronted the arrogant little turd and shown him she was not impressed. This was a different matter. Better just to keep out of his way. The last thing she needed was a clash with a local cockerel.

She shoved open the door, blinking in the harsh sunlight and noticed three of the surfers sitting on the church steps. Her radar twitched as they turned in her direction. They were bored, looking for something to amuse themselves and she was something unusual. This was exactly the kind of situation she could defuse with a wisecrack if she were on a Tower Hamlets estate, because she would have authority on her side. Here, she was a vulnerable woman on her own, an object of interest because of her very foreignness. That could mean trouble.

"*Bom dia,*" she said, and attempted to descend the steps to the road. One of the three uncurled from his lounging position to his full height and stood directly in front of her, blocking her path.

"She does speak Portuguese, Nuno was right. So why haven't you said hello before, lady? We've seen you watching us surf, but you never came to say hi. You just like watching young men, is that right?"

She couldn't see his eyes behind his sunglasses, but she was aware the other two had also got to their feet and come to stand either side of her. One of them was snickering with laughter.

"Well, we don't mind you looking at us. So long as we get to do some looking of our own." He leaned back and gave her an insolent once over. He was trying so hard to be cool and nonchalant, it was laughable. But laughter in the circumstances was a very risky move.

One of the other two turned away and lit a cigarette. "*Deixa ela pra là*, Pedro."

She didn't react but those few words offered hope of a

graceful escape. *Leave her alone, Pedro.* First, he was withdrawing from the sexual intimidation. Secondly, he'd given his mate a name. Names were powerful. And most importantly, he'd shown her the pecking order. Pedro was not number one. That didn't surprise her, because the mouthy show-offs were still jockeying for position. Those secure in their status didn't need to prove it by picking on those weaker than themselves.

"Pleased to meet you, Pedro. Yes, I am impressed by your skills on the surfboard. All of you have far more confidence in the sea than I could ever have. The blonde girl in particular seems to know no fear."

The snickering kid took the bait. "Serena's crazy. In a good way."

Ann smiled at him, turning away from Pedro's sneer. "In a good way, I agree. It must be hard for you, having the beach to yourselves for months and now all the tourists come."

"It has its advantages," said Pedro. "For one thing, there are a lot more hot girls. We like hot girls, especially foreign ones." He reached out a finger to touch her hair and she took a pace backward. Wrong move, she understood that immediately.

"What's the matter? I'm only being friendly. No need to be afraid of me. You know something? I'm curious. Why do you carry that backpack everywhere? Even into church. What have you got in there that's so important? I think it's time we had a look." He leaned to reach behind her.

Time to step up a gear and mark her boundaries. She caught his wrist and pushed his hand away, her grip businesslike.

"One thing you need to learn about women, Pedro. Never look inside a lady's handbag. True, my handbag is bigger than most but the same rule applies. Not even my husband would dare open it without my permission." She flashed a look at her wedding ring and at the blank screen of Pedro's sunglasses.

She'd wrong-footed him, she could see that, and now the ball was in his court. His snickering mate looked from one to the other as if he was watching a tennis match. The third member of the trio broke the tension by spitting a curse. With a turn of speed Ann had not thought possible, the three scattered in different directions and disappeared from view. At the same time, the sound of a motorcycle echoed off the walls of the church.

The bike came from the direction of the beach, heading towards the village. Ann continued down the church steps, keen to outpace her testosterone-fuelled welcoming committee. The bike drove up, spinning reddish dust in its wake and came to a halt right in front of her. The rider switched off the engine, kicked down his stand and stared directly at Ann. Her thought processes followed the same pattern as the previous evening. A motorcycle rider? She only knew one and that was Fátima's boyfriend. He pulled off his helmet and Ann understood why the surfers had fled. Everyone in this village was terrified of the cops.

Gil Maduro wore aviator sunglasses and a biker jacket over a blue shirt. The warmer, drier weather had done nothing for his personality, however. He gave her a stony stare.

"Who were they? The guys you were just talking to?"

"Surfers. I've never met them before but apparently they have seen me. I suppose they were curious, that's all."

The police officer put his sunglasses in his breast pocket and looked directly into her eyes. "They harassed you?"

"No. As I said, they were just asking a few questions. I was in the church, lighting a candle for Nelson, you see. They were here when I came out."

His eyes narrowed. "On their own?"

Somehow, Ann knew exactly what he meant. It was tempting to tell him that while the rats had fled the Pied Piper was still inside. But she had no idea how far the surfers had gone and whether they were still in earshot. She played it safe. "It seemed to be just the three of them, yes. Are you here looking for more evidence, Inspector Maduro?"

Instead of replying, Maduro swung his leg off his motorbike and came to stand below her on the church steps. He leaned his head towards hers and dropped his voice. "I came to see the family of the deceased. Unfortunately, I have bad news. The autopsy confirmed Nelson Leal's death was not an accident. This is now a murder investigation and I'm afraid I will need to ..."

The church door opened and by the expression on the police officer's face, Ann guessed who had come out. Maduro made no move but his entire body hummed with tension, his stare fixed above Ann's head. She looked over her shoulder to see the creep in cowboy boots, his eyes locked on Maduro. The church bells clanged, announcing midday, and broke the moment. The sharp-suited guy sauntered down the church steps and turned in the direction of the beach. The motorcycle cop's eyes never left his back.

"Who is that guy?" asked Ann. "I've seen him more than once."

Maduro replaced his sunglasses and remounted his motorcycle. "That guy is a piece of shit. Keep away from him and his little friends. We need to ask you some more questions, now that this is a case of homicide. Can you come to Soure police station tomorrow after lunch?"

Oh, shit. Remember, you're a helpless, hopeless gringa who knows nothing. "Certainly. Umm, what time exactly is after lunch?"

The officer buckled his helmet and kick-started the bike. "Any time after three." He drove away slowly, weaving his motorcycle between pedestrians, past buffaloes and around potholes. She followed his tracks as far as the bakery and then took a left, treading her familiar path back to the hut.

Her mind occupied with that morning's conversations, she

was more alert than usual to any threats on her journey home and planned for the inevitable confrontations to come. The surf boys were a minor nuisance. If they attempted to play the machismo card again, she would try to banter her way out of it, unless it went too far. Then she would teach one of them, probably Pedro, a punishing lesson. He might be lean, fit and muscular but she doubted he could match her combat training. Only if the worst came to the worst would she use her knife.

The police interview was far more concerning. She was rehearsing some clumsy answers to their inevitable questions when she became aware she had company. Padding along in her footsteps was Branca, still dirty, still wearing her bandana. When she saw Ann had noticed her presence, she wiggled and wagged ingratiatingly, peeling her lips back as if in a cheesy grin.

Ann crouched and stroked the dog's filthy coat. "You have to go home, Branca. I can't look after you. Come, I'm taking you home and this time you have to stay there. Good dog, this way."

Ricardo was in the same spot as Ann had last seen him, but with far more cigarette butts around his feet. Unlike a couple of hours ago, the house was completely silent and empty of all the relatives, neighbours and well-wishers. He lifted his head as she approached, his stare aggressive.

"I brought the dog back. She followed me."

Ricardo's expression sagged. "It's true. They killed him. Someone murdered our son."

"Yes, I saw the police officer. I'm so sorry, Ricardo, for you and your family. Is there anything I can do?"

He didn't reply, staring at the glowing end of his cigarette.

"Of course not." She answered her own question. "There's nothing anyone can do. I'm sorry to disturb you and if you like,

I'll take Branca with me, for the time being. I'll bring her home whenever you want. Goodbye."

Ricardo's voice creaked like the door of the church. "They gave Dulce some tablets. She's sleeping now. That woman loves too much, you know. She loves them all like a mama cat with her kittens, but Nelson? She loved him like a tiger. It was just the two of them against the world before she met me. She carried the scandal of being an unmarried mother and a child who no one could pretend was a Brazilian. He was ugly, God, he was ugly. Red hair, red skin, colourless eyes and the biggest mouth with the biggest scream you ever heard. That kid was back of the queue when they gave out good looks, but he was right at the front when it came to his parents. We loved him, both of us. I married her and took him as my own without a second's hesitation. Nelson has always been my son and I am more his father than anyone else. Sure, the American sends cheques but that's not parenthood. He's not the one who taught the boy how to stand up to bullies, who encouraged him to study for university, who made him into a decent human being. I poured my heart into raising that boy and now both are gone."

Ann swallowed, her throat aching.

"Do you have any cigarettes?" Ricardo asked, in the same deadened tone.

"I don't smoke, but I could get you some?"

He shook his head, went inside and closed the door.

Branca looked up at Ann's face and wagged her tail once.

"OK, *doggita*, you'd better come with me."

7

Nelson's dog follows that Englishwoman out of the village. Guess it has to find food elsewhere now he's gone and everyone knows the Brits are famous for being sentimental about animals. Clever dog.

Serena wraps her arms around her knees and watches their progress, resisting the urge to run after them. As if that's a realistic escape route. She chews the side of her thumb, imagining what she would say, trying to summon the English words. 'Hello lady, I have something for to tell you.' That sounds wrong.

Nelson would have known. He'd always been first in their class at English. She shakes her head. Why does everything today remind her of him? She knows why. Serena presses her hands over her eyes and once again, the scene plays out in horrific detail. She shouldn't have been there; she shouldn't have witnessed what happened. But she was and she had. For the stupidest reason in the world.

When she opens her eyes, Xander and Rubem are strutting down the beach, preparing to surf. The last thing she wants is to be seen and she hunches herself deeper beneath the stilts supporting the bar. Where's Pedro? You never see those two without the third wheel. Locals call them The Three Muske-teers. More like The Three Mosquitoes. None of them could admit the fact she was the best surfer and constantly bugged her with challenges she always won. You'd think they'd learn when they were onto a loser, but that's teenage boys for you. Nelson wasn't like that. He used to talk to her as his equal, even if she was the same age as his younger sister.

Nelson again. A voice inside is sending her a message, loud and clear. She has to tell someone what she witnessed. Her guts contract in terror. Not the police, no way. Cops will make her go to court and be on television and those awful people will find out her name and come back to punish her. A snake in the grass, a snake and a grass, they'll cut out her tongue. Nope, not happening. She can't report it to anyone who can do something for fear of the consequences. A tear escapes and she wipes it away in irritation.

Xander launches himself into the surf, with Rubem right behind. Still no sign of Pedro. The sea's pretty gentle today compared to last week, but every sixth or seventh breaker is worth riding. Her body wants to be out there on her board, her mind cleansed of anything other than the thrills and joys of the ocean. Cleansed, purified and absolved.

Absolution. She has no sins to confess, because all she did was keep quiet and watch. A confession to the priest and she could hand over all responsibility. A flicker of hope lights in her chest and she scrambles out from the stilts towards the rear of the building.

The Englishwoman and the dog are a long way down the strand now, two tiny specks in the heat haze. Serena is glad someone's looking after Branca. He loved that animal. Nelson was a decent guy and she owes it to him to tell the truth. She dodges through the patchwork of light and shade thrown by the food shacks and heads in the direction of the church.

"Serena!" A shout echoes across the beach. Either Xander or Rubem is trying to attract her attention. She pretends not to hear and ducks behind the mescal hut. By the time they get out of the ocean and run up here, she'll be long gone.

She sprints across the sand and only slows when she gets to the road. Her breathing returns to normal, she greets Tia Maria with a wave and by the time she gets to the church, she's calm. At least on the outside. She ascends the steps and reaches out a hand to push the door. It swings open before she can make contact. Standing right in front of her is a cop, carrying a motorcycle helmet, a gun in his belt holster. She moves aside, panic urging her to flee from the enemy, but she stands her ground. The guy nods and continues past her. Behind him comes the priest. He thanks the cop and promises to contact him if any other information comes to light.

After the motorbike drives away, Father Aldo notices her. "Serena, nice to see you. Come inside. Did you want to light a candle for Nelson Leal?"

She swallows. "Yes, please, Father, that's exactly why I'm here."

8

The whole morning Ann had been gone and yet she'd achieved nothing, unable even to return the dog. She corrected herself. No, not nothing, she had said a prayer for Nelson, narrowly missed a run-in with the local hoods and scored herself an invitation to enter a police station. Of all the places she most wanted to avoid, the local cop shop topped the list. For three months she'd managed to keep away from other people and now she was practically a social butterfly. Once again, she wished for the return of the rains.

As they walked through the surf on the way to her hut, she half-heartedly encouraged Branca to get in the water in the hope she might find out what colour the animal was beneath all that grime. The dog trotted alongside but showed no interest in having a swim. Waves rushed over Ann's feet and retreated, over and over, a soothing feeling. The afternoon heat caused her to break into a sweat and the dog had been panting before they left the village. On the approach to the shack, Ann's stomach told her it was past lunchtime and her thoughts turned to beans and rice. There was no white heron on the roof today but one of her markers dangled from the veranda.

With a word, she called the dog to her side and stood two paces from the steps, scrutinising the front door. Whenever she left the building, she tied a length of white cotton across the top step, each end looped around a nail. If someone came to the door, they would break it, as Nuno had done when delivering her mosquito net. But now there was no package at her front door to explain why the length of white cotton was broken and blowing in the breeze. She crouched to look under the stilts and but there was nothing other than sand and shade. Branca took advantage of the latter and flopped beneath the house.

Ann left her backpack beside the dog, crept up the steps and saw the flour on the door handle was smudged. Worse, the sticky tape in the top right hand corner of the door had gone. Not only had someone come onto the veranda and tried the door, but they had somehow entered the house. She stood still for a full five minutes, listening for any sound other than the creak of the palm trees and movements of the sea. Eventually, she took three separate keys from her bundle for each of the locks. They turned as normal and she pushed open the door, taking a step back. The house looked exactly as she left it, but there was only one reason two of her markers had moved. She pressed the door open as far as it would go in case there was someone hiding behind it. Her right hand on her flick knife, she stepped over the threshold.

Behind the curtain between the living area and bedroom was the obvious place for someone to hide. Ann dropped to a crouch in order to check for a pair of legs or someone curled up beneath her cot. Nothing. If the intruder was on top of her cot, she'd be none the wiser. She stood just inside the doorway, listening and taking deep inhalations. No tell-tale aromas of sweat or aftershave were present in the air and she could see from her position there was no one hiding in the tiny bathroom. All the windows seemed secure and the washing-up from her breakfast still lay on the draining board, as she had left it.

Legs bent like a runner in the starting position, Ann pulled back the curtain in one swift move. The mosquito net rippled in response to the sudden movement of air, but it was clear no one was in her bed. The place was empty. Whoever had forced their way in was a professional, leaving almost no trace. Almost. She closed the front door and checked the machete was tucked behind the curtain. It was but facing the opposite way. Ann always placed her weapon with a handle facing left, so she could grab and use it in a second. The knife was propped up behind the door, as always, except the handle now faced right.

Ten minutes later, she had completed a thorough and methodical inventory of her living space. In addition to the outside markers, three internal signs showed her someone had opened her bedroom drawer, removed her suitcase and opened the water tank. The fake floorboard had been lifted and the space beneath disturbed. However the tiles behind the kitchen sink were still in the same pattern and behind them, the gun was exactly where she had left it.

A sound from outside made her freeze until she remembered the dog. She filled a bowl with rainwater and took it out onto the veranda, where Branca drank like a camel. Ann made them both some rice, beans and vegetables and then sat at her dining table, chewing over the implications of her break-in. To open all three locks without causing any damage spoke of a skeleton key and the intruder had been meticulous in covering his or her tracks. Only someone as security conscious and frankly paranoid as herself would notice the tiny traces of another presence. The possibility of a bug crossed her mind which she dismissed just as quickly. She lived alone and was hardly likely to open up about her past to a small grubby canine. She was unlikely to talk about her past to anyone at all.

Branca checked the metal tray for the fifteenth time and, finally convinced not a grain of rice remained, she came to lie at Ann's feet. Less than a minute later, she was on her paws, barking furiously out of the front door. A figure was approaching, hand held high in greeting. Fátima again. Ann calmed the dog and reached up to the kitchen shelf for Fátima's whisky. Whatever her excuse for calling today, retrieving her whisky would undoubtedly be one of them.

She started speaking halfway up the path, before she was even within earshot. "... fool knows a cut like that could go septic and how am I supposed to remember the last time I had a tetanus shot. On top of that, I had to walk home in the rain, bleeding and frightened and worried about you. What are you doing with that mangy animal? And then when I got home, he was passed out drunk on the bed. What if I needed to go to hospital? The man is a waste of oxygen, I don't know why I bother. Tell me what that cop said. He didn't stay long, I saw him leave. Word is you were talking to him again today, outside the church. What was that about? Here, I've brought you a coconut."

Branca sniffed their pink-clad visitor and went outside to check the metal tray one last time.

"Hi, Fátima. Have a seat. Do you want a coffee? You left your whisky here last night, by the way." Ann got to her feet to boil some water.

"I know I did! Because that was the one thing I wanted when I got home, to dull the pain. But no, it was here, on your kitchen table, in front of that cop. There wasn't even any beer because that mutton-headed lump drank it all. What's this? You don't need to mark the bottle! Hell, Ann, I don't know much about you but I trust you not to drink my Scotch."

Ann's head snapped around and she reached out for the bottle. Sure enough, there was a black line beside the label, marking just above the current level. She hadn't done that. What puzzled her is why anyone else would bother. Unless they intended to come back. She was about to make a breezy excuse to Fátima but the woman was already on to the next subject.

"So now they're investigating murder. You know what this means? They'll be sniffing round the village, poking into our business, asking questions that have nothing to do with the death of Nelson Leal. I mean, I feel sorry for the kid of course, but this is something we could do without, especially in the tourist season. Is that what the cop wanted? To quiz you about finding the body? But you didn't even know Nelson had been killed, did you? It was me who told you that. Don't tell me you're feeding that scabby mutt, it will never leave you alone. Come on, tell me what he said."

Ann placed two coffee cups on the table. "Not much. He asked how long I've been here, if I knew Nelson personally and how long I'm planning to stay. When I met him outside the church this morning, he asked me to go into Soure tomorrow to answer more questions. You know what, I wish I'd never gone to see what was the matter with that dog."

"Tomorrow? We can go together. Shithead has the week off so I'm taking his motorbike and going shopping. You can ride pillion. Normally you could sit in the sidecar but I'm taking two sacks of coconuts to sell to the tourists and I plan to fill it with groceries on the way home. What time do you have to be there?" She poured some whisky into her coffee and offered the bottle to Ann.

"Not for me, thanks. Sometime after three. I'd appreciate a lift because it gets pretty muggy in the afternoons. I'll give you some money for gasoline. Fátima, were you at home this morning? You didn't see anyone coming down this end of the beach, did you?"

She stopped in the act of screwing the bottle top. "Why? Did something happen?"

"No, nothing happened. There were footprints in the sand. I thought maybe somebody came up the path, looking for me."

Fátima downed her coffee in two gulps. "If they did, they came from the jungle. I was on the porch all morning and I didn't see anyone." She got to her feet and shoved the whisky bottle into her handbag. "Come up to my place at three tomorrow and we'll go into Soure. Don't worry about gasoline, it's the least that useless chimp can do. I wouldn't say no if you wanted to buy me a beer for doing the driving, though. Hey, we could go somewhere fancy, like one of the hotel bars! I'm gonna put on something extra special because you never know who you might meet. See you at three and remember what I said about feeding that bloody dog. *Tchau.*"

"*Tchau.*" Ann watched her go down the path, her flip-flops slapping against her feet. Ann stared at the horizon for a long time, working through the implications of someone entering her shack, inspecting her belongings and leaving a mark on the whisky bottle. The whisky wasn't the only alcohol in the house. She moved aside a bottle of oil to find the cachaça she bought last week. It was around a third empty and nowhere could she see any kind of mark. Why would anyone want to know how much whisky she drank?

9

Branca was an outdoor dog, perfectly happy to sleep under the stilts but equally at home dozing beside Ann's feet. The question was, how would she react to being locked indoors while Ann travelled to the city? It was a risk Ann decided to take. If, as she suspected, the person accessing her house yesterday was Inspector Gil Maduro, he would be unable to return today as he had an interview to conduct. If the intruder was someone else, they might think twice about entering the building with the dog in situ. The one inarguable fact about Branca was that she had quite a bark. Ann left her water and some stale bread, secured the hut and arranged her security markers before trekking up the beach towards Fátima's place.

For someone who had sworn off contact with people, Ann was curious to meet the boyfriend, after the number of insults Fátima had aimed at the guy. When she got to the house, however, only Fátima was present, cramming far too many laundry sacks into the cigar-shaped sidecar. In their short acquaintance, Ann had grown accustomed to Fátima's tendency towards highly coloured clothes. Today, her outfit took bright to a new level. Her miniskirt was swirls of purple, pink and blue, with a cerise blouse knotted over a yellow vest. Instead of her floral Havaianas, she wore denim wedges on her feet. She lifted her head from cursing at the sidecar and gave Ann's cotton trousers and green T-shirt a contemptuous look.

"You look like you're going to do military service. Listen, I can't fit all these in here. We'll have to carry one bag between us on the bike. Just hold tight to me. Are you ready?"

Ann could have sworn the last time she travelled to Soure in the back in Zé's truck, the journey had taken around fifteen minutes. Yet with Fátima driving the bike, they were downtown in ten. The laundry sack filled with green coconuts wedged between Fátima's back and Ann's chest could have contained live animals as it seemed hell bent on trying to escape. Hanging on to the sack with one hand and Fátima's waist with the other, Ann battled cramp, nerves and fear for her life on particular bends. She told herself this was a good thing and it would take her mind off her upcoming police interview. Even so, she exhaled a huge shaky sigh of relief when the bike finally came to a halt.

"Give me that. I have business to do while you talk to the police. Meet me here at five o'clock and we're having cocktails at Hotel Mesquite. God knows if they'll let you in looking like a refugee. Good luck and tell that cop he can go screw himself." She dragged the laundry bag up the path to the nearest building, which to Ann's eyes, looked derelict.

The police station was two streets away and Ann was in no hurry. She stopped off at a supermarket for some essentials, including dog food. Purchases stowed in her backpack, she dragged her heels up the street and presented herself for interview. No one was at the unmanned reception desk and not a sound came from behind the four closed doors. Ann compared the abandoned building to her open-plan workplace in

London, with its incessant jangle of ringing telephones and shouted conversations across the office.

While she stood there debating what to do next, a woman carrying a bucket of water crossed the garden. On hearing Ann's enquiry, she scrunched up her face as if offended and jerked a thumb at the side of the building. Without a word, she proceeded on her way. Ann followed the none-too detailed instructions and found a tarpaulin stretched like a roof over the rear garden. Beneath it lay four water buffalo, chewing the cud. Beside them sat two uniformed officers in plastic chairs, smoking and listening to a football match on the radio. She introduced herself and asked for Inspector Maduro.

They shook their heads. "He's not here," said the first.

"Come back tomorrow," added the second.

"Tomorrow? Inspector Maduro wanted to speak to me today regarding the murder at Praia do Pesqueiro."

The name of the village had a galvanising effect. Both men got to their feet, apologising and escorting her into the shade of the building. They sat her at a table in a small room, brought her a bottle of water and promised to be with her as soon as possible. She waited twenty-five minutes before they returned, now wearing police baseball caps, carrying notebooks and a tape recorder.

"Inspector Maduro has been called away on a matter of extreme urgency, but Officer Basio and myself, Officer Nestor, are ready to take your statement."

Ann recognised bluster when she saw it, but pretended to be humbled. "That's very kind of you. Please excuse me, I don't speak good Portuguese. But I brought a dictionary for when I don't know the words."

"We understand. Take your time."

The interview was polite, thorough and took over an agonising hour. Every few minutes, Ann wondered where Gil Maduro might be and whether Branca would keep him at bay.

She gave the junior officers detailed answers, relying on her dictionary when her vocabulary failed her. In a way, that was a good thing. Professional focus on the salient points of interest made her a little too efficient a witness for your average beach-dwelling hippie. Her linguistic fumblings masked her expertise. The Soure cops were patient, even a little patronising, which suited Ann very well. It was obvious she could help no further, so when the questions dried up, she waited patiently for them to let her go. Eventually they did so, reminding her to think very hard about her answers and if she remembered anything else to contact them immediately. The older of the two asked how she was getting home.

"My neighbour has a motorcycle. She gives me a ride and we go home together. I'm sorry I can't be more helpful and I apologise for my bad Portuguese. I wish you a good afternoon."

Her relief at escaping the police station washed over her like fresh air and she walked the two streets to Fátima's parking spot with a light step. It was almost five and she was ready for a beer or why the hell not, a cocktail. When she got to the place where she had disembarked what seemed like three hours earlier, there was no sign of the bike. She walked up and down the street in case she'd mistaken the building, but while motor-cycles were present, not one was accompanied by a sidecar.

A voice from under a palm tree made her start. "I told your friend not to wait. I'm driving you home." Gil Maduro was leaning against the trunk in his blue shirt and aviator shades.

"Why would you do that?"

"Because I want to talk to you."

"Oh, really? I came to the police station for an interview, prepared to give you a full statement. Apparently, you were too busy and yet you're hanging around here, interfering with my plans to go for cocktails with my neighbour." She reined in her irritation. She'd already said too much and far too fluently.

He straightened up and took off his sunglasses with a

shrug. "I had something else to do. My colleagues took good care of you, I'm sure. Have dinner with me tonight." His voice contained no question intonation.

The inspector asking her out was something she had not expected. Immediately her suspicions were aroused. Was he seeking female company or did he plan to interrogate her when her guard was down? Either way, she didn't want to find out.

"I'm sorry, not tonight. I need to get home." She watched his face for a reaction, wary of provoking any hostility.

His indifferent mask didn't slip an inch. "Of course you do. The least I can do is buy you that cocktail. Did you have a bar in mind?"

She regretted having such a big mouth. "I didn't, but my neighbour suggested Hotel Mesquite."

"That doesn't surprise me. Mesquite is pretentious and overpriced. I have a better idea." He replaced his aviator sunglasses and opened the door of a black Jeep. "Let's drink a martini and I'll take you home."

Pousada Figueira lay on the route out of the city. A collection of palm-thatched cottages surrounded a central building with an air-conditioned restaurant, swimming pool and chic-looking cocktail bar. Ann ordered a Buck's Fizz, conscious of the fact it contained plenty of orange juice and ice. Her companion opted for a vodka martini with a twist. They sat with their backs to the bar, looking out over the pool.

"I'm sure you can't say very much at this stage, but I hope you're making progress in finding who killed Nelson Leal," Ann began. "His parents are completely devastated and I can understand why. He was a nice kid, popular with everyone."

"Not everyone, obviously." Maduro's attention was on the pool, watching a young family playing in the shallow end. The seconds ticked past and Ann sipped at her cocktail, waiting for him to respond.

Finally she broke the silence. "You said you wanted to talk to me?"

"Yes. I wanted to talk to you. Why does a woman like you come to our region to live in that awful hut? And why was it you who found the dead boy in the water?"

Her defences up, she was about to speak before she noticed his body language. When probing a witness, a good cop watches for a reaction. Maduro's eyes roamed over the gardens, as if his heart wasn't in it. Perhaps his professional interest in her was anything but.

"I'm a poet, looking for peace, quiet and inspiration."

"Yes, we've all heard your story."

He didn't seem disposed to say any more and Ann could see no way to advance her opening gambit. She waited, watching the play of sunlight on the clean water of the pool. More clients arrived at the bar, mostly tourists starting their evening's entertainment with a sundown cocktail. A man with a heavy paunch stood next to Maduro and ordered a round of beers in English. As he waited for the barman to pour glasses of Antartica, he turned to them with a friendly smile.

"Beautiful evening."

Something about the tension in Maduro's face made Ann act on impulse. She gave the man an insipid smile and said, "*Desculpa. Não falo inglês.*" She slipped off the stool, scooped up her cocktail and beckoned Maduro. After a second's hesitation, he picked up his martini glass and followed. They walked along a *calçada* path to some tables shaded by umbrellas. At this end of the pool, there were no chatty tourists or anyone else to disturb their conversation. Ann moved a chair to face away from the hotel, to admire the view and the sunset.

"Why did you tell him you don't speak English?" he asked.

"It's a bad habit. When I'm abroad, I always avoid people from my own country."

Maduro's chair faced the pool so that he and Ann were sitting side-by-side yet facing one another. From a security perspective, the arrangement was optimal. No one could approach without being seen by one or the other. For the first time, Ann was able to look at the man from an objective view-point rather than from the defensive perspective of her own fears. He was older than her, she estimated, by a couple of years. Or maybe the sun and stress had added those lines around his mouth and forehead. His skin was the colour of cork, not brown, not beige but that warm place in between. He had good bone structure and a smile made more alluring by its rarity. But the energy emanating from his eyes was what made him attractive. Not that *she* was attracted, but it was clear how he could lure in someone more vulnerable.

His eyes bored into hers for a second, then flicked away. "You lit a candle for the Leal boy. That's a nice gesture. Are you a Catholic?"

"I don't subscribe to any religion. His father asked me to say a prayer for his soul, so I did. If it's meant from the heart, I don't think my lack of faith matters. Regarding Nelson, wouldn't it be more likely he was killed because of some involvement – or lack of it – in a drug-related local business?"

"Ah, you mean because of Mauricio Gonçalves? You saw him in the church?"

Her mind replayed the encounter with the guy in the sharp suit at the altar. "His name is Mauricio? Yeah, it suits him. He came up behind me while I was praying and gave me the Big Dick Stare."

Maduro exhaled a laugh through his nostrils. "The what?"

Ann demonstrated, imitating the man's sneer and overt stare over his shoulder as she had walked away.

"That's a pretty good impression," He gave another quiet

laugh. "No, I don't believe the Gonçalves family have anything to do with this case. They grow and sell marijuana from the family farm. We turn a blind eye, because the old guy has always traded the stuff like any other crop. He was also generous to the community. Rui Gonçalves was a decent man. In a way, I was sad to hear he'd died."

Ann thought about the surf kids following Snakeskin Boots around like puppies. "The police turn a blind eye to a drug dealer? Really?"

Maduro rested his chin on his fist. "If you have a free afternoon next week, maybe you could stop by the station and give us your professional poet's opinion of how else we can improve law enforcement on this island. As I said, my focus is on a different angle. We're not looking for a local."

"And why would that be?"

He gazed into his martini and she knew better than to try and fill the silence. Eventually he twisted to face her. "What do you know about Franck Fischer? Son of the famous Cinthia Fischer."

The name drew a blank, even though Ann gave it serious consideration. "Nothing. I don't think I've heard of either. That name doesn't sound very Brazilian."

"Oh, she's definitely Brazilian. One of Pará's most famous exports. A very savvy woman who made the most of her family's money, married strategically and when her husband died, she invested his fortune into mining. She is one of the richest and most influential women in South America. Her son is spoilt, arrogant and I believe, dangerous. Someone reported seeing his boat upriver the day Leal died."

Ann absorbed that information, her gaze on the lilac skies. "I'm not sure I see the connection."

He took a sip of his martini and tightened his focus from the pool area to her face. "Yes, that's true. I asked you a question but provided no context. Are you really a poet?"

"I'm striving to be. The context?"

"The context is nothing more than circumstance. We're pursuing a line of enquiry, that's all. How's your cocktail?"

His evasive offer-and-dodge strategy was beginning to irritate. "Refreshing. Do you have reason to believe the Fischer woman or her son had something to do with Nelson's death?"

"Yes, I have reasons. I'd like nothing better than to see that odious little shit in jail. But with no witnesses willing to testify, that's not going to happen. Where did you learn Portuguese?"

She reminded herself to speak less and listen more. She evaded the question. "I've always been good at languages. Witnesses to what?"

He assessed her for a moment and seemed to make a decision. "After an anonymous tip-off, we impounded Fischer's boat in the harbour this afternoon. Forensics found Leal's hair and fingerprints aboard."

Ann was already thinking like a prosecutor. "Circumstantial. He might have joined one of their parties."

"He might. Let me tell you something about young Mr Fischer. Two years ago, a sixteen-year old girl died in the Caixuanã Forest. Locals saw her leave a bar with Fischer and his friends and two days later, she was found hanging from a tree. The case went to a tribunal but collapsed due to every witness pulling out."

Ann said nothing, trying to see where this was going.

"This happened only eight months after Fischer and another member of his fraternity were charged with causing a fellow student's death in an initiation ritual. The boy who died was seventeen and the only black member of that house. Both the accused were acquitted by an all-white jury."

The pieces of his story began to interlock. "The girl was ..."

"Her father was one of the indigenous Kayapó people. Her mother was white. What would a poet make of this, Ann Sheldon?" His tone was calm and precise with an underlying strain.

She considered both sides of the fence and sat in the middle. "Hazing or any other all-male initiation ceremonies often go too far. No one wants to be the weak link and say stop. On the other hand, if there was a racial agenda ..."

"The racial agenda is in no doubt. Early interviews in both cases tell of a tribunal, where Fischer and his friends pronounce judgement on someone's ethnicity and sentence them to death. All witnesses withdrew their statements or refused to testify in the months leading up to the trial. Franck Fischer is a psychotic right-wing megalomaniac who murders people who don't fit his vision when he has an opportunity. His mother's money and position ensures he doesn't get caught. My belief is he objected to Nelson Leal's parentage, tried him and threw him overboard."

Ann listened to the facts and the spaces between. She kept her tone soft. "You know a lot about him, Inspector. Neither of those incidents happened on your patch."

He shook his head. "No. But this incident did."

Ann reverted to innocent foreigner. "I'm no expert, but aren't the reasons behind real crimes usually less glamorous? Mundane things like money, gang-related, getting involved – or refusing to – with the wrong people. Psychopathic murderers are the exception, even if the media make us believe the opposite."

"You forgot one of the most mundane reasons to kill some-body. Hatred."

They sat in silence for several minutes until Ann ventured one last attempt. "If you believe he's got away with that twice, can you make this one stick?"

"Yes, I believe I can. Or maybe I saw it in a dream. Would you like another?" Her champagne and juice was almost empty and with one last gulp, he drained his martini.

She considered the pull of sitting in relaxing surroundings, enjoying a drink and stimulating conversation, but was wary of the trap. Maduro had given a lot away and would expect her to open up in return.

"That's very kind of you but I really should get home. Thank you for the drink and for your company. It was unexpected but very pleasant."

His gaze fell on her backpack. "Yes, of course. Your groceries need to be cooled. Let's go. The Jeep's too heavy to drive along the beach, but I can take you to the village. Do you feel safe down there in that little shack?"

She followed him past the pool and out to the car park. "I'm pretty security conscious. Where do you live?"

He started the vehicle and the lights illuminated a burst of red flowers growing up the wall of the building. "Soure, while I'm working. What do you think of it?"

"Like nowhere else I've ever been," she replied, truthfully. "Brazil is full of surprises."

They drove in silence to the village, the embrace of warm and fragrant evening air coming through the windows. On entering the village, Ann noticed the resentful glares and suspicious glances at the police vehicle. Maduro drove to the end of the track where it met the beach and turned off the engine.

"Two things you should know. Drugs, by which I don't mean growing weed, come under the remit of the Polícia Federal. We can't go after Gonçalves and he knows it. The second thing is that I plan to take Franck Fischer in for questioning and charge him with the murder of Nelson Leal. If you're interested, check out his history." Maduro exhaled as if he'd just got something off his chest. "Do you want me to walk you home?"

"That's not necessary, thanks. I live here and I'm used to it. I appreciate the drink and the lift. It was interesting talking to you." She clambered out of the Jeep, reluctant to meet his eyes until there was a good distance between them. "Goodnight, Inspector Maduro."

"Call me Gil. Goodnight, Ann." He started the engine and reversed up the track.

She couldn't see his face over the glare of the headlights but waved anyway, before heaving her pack onto her shoulders and beginning the trek to the shack.

10

The moon rose over the sea, a friendly guiding light as she tramped along the shore, closer to the waves where the sand was firmer. She was hungry and more than a little concerned about Branca. In the dunes, a fire was burning. The strains of guitar music drifted down the beach and a gust of male laughter followed girlish squeals and giggles. Teenagers kicking back and relaxing after a day on their surfboards, she imagined. Ann could make out the lights of Fátima's place and quickened her pace, eager to get home. From the bonfire, two shadows scrambled down the beach in her direction.

"*Olá, Ann. Tudo bem?*"

The voice and its informal address were familiar. She recalled the surf boys on the steps of the church. A cocky one called Pedro, his leader who had only said a few words, and a sniggering sidekick. These were the latter two, although it was impossible to see their faces in the moonlight.

"*Olá.* I'm fine, and you? Good surf day?"

"The best." The two young men fell into step with her, one

either side. "We showed the city kids how to do it, right, Rubem?"

"Yeah. We shamed them." His nose-laugh sounded like some vaguely remembered cartoon character. "They won't come back in a hurry."

"Why don't you come have a beer with us?" asked the first guy, who clearly held the authority. "We like to get to know our neighbours."

Ann didn't break stride. "One of these days I will, thank you. I'm not usually one for socialising but a beer on the beach sounds like a great idea. Not tonight, though. I have plans. Hey, I didn't catch your name. This is Rubem, your friend is Pedro and you are?"

"Xander." He took three rapid paces ahead and whipped around to face her. "Listen to me, lady. We invited you to drink a beer because you need some friendly advice. This is a message from Mauricio. We don't like the friends you keep. Hanging out with cops is not cool. Bringing them to the beach is not cool. You hear me?"

Rubem stood right behind her, preventing her from taking a step away from Xander's aggressive finger. Her whole body tensed, ready to protect herself and her backpack.

"I hear you. The truth is I'd rather crawl over broken shells than talk to the police, but I found the body, remember? Today I gave a statement and now they'll leave me alone."

Xander lit a cigarette, the flame lighting his face for a second. His eyes didn't leave hers. "I hope so. For your sake." He blew out smoke in a stream towards the sky. "*Boa noite.*" He pushed past, bumping into her shoulder despite the acres of empty beach around them.

The soft crunch of feet on sand told her Rubem was retreating, leaving her alone on the shore.

"*Boa noite,*" she called and continued on her route. Twice she slowed to listen for following footsteps and once looked over her right shoulder. The two shapes were not making for the fire in the dunes as she had expected, but heading in the direction of Fátima's place. She watched as they called out a greeting and Fátima, with much noise and enthusiasm, welcomed them onto her porch.

When she reached her own shack, Branca welcomed Ann with twice the enthusiasm and a tenth of the noise. There was no mess on the floor and no signs of any intruders. She let the dog out to roam while putting her purchases away, worrying about the close-knit village and her own role as troublemaker. Once again, she considered the benefits of an early departure, while boiling water for spaghetti. She heated canned meatballs and when Branca returned, emptied a can of dog biscuits onto the metal tray. The dog wolfed the food, her tail keeping up a constant wag. Ann ate her own meal on the porch, processing the events of the day. Once fed, the two sat facing the night ocean, satiated and comfortable in each other's company.

Maduro had set off several chains of thought by raising the idea of the cannabis farmer. If the old guy had died and his son harboured ambitions to be an arriviste baron in Class A drugs, he'd have to find a market. Beach villages like Praia do Pesqueiro during rainy season were a waste of time, but when all those rich and idle youngsters poured in, that was a different matter. During the summer, demand would skyrocket and Gonçalves could supply. The missing link was his sales force. His presence around the village on market day was as a recruiter, Ann was convinced, and the surfing teens had stepped up. She recollected Mauricio's attempt to convene his troops on the terrace of the bakery and Viviane's forceful refusal.

Drug lords, just like any other organised criminals, demanded absolute loyalty from their distribution chain. There were two ways to guarantee that. One, a performance-related bonus, probably more money than these kids could earn in a year's worth of bar-tending or hawking fish. Two, abject terror of what the boss would do when crossed. Someone would be made into an example, summarily executed as a warning to the foot soldiers. Killed in front of them or the body discovered in full view for all to see the consequences. No wonder Ann had quailed when she saw Nelson's bound hands. It was a message, but her immediate assumption she was the intended recipient was possibly wide of the mark. The question remained, why Nelson? Was he targeted due to Viviane's public display of aggression? Or was her assumption correct – he'd refused to join the ranks of the new recruits?

In Maduro's shoes, that would be her main line of enquiry. Yet he seemed more interested in some rich playboy kid. The obvious gap in his reasoning was motive. She didn't buy Maduro's racial angle. If the speedboat had mown down a swimmer or the truck run over an unfortunate villager, Franck Fischer could be charged with manslaughter, but Ann could see no reason why a trust-fund teen would cynically murder a local waiter. Unless Maduro wasn't telling her everything. *Check out his history.* How was she supposed to do that?

One other comment, composting away in her subconscious, floated to the surface in Ricardo's agonised voice. *Sure, the American sends cheques but that's not parenthood.* Whoever had fathered Nelson was still taking financial responsibility for the boy. If, as Ricardo had said, Nelson intended to go to university, would the biological father be expected to foot the bill? The child's death would certainly release him from any claims on his cash, but after paying for seventeen years, why kill him or have him killed now? It didn't stack up, and Ann wished she knew a little more about the circumstances. The one person who might be able to tell her was Fátima. She pondered the surfers' visit and how they seemed to be old friends as Fátima had greeted them by name. Better trust no one, ask no questions and keep out of it all. It was, she told herself for the hundredth time, none of her business.

She went inside, Branca at her heels, and was about to pour herself a nightcap when she remembered the black line on the whisky bottle. *Think it through*, she told herself. *Why would anyone need to know how much you drink?* As she performed her usual checks of windows, doors, machete and folded a towel to serve as a dog bed, she posited several theories. One, it was a gesture designed to scare her, suggesting the intruder could and would return. So why so subtle a mark? Two, someone wanted to measure her alcohol consumption, perhaps to judge when her reaction times might be impaired. And then what? Three, the contents of the bottle might already contain something other than alcohol and the reason for the mark was simply to indicate how much it had taken to kill or incapacitate. She left the cachaça where it was and brewed an infusion of *jambú* leaves instead. As promised, the 'toothache plant' delivered a citrusy tingle with numbing after-effects.

She was dozing off under the net, listening to Branca's snores and the nocturnal sounds of the jungle when her eyes opened wide. If the cachaça had been doctored, so had the whisky. Tomorrow she would check on Fátima, make sure she'd suffered no unpleasant reactions and ask a few casual questions about her friendship with the surfers. That is if her tongue had recovered by morning.

Ann jolted upright, gasping at the unexpected noise. Branca was on her feet, barking the same urgent alarm call which had drawn her to the river and Nelson's body. Silvery rays lit the sky although the sun was yet to breach the horizon. In a pause where the dog took breath, Ann heard male voices approaching. She dressed in a hurry, now fully awake and ready to deal with dawn visitors. When footsteps creaked on the porch and knuckles rapped on the door, Branca went into overdrive. Ann put one hand on the dog's bandana and the other grasped her machete.

"Hush, Branca, hush now." She raised her voice to an authoritative, confident level. "Who is it?" she called, in Portuguese.

"Ricardo Leal. I have someone here who wants to meet you. It's early, I know, but he doesn't have much time."

Ann opened the door, releasing Branca to greet her owner. The dog stood, stiff legged, growling and licking her teeth in a manner so alarming that both men reversed down the steps. It seemed she had taken Ann's guard dog suggestion to heart.

"Just stay there a moment, I'll put her inside and make coffee. It's warm enough to drink it on the porch." She looked down at the two men hovering at the bottom of the steps. The man with Ricardo was tall and well-built, with strawberry blond hair and teeth which must have cost him several thousand dollars. His smile was uncertain but his stance humble, as if apologising for his very presence.

Ann guided the dog over the threshold and gave her a reassuring pat. She boiled some water, made coffee and took the pot with three cups out onto the veranda. Ricardo was leaning against the railing while the man in the suit sat in her chair. On seeing her, he scrambled to his feet.

"Sorry, I'm in your seat. You speak English, right? My Portuguese is lousy as Ricardo will confirm. Let me help you with that. The name's Mike Ferguson and I am Nelson's biological father."

He took the tray from Ann and placed it on the wooden table. Then he held out a hand.

She shook it. "Ann Sheldon, pleased to meet you." She switched to Portuguese. "Ricardo, you want some coffee?"

Ricardo lit a cigarette. "Yeah, coffee's fine. You need to listen to this guy. He's got money and he can make things happen, OK? Speak English, I don't mind, I know what he wants to say." He took a cup of black coffee and went to sit at the top of the steps. Branca came out of the house, paced daintily around him and wandered down the path towards the beach.

The American took up Ricardo's position against the railing and faced Ann. His expression was worn and tense but he made a real effort at imbuing his smile with warmth. "We woke you. I'm sorry about that. I wouldn't normally call on someone at this early hour, but I have a flight to catch. Ricardo and Dulce think you can help, so I came down the beach to throw myself on your mercy. You're from England, right?"

"I'm a Brit, yes, and your accent says you come from the United States. I don't imagine you want my life story any more than I want yours. Why do you think I can help and with what?"

He took a sip of coffee and even his polite veneer couldn't disguise his revulsion. He replaced the cup and tried another smile. "I know you don't want my life story but I'm gonna give you an executive summary. For no other reason than it's relevant. Eighteen years ago, I came here on spring break to surf, drink too much and flirt with pretty girls. Dulce was young, beautiful and spoke some English. Yeah, we had a holiday romance." He glanced at Ricardo, whose focus was on the sea. "We kept in touch for a while, sending postcards and pretending we had a future. Then she told me she was pregnant. I offered to support her in whatever decision she wanted to take. The way I see it, she took the bravest route of all, having the baby and bringing him up alone. She endured the toughest time. I supported her financially but no way is that the same thing as being a parent. In real terms, Ricardo has always been Nelson's father."

Ricardo looked over his shoulder and gave Ferguson a nod of acknowledgement. He flicked his cigarette butt high into the air and strode off down the path. When he got to the beach, he met Branca on her return journey. He spoke to the animal and patted his leg, but Branca ignored him completely and trotted in the direction of Ann's shack. Ricardo shrugged, waved a hand at the veranda and trudged along the beach in the direction of the village.

"He's a good man. Nelson's death just about broke the guy."

Ann nodded her agreement, deleting Mike Ferguson's name from her list of suspects. *Suspects? Who did she think she was?* "I know and they have my sympathies. Mr Ferguson, I'm not sure how you think I can help. To be honest, I came here to retreat from the world and turn my focus inward. I'm sure it sounds esoteric and self-indulgent to you, but it's the way I want to live my life. One thing I don't want to do is get dragged into a situation which has nothing to do with me. It's already brought trouble to my doorstep."

Mike Ferguson massaged the bridge of his nose. "Call me Mike. You know something? Circumstances don't necessarily fall into line with what we want. I'd like to be sitting in my air-conditioned office in Austin, smiling at Nelson's graduation photograph and signing another check. But I'm here, in a country where I don't speak the language and everyone but Dulce and Ricardo treats me like the devil incarnate. All I want is to find out what happened to that boy. Nobody in this village trusts the police. Whether that's justified or not, I have no idea. What I do know is the police are my only hope of catching Nelson's killer. Ricardo tells me you're in contact with the local detective. I'm not a wealthy man, Ann, but I'd be willing to hire you as my agent on the ground. You're someone who can communicate with the cops, put pressure on these guys not to let this slide and keep me in the loop. It's vitally important to me. That was a disgusting, unjustified murder and I want to know who's responsible. Can I count on you?"

Seagulls and other water birds formed an operatic chorus behind a returning fishing boat. The sun broke over the horizon, lighting up the beach like a supernova. The jungle erupted into voluble life, announcing the day with screeches, calls, songs and howls. Ann tried to see the scene through Mike Ferguson's eyes. Nature at its most fecund and alive was impressive but intimidating.

Can I count on you? The American had no idea how those words twisted Ann's emotions. The answer was no. She was a liar, a deceiver, a quisling and a deserter. As reliable as British weather and about as uplifting. Pages and pages of her repeated and half-believed story blew away like cobwebs, revealing the truth about why she'd run to a run-down shack at the end of a beach on remote island in rainy season. She deserved nothing better. Her hermit-like existence was a self-inflicted punishment. Until people, like mosquitoes, made their way through her flimsy defences and pierced her flesh.

This man had no claim on her loyalty simply because they spoke the same language. She owed him and Nelson's family nothing. The whole point of hiding was to remain concealed, not thrust oneself into the spotlight. To stick her head above the parapet now could mean a sniper's bullet, a knife between her ribs or plastic ties around her wrists and a dip in the river. And yet, unravelling a puzzle was in her DNA. She made a decision, knowing she'd regret it.

"Mike, like you, I want to know what happened. Nelson was a good kid and I feel for his family. You can't hire me, I'm afraid, because then I am beholden to you and all I want is to keep my head down and go about my business. What I do promise is to listen. If I hear anything, I'll pass it on. It's not much, because I only have an hour at the Internet café once a week. Even so, I commit to sharing everything I find. That will have to suffice. When is your flight?"

"An Internet café? You're kidding, right?" He checked his

expensive timepiece. "Look, I gotta go. Marajó is incredibly difficult, don't you think? It takes two days to get to this place and another two days to get home. It's not just the language, the weather, the insects and all, but the fact we're outsiders. What the heck brought you here, Ann, I can't imagine. OK, if you won't accept a stipend, I'm gonna gift you a tablet. Set yourself up with an email address and do what you need to do to send me a daily update. I guess you'll need a phone too. There's no way you're getting a Wi-Fi signal all the way out here."

"I don't want a phone or a tablet, Mike. That's exactly what I'm ..."

"Hiding from?"

"Leaving behind. I'm off grid and want to stay that way."

"I get it. It won't be for long, just till they find who did it. Ann, I'm asking for your help. You're my only route in and I'm relying on you. Here's how you can get a hold of me." He took a card from his shirt pocket and tucked it under the tomato plant. "Someone killed my boy and I want justice. Thanks for the coffee."

Ann was still considering her response when Mike Ferguson creaked away down the steps, sweat patches visible on his shirt. As she watched him trudge up the beach, something floated into her vision, settling on the top step. A long white feather. The heron often left less welcome deposits after its visits, but this one was pure and perfect. She picked it up and played the tip across her fingers. White feathers meant different things to people. Her dad believed they were tokens from your guardian angel or a reminder of a lost loved one. Ever-practical Katie would say it was something discarded by a bird with no more significance than a strand of hair. To Ann, a white feather represented a symbol of shame and cowardice.

No more than she deserved.

11

For two days, Serena has feigned a stomach-ache, so she can hide from everyone. The only person she sees is her mother, who makes no secret of her impatience. *What did you eat? Drink more tea, that's the best. A walk would do you good. Hanging round the house all day, you could at least help with the chores. Dolores is at the door, why don't you say hello? If you're not better tomorrow, I'm bringing in Tia Maria.*

On the third day, Serena is no closer to making a decision, but claustrophobia is making her feel genuinely sick. She has to get outside. As the sun rises, she throws on shorts and T-shirt over her bikini, grabs her board and runs down to the beach. Dawn patrol: the only time of day when she can have the place to herself. It's not right, surfing alone; she should have a buddy in case something happens. But other people muddle her head and she needs clarity. She gazes out over the ocean and asks the gods to help her choose the right course.

Someone must make them pay, but neither the police nor the church can be trusted. Every possible scenario has more downsides than up. An anonymous note is pointless because she has no proof other than what she saw with her own eyes.

She's the only evidence, which means exposing herself. How to see justice served without getting involved? Three days she's fretted over the problem and hit nothing but walls. She wishes with all her heart she hadn't been there, but how else will the world know what they did to Nelson?

She steps out of her shorts and T-shirt, tossing them on her Havaianas and clips the leash to her ankle. The waves are pleased to see her, caressing her legs with cool water and sea foam bubbles while the spray fills her nose. This is home. She bodysurfs a kilometre out, with no one to call her a clam-dragger, welcoming the thud of each breaker over her board. Hair and skin wet and energised, she watches the swell and chooses her moment.

No one taught her how to surf, at least not that she can remember. It came naturally, as if by instinct. A set builds and she readies herself, crouching, left foot forward, until the bomb breaks. Nowhere near big enough to barrel, she opts to catch it and go off the top, riding the lip as long as the momentum lasts. The exhilaration and concentration takes her out of herself, her mind focused on the here and now, working every muscle to ride the wave.

For twenty minutes, she catches and carves breaker after breaker, aware of nothing but the moment. When she spots figures arriving on the beach, she drags the board back to shore, relinquishing her solo status. Lounging by a palm tree is Xander, watching her progress, smoking from the corner of his mouth and holding the cigarette between finger and thumb. She walks straight past, not interested in his bullshit. He smells of alcohol and probably hasn't been to bed yet. He thinks he's a hellraiser. He should grow up.

"Don't say hello then," he calls.

"OK," she says, without turning around.

"Where've you been?" He's following her.

"Sick. I'm better now." She pulls on her shorts and wriggles her feet into her Havaianas. Her T-shirt is missing. She scans the area, knowing it hasn't blown away.

"I can see that. You were looking pretty good out there. Matter of fact, you're looking pretty good right here." His gaze takes in her bikini top.

"Piss off, Xander, and give me my T-shirt. Perving over fifteen-year-olds is not a good look. Are girls your age too mature for you?"

He shrugs, too drunk to argue, and stamps out his cigarette in the sand. "Come on, Serena, I was just kidding around." From his jacket he withdraws her blue cotton top. "Here you go. Listen, we're having a fire and some drinks tonight. Down the beach a little way, so we can relax and smoke some shit. You should come along."

She shakes her head and pulls her T-shirt over her head. "I'm busy tonight, but no thanks."

"Why not? It's just a few beers, maybe a joint or two with the usual crew."

She walks away, hitching her surfboard under her arm. "Thanks for inviting me, Xander, but I really don't feel like it right now."

Xander walks alongside her, uncharacteristically quiet. As Serena's house comes into view, he speaks. "Are you avoiding us?"

Of course she's avoiding them and it's pretty obvious why. Serena searches for the right words. "Hanging out with you guys used to be fun. Not anymore. You, Rubem, Pedro, you've changed." Her head is hot and she wants him to leave her alone.

"Pedro's in trouble with Mauricio." Xander's tone is fearful and his gaze never leaves the ground.

Serena's anger cools. "Mauricio Gonçalves? Why? What did he do?"

"Dunno. But Mauricio took him to Quinta dos Rios and no

one has seen him since. The thing is with Pedro, he's a good guy, but reckless, you know? Believes he can take whatever he wants with no consequences." He lifts his gaze to meet Serena's. "Nobody does that with Mauricio. The guy runs his business like a military operation. You screw up, you pay a price. But it's not like confessing your sins to Father Aldo and doing ten Hail Marys. Mauricio fits the punishment to the crime."

Serena can tell by his voice he's telling the truth. "Xander, what did Pedro do?"

His eyes are glassy and he takes a moment to react. "How do I know? I'm not his keeper! Look, are you gonna join us for a beer tonight or not?"

"Not. While you're hanging with that crowd, I have other friends. Go home."

She pushes open the door of her house and starts thinking.

12

W oman and dog sat on the porch, surveying the beach as the sun raced higher into the sky. Branca gnawed at her paw while Ann ate a couple of pancakes and drank more coffee. The problem with investigating a crime such as this was a complete lack of reliable information. Every question she asked would expose her to why-do-you-want-to-know and earmark her as someone with a particular interest in the death of Nelson Leal. The only way she could enquire while maintaining an air of disinterest would be to come at the problem from a different angle.

For example, start close to home. Ann could walk up to Fátima's place with an apology for missing the cocktails in Soure. She'd offer a certain amount of detail on her conversation with Gil Maduro, but reveal nothing significant and make some casual enquiries regarding the surfers, their connection to Maurício Gonçalves and affect a lack of interest in local gossip. The noise of Branca licking her paw infiltrated Ann's consciousness. With the bribe of a slice of pancake, she persuaded the dog to let her examine the offending leg. A livid red patch with broken skin just above her pads was the source of the problem. Ann's veterinarian knowledge was on a par with her familiarity with brain surgery.

If only Katie were here. She dismissed the thought immediately and lured the dog inside with the remains of her breakfast. With some difficulty, Ann encouraged her into the shower and applied her tea tree oil shampoo. Her philosophy was antiparasitic is best.

Branca, contrary to expectations, seemed to enjoy the experience, wriggling under Ann's fingers as she massaged her fur. Years of dirt and grease seemed to melt away and the dog finally lived up to her name. She really was white. Ann released her to hare about on the sand, shaking and rolling to dry herself. A thought occurred as she hung the dog's tatty bandana on the railing to dry. Branca had never once injured herself on the buried broken bottles. Perhaps she was too light to apply sufficient pressure. Once dried and covered with damp sand, the dog padded up the path and climbed the steps, ears pricked and nose alert for any remaining pancake. Ann took some antiseptic cream from her essential medicines bag and applied it to the sore patch, wrapping a self-adhesive bandage around the dog's paw. She doubted it would last more than five minutes but it was better than nothing.

Her practical side rolled her eyes. Emergency supplies wasted on somebody else's dog? She ignored that part of herself. After all, when had Ms Play-It-By-The-Rules brought her anything but grief? Today she decided to let the dog roam free while she pursued her own agenda. House secured, backpack on and markers in place, she and her freshly washed canine companion wandered down the path. As if she knew her company was superfluous, Branca paced away towards the left and the jungle. Ann turned in the direction of the village, rehearsing her questions to Fátima.

At the other end, the beach was already filling up with surfers, holidaymakers and day-trippers. Few made it this far down the beach and she was happy about that. On the approach to Fátima's hut, she noted the motorcycle with sidecar was still parked at the front. In Ann's limited experience, Fátima was always outside unless it was raining. This morning the shutters were still closed and the porch empty. Possibly she was still asleep after entertaining the surf boys last night. Maybe she had already gone into the village in search of coffee and gossip. Ann climbed the steps and rapped on the door. No reply. She wasn't surprised. She turned to look at the beach, appreciating the difference in angle and how her own shack was largely hidden from view by the greenery along a creek.

A noise behind her caught her off guard and her right hand flew to her back pocket which concealed her flick knife. The front door opened and a barefoot man in shorts and a vest stood blinking at her with an expression that said 'hangover' in capital letters.

"*Sî?*" His voice was little more than a growl.

Ann launched into her clumsy Portuguese. "Good morning. Many apologies because you are awake. I call myself Ann. I want to say thank yous. You borrowed us your bike yesterday. It was very good. Fátima isn't at home?"

The man yawned and stretched, showing ivory teeth and hairy armpits. "She's not here. I'm going to make coffee. Want some?" He turned back into the house, scratching the waistband of his boxer shorts. He was a fine-looking man and Ann began to see why Fátima stayed with a guy she professed to despise.

With a quick assessment of the situation, Ann chose to be sociable. She admitted her curiosity and sat on the porch, waiting for him to return. While she listened to him clattering about inside, she racked her brains, wondering if Fátima had ever mentioned her boyfriend's name. She remembered all the insults and disparaging remarks but could not recollect what he was actually called.

"You want something with your coffee?" He now wore jeans over his boxers and flip-flops on his feet. He slumped into the chair opposite and ran a hand over his face, before tipping a slug of whisky into his coffee cup. He raised his eyebrows and offered it to her. It was the same one she had bought Fátima as a thank you for the chickens, and still bore the black mark high above the current level of alcohol.

"No thank you, too early. Excuse me, I don't know your name."

"Too early for me too. Drunk and stoned, I don't know what time I fell asleep. When I woke up, she was gone and you were banging on the door. Those beach bums are bad for me. Bad for her too but she likes to pretend she's still a party girl. My name's Nando. And you're Ann, I know that much."

Ann sipped at the coffee. It was rich and strong, but she was already buzzing from too much caffeine. "Mmm, that's good." She set the cup on the table, intending to drink no more. "Fátima said where she was going? I have a need to talk to her. Not urgent, but maybe today is good?"

He didn't answer and began rolling a cigarette. His hands were long and smooth, more office worker than stevedore.

She tried again. "You work on the ferries, Fátima says? It's a hard job, no?"

"Life is hard for everyone." He lifted his gaze from the paper and tobacco and focused on her face. "Hard for a poet, hard for a sailor, hard for someone who has too much time on her hands. You found the body of Nelson Leal. How do you write a poem about that?"

Ann dropped her gaze. This was not what she was expecting. "I don't think it's possible to write about that. For a good poet, maybe. Not for someone like me."

He lit his cigarette and inhaled, closing his eyes. "Bad poets are the worst. Especially if they are teenage boys." He opened his eyes to lizard-like slits, amusement lifting his lips. He looked exactly like a gecko. "Oh yeah, I've been there."

She laughed, once again caught off balance, and could think of plenty of witty replies, none of which she could translate into Portuguese.

"You have a *garça*," he said.

She tilted her head, not recognising the word.

"The white bird that sits on your roof. How do you say *garça* in English?"

"Oh, I see. A beautiful creature. In English, it's called a heron."

"Heron. Yes, it is beautiful and also lucky. Everybody knows a *garça* brings you good fortune. Or babies, if you like that sort of thing. Heron." He rolled the word around his mouth. "God knows when Fátima will come home. She's hanging out with those bums, I expect. That Xander, you know him? Slippery as a dose of diarrhoea. He can make her rich, he says, he can give her everything she wants. Everything she wants? Not enough money in the whole of Brazil to give her what she wants. And all of it in purple. Those bums are in trouble, now most of them are under Mauricio's control. They think the sun shines out of his arse. You sure now?" He tilted the whisky bottle in her direction.

She shook her head, calculating her next move. *Side with him, show vulnerability, invite confidence.* "I'm not a drinker, not really. A woman alone needs to be careful. Nando, those beach guys ... last night they stop me. Only talk, friendly but not friendly. That's why I want to ask Fátima. To understand if dangerous."

He stubbed out his weedy little cigarette. "The bums aren't dangerous. All mouth and attitude. Their boss? Mauricio Gonçalves is pure poison, a danger to everyone. I need a piss. *Até logo*."

"See you later," she echoed, watching him enter the house. She hoisted her pack over her shoulder and started down the splintered steps. Maybe Fátima being out of the house wasn't such a bad thing.

Nando's voice from the shady interior stopped her in her tracks. "Poet lady! Get yourself a bike! Ride along the tree line and avoid those surfer assholes. Stay out of it, '*tá bem*?"

"OK," she called. "Thank you."

A bike was such a great idea she could have kicked herself for not thinking of it before. Faster to visit the village and she could cycle into Soure when necessary. The next question was how to acquire two wheels. Money was always going to be an issue living as she did. She'd known that from the minute she chose to run, but her 'essentials' fund would not be seriously depleted by the purchase of a second-hand bicycle. A memory ambushed her as she picked her way over powdery white sand and by the time she reached the path to her place, her face was wet with tears. She sat on the steps and closed her eyes, allowing the vision to play itself out. The more she submitted to these involuntary recollections, the weaker their power. At least that's what she told herself.

Katie's laughter was halfway between a gasp and a giggle as she pedalled along the driveway, Dad holding the saddle. Her concentration was such that she didn't notice when he let go. Her big sister clapped her hands in appreciation. Mostly for Katie, but also for Dad's cunning. He'd done exactly the same thing two years before with exactly the same bike. He glanced over and they shared a smile. 'Everyone learns at their own pace,' he said to Mum when she expressed impatience at Katie's timidity. Second Born was a quiet baby and cautious toddler, fearful of causing harm to herself or anything else. Dad never hurried his little girl while she built up courage to take a step into the unknown. Whereas his oldest hurled herself at every challenge going and took pride in the scars. San Fairy

Ann, Dad used to say as he dabbed Dettol onto her knees, plucked shards of glass from her forearm or held her hand while a nurse set her leg in plaster. In and out of hospital, constantly terrifying her parents and little sister, First Born was fearless. How do you define yourself when you lose your defining characteristic? San Fairy Ann. She used to think it was her nickname. That was one reason she'd chosen her new identity.

What I do promise is to listen, she'd told the American. Listen to what? She wasn't going to hear much from her porch, other than the screeching heron, crashing waves and continuous chatter from the jungle. For the rest of the day, no one came to the hut. Ann couldn't face trekking into Soure to enquire about bike shops and found plenty of reasons to avoid the village. She cut up stale bread and fried it in chilli oil to throw into her vegetable stew, which thanks to a handful *cipo d'alho* had a fragrant, smoky flavour. *Look at me now, cooking with stuff I don't even know how to pronounce! Six months ago, I disdained anything from M&S with instructions other than microwave for 3-4 minutes.* The sun hung low in the apricot sky and palm trees cast long shadows, silhouetted fronds stroking the white horses' manes as they rushed up the shore and melted into nothing. Branca emerged from under the stilts and ate another cup of dog food as if hyenas were prowling to snatch it from her jaws. Fed and watered, she curled up in a patch of sun by Ann's feet, her coat turning saffron in the sunset.

The corner of Mike Ferguson's card poked out from under the tomato plant. She should take it indoors and place with her safe items. Except she still hadn't decided how to handle his request. Daily updates? Ha! Even if he made good on his offer to send her a tablet, she wasn't going to fall into the trap of creating an online identity. Hadn't she erased herself completely from the virtual world? She'd ditch the card next time she was in the village. Not that it was necessary. She'd already memorised the email address. It wasn't difficult: m. ferguson@macquiver.com

That cognitive impulse flared again. *Macquiver.com? Why not look it up online? Ah.* Learning to use the Internet was a million times easier than trying to unlearn a dependence on digital information. Thousands of miles away from any other reliable source of verifiable facts, she had little alternative. But Ann Sheldon was a non-person, a blank, an absence with no digital footprint. It had taken blood, sweat, stress and an ocean's worth of tears to get this far. She had no intention of diving down that worm-hole. Never again.

She switched her attention to another individual: Cinthia Fischer. When Gil Maduro had asked her whether she recognised the name, she'd said no. It was the truth. She didn't know who Cinthia Fischer was but somehow she did know how to spell it. In English, it would be a natural assumption to spell her first name with a Y and her surname without the C. Cynthia Fisher. Perhaps some part of her subconscious had translated the Anglo-Saxon version into Portuguese. Or maybe she had seen it somewhere. She stretched out her legs, resting her heels on the veranda railing and staring up at the endless acres of blue sky. She allowed her mind to wander, retrieving memories of reading names: painted on signs, printed on cards, suggested by search engines or splashed in neon letters across the front of a tabloid.

She collected the trashy gossip mags from beside her bed. When she'd bought them, her intention was to learn better Portuguese by reading the simple stories. The problem was Ann found herself unable to sustain an interest in a telenovela's first gay kiss or which actress's body was showing signs of cellulite. The name Cinthia Fischer was one of the headlines. The story wasn't big enough for the front page but relegated to a small feature on page 10. With the aid of pencil, paper and her dictionary, she translated the article, such as it was, in around fifteen minutes.

CINTHIA SINGLE AGAIN?

On Tuesday afternoon, a private jet touched down at Belém airport. Passengers included Cinthia Fischer, her playboy son Franck and his Instagram influencer girlfriend, Shelbee Spicer. The question on everyone's lips? Where was Cinthia's fiancé, Damon Wright? Only four months ago, the couple announced their engagement on Valentine's Day with a promise of a summer wedding. Wright's words on social media were: 'She's beautiful! Inside and out!', yet no date was settled for their nuptials.

Now she arrives for a month-long sojourn in Brazil alone. Cinthia gave no interviews but in an answer to a journalist's question at the airport, she said Wright was working. Really? One of the wealthiest men in telecommunications can't take a holiday?

Tongues were wagging before her sad and lonely walk from private jet to limousine. Last month, Wright hosted a charity event for single parents in Fort Lauderdale, Florida. The woman by his side was not his new fiancée. Instead his eldest daughter assumed the role of hostess (see pic), leaving guests wondering at Cinthia's absence.

Since losing her husband in 2008, poor Cinthia has been unlucky in love. Devastated after Woodward R. James went back to his wife, a whirlwind romance with notorious heartbreaker Mick Mulligan (now rumoured to be dating an Albanian dancer the same age as his niece), she met and fell in love with the sexiest of CEOs (see pic.) Billionaire Wright is the twelfth richest man in America while Cinthia Fischer is the twentieth richest woman in Brazil. A match made in heaven? Or is Cinthia yet to meet her true 'Mister Right'?

Ann studied the pictures, particularly those of Franck Fischer. Something about him raised her hackles. Not the highlighted hair pulled back in a ponytail or the proprietorial hold on his girlfriend's hand, but the expression on his face. Smug and untouchable, he oozed contempt. Maduro's dislike of the young man made a lot more sense now she had seen the kid's face. She reminded herself Fischer Jr. had just come off a long flight and was faced with a phalanx of photographers, intent on invading his mother's privacy. Still, he did give the strong impression of being, in Maduro's words, an odious little shit.

Branca let out a volley of barks, giving Ann such a fright she dropped the pencil she'd been tapping against her lip. In the late afternoon light, Fátima approached, carrying another of her laundry bags.

"*Olá*, Ann! You were looking for me, according to that waste of space. Shut that scabby dog up, will you! He says you want a bike? Are you crazy? You want calves like watermelons? Talking of watermelons, I brought us a cocktail. Why is this animal still here? Thanks to that interfering cop, we missed our piña coladas at the hotel. Who do those assholes think they are? Screw him. I brought the ingredients so we can make our own. No rich guys at the bar for us to impress, just a filthy flea-ridden... what's that around its leg? You're nursing the damn thing, aren't you? I said it before and I was right. You need your head examined."

Before she had finished her monologue she arrived at the top of the steps and dumped her carrier bag on the table. "It's happy hour! You got any nuts?"

"Hi, Fátima. How was your day?"

"Same as every day. Disappointing. I need a drink. You have ice and cachaça, right? I brought a watermelon, the rest of that whisky and some coconut. You can make a piña colada out of that, I'm sure, and don't worry about the umbrellas." Her gaze fell on the magazine. "Oh, I haven't read this yet. Can I have a look while you fix the drinks?" She scooped up the magazine and sat on the top step, already snorting at the pictures.

Her forceful personality was something Ann admired while realising it robbed her of a voice. The more she allowed this woman to dominate their conversations, the more power she relinquished. Time to step up.

She took the magazine from Fátima's hands with a smile. "As a matter of fact, I'm done with it. You can take it home if you like, after we've had a drink and a chat. Come inside while I make the cocktails because I want to ask you a question. Those guys on the beach last night, they made me feel pretty uncomfortable. Even worse, once they'd intimidated me, they came over to your place. I have to say, Fátima, I'm wondering who my friends are? And by the way, there's no whisky in a piña colada."

For somebody who rarely stopped talking, Fátima's response took a while. With great deliberation, she got to her feet and looked Ann in the eye. "Your friends are people who bring you chickens. Your friends are people who warn you when you're going to get into trouble. Your friends give you a ride into the city. Your friends have your back. I'm not the one who prefers to have cocktails with a sleazy cop instead of sticking to the plan. The surf boys know what it means when the cops start sniffing round here. We keep ourselves to ourselves and we never talk to the police. Remember that. You're wondering who your friends are? Let me tell you, it's not the goddamned police." She sighed. "Actually, I don't care what's in a piña colada, just make me a drink."

Ann took the magazine with her into the kitchen along with Fátima's laundry bag. "The reason I had to go into Soure was to meet that detective. He wasn't there and I spoke to his juniors. When I came back to meet you, he asked me out to dinner."

"To dinner?" Her eyes flashed with curiosity and she sat down at the kitchen table. "He asked you on a date?"

Ann mashed watermelon chunks through a sieve. "I don't know if a date was what he meant. Anyway, I refused. The only reason I agreed to a cocktail was because I wanted to ask about his investigation. Listen, I'm just going to put cachaça and coconut in this and we can call it whatever we like. *Melancia colada*? The cop gave me almost nothing but he did warn me about Mauricio and his drug runners."

"Yeah, *Melancia colada* sounds pretty good. You don't want to listen to the cops about the Gonçalves family. They know jack shit and you're wet behind the ears. You know one thing? That dog looks a lot cleaner than the first time I saw it. Doesn't it piss everywhere?"

Ann poured the drinks and held Fátima's gaze. "No, she doesn't. Females don't piss on their own patch."

Fátima took a glass and one of the kitchen chairs, before returning to the veranda. "This is my favourite time of year, you know? When the rains are here, it feels like we'll never live again. But the water goes, the sun reappears and we start the whole stupid cycle again. This year will be different. This year I'll meet someone special. This year I'll get out and move somewhere full of life and energy where I can make some money and get the life I deserve. Same dreams, same disappointments, no wonder we age so fast. I can't understand you, Ann. Seriously, it makes no sense. You speak English and Portuguese, you can live wherever you want. You're not bad-looking, but you really don't make the most of yourself. I'm sorry to be blunt, but it's true. Stop dressing like a soldier and you could be attractive. I'd kill for your hair like yours, but you only ever wear it up and what's the point in that? Thanks for the drink."

They drank in silence, tuning into the atmosphere and absorbing the ever-changing view. Ann noted the different dynamic. Fátima had offered several backhanded compliments, one of which was taking her own chair onto the balcony rather than occupying Ann's. She looked across the table at Fátima's hibiscus-patterned leggings and mulberry sweatshirt.

"I take your point about my boring clothes. But purple doesn't suit me."

Fátima narrowed her eyes and glared at Ann until her face softened. Her cheeks cracked into a genuine grin as she swirled the contents of the glass. "Purple doesn't suit everyone. Hey, what did you think of Nando? Don't bother saying he's stupid, because I know that already. He's great in bed and crazy in love with me but there's no future with a man who lacks ambition. I want more from life than getting drunk and having sex in a crappy shack. He can't see there are other opportunities than ferrying tourists up and down the coast. Xander has ideas, charisma and knows how to play the game. Mauricio and some of the kids who work for him are making money I can only dream of. Don't be too quick to judge."

Without warning, Ann's temper struck like a lightning bolt. "Too quick to judge drug dealers? Fátima, don't be so bloody naïve. Anyone pushing substances, whether that's Class A drugs, opioids or any other kind of painkiller, is a piece of shit. Their sole aim is to enslave those already weak. I'm not talking about smoking joints or medicinal herbs but chemical compounds designed, yes, literally designed to ruin people's lives. To the extent where they will break the law, suffer humiliation, steal from their loved ones and break every point on their moral compass just to get the next dose. Their soulless overlords grind people into the dirt just to make a profit. Mauricio and his mates are the scum of the earth."

Her speech shocked Fátima into silence but seem to awake an instinct in Branca. The dog rose from her position at the top of the steps and came to bunt her head at Ann's elbow. She ran a hand over the dog's coarse coat, reassuring and taking reassurance. She took a deep breath and tried to recover her composure. She had to change the subject as she was in danger of giving too much away.

"Fátima, my philosophy is live and let live. If the surfers

and Mauricio leave me alone, I'll do the same. As I keep telling everyone, I came here for peace and quiet. Since the rain stopped, that's harder to find. Do you want another drink?"

"Not unless you have any nuts. The whole point of cocktails is that you have nuts. Do you want to hear my idea about a bike or not? I don't care one way or another because half the year you can't use the crappy thing and it only rusts." She followed Ann indoors, Branca at their heels. "The Leal family gave Nelson's bike to his sister. Dolores is only fifteen but like Dulce, she's pretty heavy. They never have any money so they want to sell the girl's bike. You're skinny and won't go far. It'll probably cost you less than the mosquito net. No more ice?"

Ann opened the cold box and squeezed out the last two ice cubes, one in each glass. "Thank you, I'll ask them tomorrow. Here's the magazine and I have two others you can take. I used to like this type of rag in England, but here, I don't know any of these celebrities. So what's the point?"

"Fashion is the point! Where do you think I get my ideas?" Fátima flared her nostrils. "In your case, though, that's a waste of time. Better give them to me. What are you feeding this animal? It farts worse than Nando." She started flicking through the magazine, her glass in her left hand. "Not that I can learn anything from these old broilers. How is someone like her sleeping with someone like him?"

With less interest in the photographs than her own toenail clippings, Ann feigned curiosity, willing Fátima to turn the page. "She's a newsreader? Really? Who's the guy next to her? Why was he in prison? Ooh, Belém! Who's that?" she asked, aiming for guileless and naïve.

For a second, Fátima said nothing, her eyes scanning the piece. "Cinthia Fischer. Now that's a woman who understands power. Her problem is she can't hang onto it. One seduction, one step up. That's not the difficult part. Cinthia loses men and when you lose a man, you lose money. She'd better hope that

Franck Fischer turns into Elon Musk, but I wouldn't hold my breath. Is that why you're here? Because you lost your man? You came to the wrong place if you want to find a husband."

Fishing boats set off from the port, chugging out to sea on the dip-dyed horizon. Two opposing hopes crossed Ann's mind. *May your trip be successful*, she wished the occupants of those boats. The other half of her brain willed the fish to safety, escaping the nets and surviving another night. Her rational brain accepted the dichotomy with a sigh. Her neighbour kept staring and Ann knew she would have to answer the question. She gritted her teeth and stuck to her story.

"No, I'm not here to find a husband. I'm here to find myself."

Fátima rolled her eyes. Internally, Ann did the same.

13

The next morning, Ann woke with the light and had a sudden urge to swim. She grabbed a towel and locked the door, but skipped her usual precautions as she would be within view. Branca trotted alongside her. She thought the dog might sit and guard her belongings, but that romantic hope drifted away like the last vestiges of sleep. As soon as Ann waded into the water, Branca lost interest and wandered off in the direction of the jungle. The surf was boisterous but exhilarating and Ann swam along the shoreline, wary of the powerful currents further out. The sound of waves breaking over her head was pierced by another sound – Branca's alarm call. She scanned the beach. A figure was walking away from her shack, followed at a distance by the barking dog. She wiped seawater from her eyes and recognised Ricardo Leal. She waved and called out a greeting. He raised a hand in the air and then pointed to her porch, giving the thumbs-up. With that, he walked away in the direction of the village, not even attempting to summon his dog.

Curious, Ann swam ashore, wrapped the towel around herself and started up the beach, grateful for her flip-flops.

Even this early, the sand was already warm. On the porch lay a pink and purple bicycle and a cardboard box the size of a large book. She wondered for a second how news had travelled so fast but gave up trying to understand the way the village worked. Instead, she made coffee and sat on the porch to open the package. It had neither address nor indication as to its provenance, but it was heavy enough to be a hardback book. She slid a knife under the fold, using it to lift the flap, suspicious of what it might contain. No powdery residue or toxic liquids were visible so she tilted the box, easing out the contents.

It was a thin laptop, about half the size of the computer she used to own. It came with a charging cable and judging by the packaging, it was brand new. Also in the package was a smartphone, enabling her to connect to the Internet without Wi-Fi. How Ferguson had managed to get this to her so quickly was a mystery. The concern now was whether or not to use it. Though what connection Ferguson might have to the people who wanted to find her she could not imagine. She drank her coffee and assessed the risks. Two cups later, she still hadn't made a decision. Instead, she plugged both devices in to charge, locked up the shack, set her markers and wheeled the bike up to the tree line, where the ground was firmer.

It wasn't the sturdiest of cycles, clearly meant for someone younger and shorter than herself, but with a few adjustments to the saddle and handlebars, it was rideable. She set off for the village, intending to pay Ricardo and offer to return Branca. But as if she'd read Ann's mind, the dog sloped off into the jungle, ignoring all whistles and calls. With a shrug, Ann hitched her pack higher on her shoulders and began pedalling.

The ground was uneven and sometimes she had to get off and wheel the bike through deep soft sand or carry it over a creek. Even so, the journey into the village took a mere fifteen minutes. She rode directly to the Leals' house and found Ricardo outside, mending a fishing net.

"*Bom dia*," she said, dismounting. "Thank you for bringing the package and the bike. I am come to pay you for it."

He put down the net. "*Bom dia*, Ann. Did it work?"

"Yes. A bit small but I am changing the seat. How much do you want for it?"

"Not the bike, the computer. Can you communicate with Mike?"

Ann hesitated. "I don't know yet. I wait for it to be full of electricity, then I try. It was very quick, getting the machine here."

"Very quick. Mike makes things happen. It's good you are talking to him. You can have the bike. No need to pay me. It's enough you help find out who killed our son."

O nosso filho. Our son. Was he referring to Dulce and himself, or him and Mike? Ann swallowed her initial impulse to contradict him. "Ricardo, I don't know if my help will make a difference. If yes, that's good. But I want to pay for the bike. Please. Fátima suggests twenty reais. Is enough?"

"You can give me ten." He lit a cigarette. "Did that cop say anything? Do they have any leads?"

Ann handed over a twenty-real note. "Ten for bike, ten for delivery. Please take. The police don't say much. They ask about the Gonçalves family and ..."

"*Filho da puta!*" The venom he put into the curse jarred Ann's nerves. "Mauricio is nothing more than filthy scum."

Ann trod carefully. "Mauricio Gonçalves ... employs some local boys, I think. Did he want Nelson to work for him?"

"No way. Nelson wouldn't even speak to that pile of shit. Everybody in the village hates the sight of the man. Those little roosters following him around, they'll soon be sorry. If he brings a drugs war here, we'll all be sorry." He held out a hand for the money. "Thank you. Any problems with that bike, bring it to me. I fix things. It's a shame on the Gonçalves family. His father was a good man. Mauricio's older brother isn't bad either, just a bit simple." He tapped his temple. "But Mauricio is evil and will ruin his father's farm."

"Where is the farm?"

"Between here and Praia do Céu. Around eight kilometres inland. Listen to me, Ann. You keep away from there and keep away from Mauricio. What else did the police say? They asked you about Gonçalves and ..."

"Oh, yes. They asked me about Franck Fischer. You know him?"

Ricardo frowned. "Fischer? No, I don't know him. He's the big-mouth with that lovely yacht, *A Linda Lua*. Gods knows how much a boat like that costs. More than I'll make in a lifetime. Why are the police interested in him? He was here that day, it's true, making a lot of noise with his drunken mates, but that lot don't go to the bakery. They hang out at the bars on the beach or bring their own buckets of champagne."

"You ever see him before?" Ann asked, pulling a vine tendril from between the spokes of the front wheel.

"Yeah, several times last week. When they come to the village, you can't miss them. That boat tearing around the bay and then that crowd roar through the village with their trucks. They treat this place like it's their own personal playground. People like us, the ones who live here, just have to get out of their way. Did you tell Mike what the cop said?"

"Not yet. But I will, I promise."

"Thank you. You can keep that dog, if you like. It was Nelson's. Listen, when the police release his body, we will have the funeral at the church. You must come."

It wasn't an invitation but an order. "Thank you. Of course I'll be there. And thank you for the dog. She makes me feel better."

Ricardo stubbed out his cigarette and returned to his net. "About all it's good for is barking. May as well stay with you, where barking could be useful. Let me know how it goes with Mike."

"I will. How's Dulce?"

He shook his head but said nothing.

She said goodbye and rode up the street towards the bakery. Eight kilometres inland. That was about as vague as it got. Not that she had any intention of trying to cycle to the farm. She wasn't that stupid.

She bought a bag of tomatoes and fresh anchovies and persuaded the fisherman to throw in some guts for Branca. At the bakery, she queued to buy four soft bread rolls, already planning lunch. There was a new waitress working the tables. Ann recognised the girl as Nelson's sister, the one who had served coffees to the sympathisers on the day of his death. She'd stepped right into her brother's shoes, riding his bike and now doing his job. She didn't have the confidence of her half-brother, but who could expect her to be anything other than downcast after what had happened.

Viviane served Ann her bread and talked her into buying two *natas*. Ann agreed. It was always best to agree with Viviane. While she was wrapping the pastries, Ann took a chance.

"I bought a bike today, from the Leal family."

"I know, I heard. It belonged to Dolores." She indicated the waitress. "Poor girl."

"Yes, poor girl. Poor family."

"I curse the soul of whoever killed Nelson," she hissed. "May that black and murderous bastard rot in hell forever. Don't you want any coffee?"

"No, thanks. I want to try out the bike. How far is Praia do Céu from here?"

"An hour, maybe. Not much to see and the road is dangerous. Here."

Ann paid and took her purchases outside to stash them in her rucksack. Her bike was as she had left it, leaning up against the terrace. She sensed someone watching and looked over her shoulder to see Nelson's sister standing in the arch. Ann patted the bike and placed a hand to her chest, mouthing the word, '*Obrigada*'. The girl shrugged with a shy smile and returned to her work.

The backpack was heavier than on the outward journey and the sun a lot hotter. Weaving through the palm trees, Ann considered her morning a success. She was becoming a part of the village and despite her own intentions, it was a feeling she liked. She pedalled faster behind the beach shacks and sea-facing restaurants, all of which were open and welcoming tourists. Snatches of American English reached her ears between the sounds of the sea and some tinny speakers playing salsa music. Once the shacks petered out, the sand got softer so she steered a course closer to the tree line, eager to get home and eat.

She dismounted to lug the bike over a creek and heard an echo of her own grunt as she placed it on the ground. She stopped, listening and rotating her torso 180°. No one was behind her, but the jungle could be hiding all kinds of creatures. Staring at the thick greenery, another colour caught her attention. A scrap of bright red fabric lay a few paces from her feet. All her senses switched to full alert. She kicked down the stand to rest the bike and reached for her flick-knife.

The scrap was not red fabric as she'd assumed, but a blood-soaked tissue. She searched the sand and saw a smattering of spots, much darker than the tissue, leading to the trees. At that moment, the grunt came again. She slipped off her pack and crept forward, wary of a trap, ears straining to identify the origin of the sound. Once in the shade of the palm fronds, her eyes adjusted to the gloom and she made out a lighter shape curled at the base of a tree. Branca?

She dared go no closer but took a piece of driftwood and threw it at the shape.

"*Ai*!" The body twisted around and the fearful eyes of Pedro, the arrogant surfer, stared at her. His breathing was ragged through his mouth and he clutched his left hand around his right. Blood soaked his T-shirt.

Ann scanned behind him and either side but could make out no other figures waiting in ambush. "Are you OK?" she called, moving no closer.

"Get out of here!" he hissed.

"You're hurt?"

"No!" He looked down at his T-shirt. "An accident, that's all. Go away."

"Let me help you." She took a pace towards him.

"No!" He raised his hand to gesture at her, his eyes rolled up and he keeled over, his head hitting the mossy undergrowth.

Ann dropped to a crouch and ran towards him, aware of what might be above as well as behind the trees. Pedro was out cold. She pressed two fingers beside his windpipe and found his pulse. His hands had fallen to his sides, both stained red. The right, to Ann's horror, was missing half the index finger and still pumping blood. She eased him into the recovery position and ran to her backpack for her mini first-aid kit and her mineral water. All she could do with such limited resources was clean the wound and stem the bleeding, then get him to hospital. Maybe Nando was still at Fátima's with his motorbike and sidecar. She could hardly carry him on her bike.

When she returned, he was still unconscious. She worked fast to wash the area, staunch the flow and bandage his finger, acting out of habit and muscle memory, despite her own shaking hands. To cut a finger off at the knuckle so cleanly was no accident. She'd seen this more times than she wanted to remember. Drug runners who sampled the goods were taught a lesson. No more sticky fingers. When she'd got this kid to the hospital, she would go directly to the police station, root out Maduro and tell him the facts. From there, he'd have to inform the Federal force because Ricardo was right. A drugs war would wreak havoc on this village.

She patted Pedro's cheek lightly at first and then with increasing firmness. His eyes squeezed together in a wince and then fluttered open.

"How are you feeling?" asked Ann.

He focused on her, his stare uncomprehending.

"I cleaned your finger but you might have other injuries. Do you remember what happened?"

He didn't reply.

"Pedro, you need hospital treatment. We must get help. Can you walk?"

He pushed himself into a sitting position with his left hand and looked down at his right. Still he said nothing.

"Fátima's boyfriend has a motorcycle. It's about half a kilo-metre from here. Can you walk with me? He can take you to hospital."

Pedro looked down at his blood-soaked T-shirt and shook his head. "*Não posso.*"

"OK. If you can't walk, I'm going to fetch him. You stay here and I'll be back as soon as I can. I'll leave you my water. *Está bem?*" She stood up and looked at him to check he understood.

For a moment he continued staring at his T-shirt until he noticed she was still there. He nodded once and muttered, "*Está bem*". Spots of red were already visible on the bandage. Ann had to act fast.

She sprinted to her bike, tossed the first-aid kit on top of her groceries, shouldered the backpack and pedalled furiously in the direction of Fátima's shack. As she drew closer, she could see the motorcycle and sidecar were no longer parked outside. With a curse of frustration, she dumped the bike in the sand and ran around to the front door, expecting to see Fátima sitting on the porch, painting her nails. The veranda was empty. Ann tapped on the door, once, twice, three times, but there was no sound from within.

The only other possibility was to get Pedro through the jungle and out onto the road where she might be able to flag down a passing truck. Whether the kid could walk that far, she didn't know. Sweat slid from her forehead into her eyes and her back was soaked. Her own shack was a kilometre away with a better set of medical supplies. Ann hesitated, weighing up the pros and cons, and came to the conclusion she should put all her efforts in getting the boy to hospital.

When she got back to the creek, right away she spotted the T-shirt. In the shallow stream running from the jungle to the sea lay Pedro's originally yellow, now yellow and red T-shirt. As clear water coursed over the fabric, some of the red washed away. A patch of sand on the other side was damp, as if someone had recently washed himself. There was no trail of footprints in any direction, at least none Ann could discern, but she knew without question Pedro had fled.

Under the tree where she had found him, there were signs of a disturbance and if she looked closely, bloodstains were visible in the undergrowth. But the injured kid, along with her water bottle, were missing. Part of her was not surprised. If what she believed had happened to his hand was true, he would avoid a local hospital at all costs. Too many questions. Somehow or other, he'd return to his family, explaining the injury as some kind of accident and refuse medical attention. She hoped he'd be lucky and the wound would not become infected. There was nothing more she could do for Pedro. But she was duty-bound to report what she had seen. Even there and then, the principles of law enforcement took precedence.

14

Her mother won't miss her. Most days Serena's up with the light and comes home after dark. Absence isn't the problem. Walking through the village, along the road to Praia do Céu and maybe even taking the turn to Quinta dos Rios is the problem. She'll be seen. Surfer girl with the white- blonde hair – people will talk. Plant the excuse before the question. *Don't forget I'm going to Praia do Céu today. I told you! I said the surf is going to be amazing and I'm not gonna miss it. I did tell you, Mãezinha, you just don't listen. I'll be home late, OK?*

Another issue is her board. If she's going surfing, why leave without it? Underneath the house, she straps it out of sight just as she did most of the rainy season. *Mãe* never checks, she trusts her little girl. When her mother finally goes to market, Serena dresses in a baggy top, jeans and trainers, scuttles behind the houses to avoid the crowd and sets off in the direction of Quinta dos Rios. She rehearses her speech as she walks, mainly to drown out a voice in her head which is screaming, 'What do you think you're DOING?'

Mauricio Gonçalves is a scumbag, everyone knows that, but he has the power to fix things. That's the way things work on

Ilha do Marajó. People here take care of our own. Nelson was a local boy and if anyone can deal with the people who killed him, it's the Gonçalves family. Serena's going to convince him that it's up to him to help their community. Who knows, maybe he'll quit all the aggression and join forces with everyone against those hateful people in their huge trucks and shiny boats and beautiful clothes. A wave of shame brushes past her. At the same moment she hears a vehicle rumbling up the track.

Serena wants no offers of a lift, enquiries or catcalls. She scrambles sideways off the dirt track, eyes peeled for snakes, and ducks into the gully. Head down, she listens as the car passes. She doesn't recognise the engine sound. Maybe it's a tourist. She takes a bottle of water from her handbag and slugs a third of the contents. A long trek lies ahead so she should be careful and save it till she really needs a drink. Her jeans are already dirty from the dust and slimy mud in the gully. That voice again. 'What do you think you're DOING?'

She marches on up the dusty road. 'The right thing is what I'm doing." She hums a song she's heard on the radio. The English lyrics don't really make sense from what she under-stands, but it's the attitude that matters. *Don't mess with me or you'll regret it.* An alligator crosses the road ahead, deliberate and armoured as a tank. Serena freezes until its tail slithers off the road and into the swampy water. She walks on, calculating another three kilometres to go. Rustling from the jungle makes her tense until she sees a wild boar with two stripey little piglets rooting at the base of a tree. *What is the matter with you, Serena? Steering clear of the jungle animals but striding with confidence into Quinta dos Rios?* She chews on her thumbnail, arguing with that inner voice.

She's the only one who knows the whole story. She has to ask for help, but from someone who can actually do something. Facing a man like him takes courage, sure, but isn't she the bravest surfer on the beach? Her insides cramp in a way that never happens when facing a wave. Not even the Pororoca, a word to make any resident of the island twitchy.

In February and March, between a full moon and new moon, the ocean penetrates the river, a tidal bore hurtling up the tributaries with the force of a tsunami. The phenomenon terrifies island-dwellers, whether they live near the water or deep in the jungle. In the old folks' language, Pororoca translates as The Big Roar, and once you've heard it, you know why. The sound announces its imminence with thunderous intent. Thousands of tons of fresh water tear up trees, wreck boats, sweeping away animals and humans alike. The danger level for a surfer is incomparable to the sea. Water density, unpredictable speed and variable wave heights mean that a single error will cost you your life. Drowned, battered by washed-away jungle detritus, attacked by reptiles or piranhas, the Pororoca knows no mercy. Professional surfers fly from California, Hawaii, Portugal and Australia to try and to master this phenomenon.

Serena da Rocha surfed it at the age of fourteen. Xander, Pedro, Rubem and the rest know that as long as they live, they'll never match such a feat. That's why they torment and tease her. They're jealous.

She smiles. She's walking faster, her head held high. Toucans call from the branches above as if cheering her on. She can do this. She runs through her story one more time, stuttering to a halt when the farm comes into view. The tarmac road curves to the left and opens into a compound. She slows, trying to assess the terrain. A big house, some concrete sheds, two cars and a pickup she's seen before. She groans. Of all the people who can't keep his mouth shut, she has to cross paths with Zé.

She hides in the shadow of a banana plant, patient as she has learned to be, watching and waiting for her moment. Beside Zé's dodgy pickup and a beat-up Ford is a pristine white

Porsche. It looks like a wild unicorn between tame buffaloes. Serena's not into cars but she is into beauty. The graceful design makes her think of waves: the surge, the crest, the flow. She wants to touch its curves, run an appreciative hand over those lines.

It takes twenty-five minutes before Zé trudges across the scrubby grass and drives his pollution machine down the road. He does a double take. She wasn't careful enough to hide her hair. He brakes and winds down the window.

"Serena? What are you doing here?"

"None of your business. Piss off, you nosy old fart!"

He shakes his head and drives away. Only then does she come out of her hiding-place and walk right up to the front door. There's no bell, so she knocks three times, like she means business. She waits and knocks again. The toucans screech but this time it sounds less like cheers and more of a warning. Someone unlocks the door.

A big man in dungarees stands there, gawping at her. He smells of sweat and old musty clothes and blinks at her as if she's not real.

Her nostrils flare and she takes a step back. "*Bom dia*. I want to speak to Mauricio Gonçalves, please."

The man shakes his head with a disbelieving exhalation. "No. You go away now."

He begins to close the door. "*O senhor*! It's very important. Please tell him I need his help." She places her palm on the wood, preventing him from shutting her out.

The door opens wide and beside the smelly guy there's Mauricio Gonçalves. She's never seen him this close. He's in a suit today, with those snakeskin boots and he has some weird facial hair, a long moustache and thin strip down the middle of his chin. His eyes assess her and he peels his lips from his teeth.

"We have a guest! How can we help you, young lady?"

"Senhor Gonçalves, my name is Serena da Rocha. I need

your help. It's a matter of life and death. Please can you spare me half an hour of your time?"

His eyes flick first to the big guy and then to his watch. "You can have half an hour. João, bring us some guaraná. Come inside, Serena da Rocha, I'm all yours."

15

In theory, Ann should have slept well. Having a swim, acquiring a new bike, doing a good deed, eating well and setting herself up for digital anonymity was enough to exhaust most people, but Ann had kick-started her brain.

She spent hours researching Mike Ferguson and any potential connection he could have to her past, in any form. She found none. That wasn't to say it didn't exist but if someone with her knowledge couldn't find it, it was at a higher level of security than she could access. So she established a communication channel between herself and Mike Ferguson. She reported everything she'd told to Ricardo Leal, Nelson's other father. She omitted her encounter with Pedro because until she was sure of its relevance, that information would only muddy the waters. She voiced a concern about hooking up to the Internet via the phone and the extortionate expense. His reply was reassuring. She could spend all day connected. The bills were covered.

Like a dependent weaned off an addictive substance suddenly given unlimited access, Ann dived in head first. When convinced she could explore the endless labyrinth of the web undetected, she was unstoppable. With added privacy layers and reroutes over the phone connection it took five times longer for sites to load than even Soure's prehistoric Cyber Café but Ann could wait. By the time she finally closed the device, performed her domestic security checks and fell into bed, it was nearly two in the morning. For somebody who went to bed with the sunset and rose at first light, this was the equivalent of pulling an all-nighter. And as she well knew, an all-nighter played havoc with her sleep.

For hours she lay enveloped in soft, warm blackness, like curling up in a seashell, listening to soothing ocean waves, snores from a contented dog and the ever-present soundtrack of nocturnal jungle activity. Her mind refused sleep, an officious postmistress busily sorting what she'd learned into piles of information. She knew exactly where the Gonçalves farm was located, how long it would take to get there and the risks involved if she tried. One road led to Quinta dos Rios and nothing beyond. Anyone taking that route had a clear intention and nowhere to hide. Presumably it was possible to approach from the jungle, if one had sufficient expertise in this terrain. For a lone woman armed with a flick knife and a pushbike, the proposition was laughable.

While the Internet was capable of pinpointing the location of the farm, it offered precious little on its owners. That came as no surprise. Where digital information failed in terms of the Gonçalves family, it over-delivered when it came to the Fischers. Cinthia Fischer must have had an entire publicity and communications team in order to spread the amount of positive stories about the woman, her business and to a lesser extent, her son.

Ann was well versed in the art of whitewashing. If a negative media story or exposé on one's client was about to break, her team released several high-profile interviews or reports on altruistic gestures to counter whatever the mud-slingers had prepared. A few hours crosschecking indicated Cinthia was undoubtedly a wealthy woman although several of her ventures had ended in spectacular failure. That said, she supported charities, donated to good causes and had established an education fund in Belém for 'female betterment'. While the phrase raised Ann's hackles, she had to admire the sentiment. The woman, as Fátima had observed, was not stupid.

As for her son, the jury was still out. His boat, *A Linda Lua* or The Beautiful Moon, was worth three-quarters of a million dollars and he only used it for a month each summer. A detail she would not share with Ricardo. Stories of this young man's excesses and hell-raising exploits abounded, countered by twice as many bland press releases on his academic achievements, sporting prowess and glamorous girlfriends. She also found the links to the two cases he'd been charged with and acquitted of both. Nothing supported Maduro's 'Vigilante Trial Theory'. A tragic accident and a suicide, at least officially. If there was one job Ann didn't envy, it was Franck Fischer's PR team.

One other element she could not dismiss as high spirits or youthful exuberance. Franck Fischer was associated with a far-right anti-immigration group. Nowhere online could she find proof he was an active member, but his social media accounts expressed tacit approval and the group themselves – First Line of Defence or FLD – quoted him in more than one of their statements. This purity of race angle puzzled Ann, as the boy's mother was Brazilian and his late father American. Possibly he'd encountered a certain extremist element while at university and, like many first-generation immigrants, become one of the most vocal against others enjoying the same opportunities.

All good reasons to dislike this figure, but why Maduro's almost-obsessive interest? Her search for the inspector's profile delivered limited results. Gil Maduro gave every appearance of being a good cop: among the best graduates of his year, impeccable record, leading community initiatives and even quoted in the international press over the Soure force's use of water buffalo. The photo didn't do him justice. That story was from 2019, but Ann noted he was unmarried.

She realised she was scrunching her toes, not an action conducive to a good night's sleep. Tomorrow she would offer Maduro a quid pro quo. Buy him a coffee, tell him about Pedro's 'accident', and ask him for more detail on the Fischer kid. She had to appear neutral and disinterested but driven by conscience to press him on the drug dealers.

When she finally slept, she dreamed of blood. Of course she did. Regardless of what she'd seen in the past and how she held her nerve in the face of the most nauseating violence, it never failed to manifest itself somehow or other in her subconscious. She had watched how one tier of the hierarchy enforced its terms on the tier below, with unsubtle and unforgettable punishments for transgressors. Every time. When witnessing such an incident, the cooler she played her indifference, the worse it haunted her dreams.

This time the blood ran from the jungle, a trickle meandering down the beach towards the sea. She watched, rooted to the spot, knowing the trickle was only a precursor of what was to come. She waited for the flood but it never arrived. Instead, the trickle stopped, changed course and flowed in her direction. She ran, but the blood, like a probing finger, grew closer and closer to her heels. The bike lay on its side outside her shack but she knew trying to cycle through sand was slower than crawling. She could not outrun this phenomenon so the only thing left was to dilute it. The waves were ferocious, pounding against the shore as if trying to restart its heart. She dived in, disorientated and gasping as the ocean spun her in worlds of sand and salty water, her limbs heavy and unable to keep her head above water. She burst out of the surf confused as to where the beach lay. She found her feet and staggered away from the clutching waves, only to see the beach was no longer white but red. On the steps to her shack lay Branca, peeled of her fur like an anatomical model.

Ann sat up, horrified by her own visions, hugging her knees until her breathing calmed and heart rate subsided. Beside her bed, Branca twitched and snored, comfortable in her own skin, waves stroked the beach with the gentle tones of a rainmaker, and jungle creatures continued their shrieks, cries and howls. Ann curled under her blanket and wondered how Pedro was doing.

The late night and graphic nightmares took their toll. She woke late, fragile and emotional, jittery about letting Branca out of the door. As if her subconscious had been through the tumble dryer, her mind pulled out random memories and sensations like odd socks. Learning to retrieve a brick from the bottom of a swimming pool while wearing pyjamas. Watching a nature programme with her father where a baby pelican was dying in the desert because the rains hadn't come. She and Katie, both choked with tears, asking, 'But why don't the cameramen help?' And her father's reply, 'You have to let nature take its course'. Looking across a circle of men and catching the same agonised impulse in her colleague's eyes as a teenager screamed in the dust. Later, asking Thanh to stop the car so she could vomit onto the pavement. His voice as he held her hair, 'Better out than in, girl'.

No. She could not, would not think about Thanh. If she wanted to retain her sanity, that subject was off-limits. She made a pot of coffee and sat on the porch, breathing the morning air and directing her mind to the present. *A promise is a promise, if only to yourself. There's no such thing as the past, only the future.* She got up and started packing for the day ahead.

The laptop, while designed to be light and portable, would

add weight to what she had to carry. On the plus side, she could use the woven basket affixed to the front of the bike to carry some of the grocery load. The computer wouldn't fit behind the kitchen tiles, with the rest of her secrets, so her deep-seated insecurity advised her to slip it into one of the many zippered pockets and take it along for the ride. She locked up, set her security markers, left a bowl of water on the porch for Branca and wheeled her bicycle up to the tree line.

Instead of cycling into the village then doubling back on the main road, she intended to take the shortcut she had discovered whilst a passenger in Zé's pickup. Riding through the jungle was out of the question but even wheeling it would still cut forty minutes off the whole journey. When she left, Branca was nowhere to be seen. Ann set off, already rehearsing her speech to Gil Maduro. Her sensible side reminded her of the risks. She had already been warned about talking to the police. She had no proof the people who had punished Pedro were drug dealers. Her ability to connect Pedro's injury to Mauricio Gonçalves's operation could flag her as something rather different to your average poet. Whether or not Nelson's death was connected to a wannabe godfather, she had nothing more than suspicion. But that was someone else's problem. *Not my circus, not my monkeys.*

The late start meant she arrived in Soure, dusty, sweaty and hot just after eleven. After a couple of wrong turns, she found the police station and parked her bike on the shady side of the street. She had no intention of marching in there for a repeat encounter with the gormless officers from last time. Instead, she intended to wait as long as it took until she could be sure of speaking to Maduro alone. She locked her bike against a palm tree, set her backpack by her feet and drank half a litre of water to compensate for what she had lost on the ride.

"Good morning, Ann." Gil Maduro stood behind her, cool and crisp in his uniform. "Are you waiting for me?"

His ability to creep up on her enraged Ann and made her snappy. "I have some information I thought might be of interest to the police, that's all. I wasn't waiting for anyone, just taking a moment to cool down."

"Yes, it is hot. Maybe we should sit in the shade somewhere and you can tell me what you have to say. By the river is pleasant. I have a few things to do in the next hour but I can meet you at midday. Take that street to the end and then go right along the riverbank. There's a bar called *Casa de Iemanjá*. If you're hungry, they do a pretty good *camusclim*." He strode away across the street, raising a hand in greeting to a passing car.

Casa de Iemanjá. House of the Sea Goddess. Ann snorted, remounted her bike and headed for the river. She was hungry after her ride and nothing more than coffee for breakfast, but having lunch with the cop was not on the agenda. For one thing, she didn't want to spend too long in the man's company. He was far too perceptive for her liking. Secondly, having been warned off against consorting with the police, it would be inflammatory to be seen breaking bread with the inspector. The whole idea was to have a quiet word behind closed doors and leave the decision up to him.

When she found the bar, it was not what she expected. This was not some street café with mismatched chairs, overfilled ashtrays and a TV inevitably showing a football match. Instead, it was a hotel with a terrace overlooking the river and an air-conditioned interior. Exactly the kind of place Fátima would love to drink cocktails. What tipped the balance was reading the description of *camusclim*. Shrimps and pasta baked in a béchamel sauce sounded irresistible, especially as everything she made was cooked on a basic hob. She ordered a beer and sat near the window, observing the well-heeled patrons of this discreet watering hole. From what she'd seen so far, Gil Maduro had pretty good taste.

He arrived several minutes before twelve, exchanged greetings with two businessmen near the bar and strolled over to her table.

"Good choice. It's always quiet inside. This is my lunch break so I plan to have the special and a beer. How about you?"

"I hadn't planned to eat lunch in town, but the description won me over. Me too."

"Another good choice." He hailed the waitress. "And seeing as you've brought me some information, lunch is on me." He gave their order and surveyed the diners on the terrace.

"That's very kind of you. Although you don't know how useful my information is going to be. This is a nice hotel. Is this where you usually come for lunch?"

He returned his gaze to her. "Sometimes. Depends where I am when I get hungry. This place calms my mind. Predictability, order and simplicity. The exact opposite of my job. Another of its attractions is the great food." He smiled at the waitress who delivered two hearty plates of *camusclim* and two cold beers. "*Muito obrigado*, Adelina."

They began eating and Ann was incapable of speech for several minutes. It was so long since she'd had something rich, creamy, full of flavour and piping hot from the oven, she could have cried. Repercussions of her late-night and bad dreams, nothing more. Still, she ate in silence, appreciating every mouthful.

"Poetry is not my area of expertise," Maduro began. "But I imagine order and simplicity both play a role. Predictability, though, definitely not. That's the point. A poet has a limited number of tools but an infinite way of using them. I apologise, I don't really know what I'm talking about."

Ann stared at him, fork halfway to her mouth. When she

recovered herself to speak, she had to fight the urge to match his honesty. "I think that phrase could equally apply to any poet. None of us know what we're talking about, we're just grasping for meaning using the medium of words. The results of a poet's work are less tangible than that of a police officer's, of that I am certain."

He took a long draught of his beer and rested the cold glass against his cheek for a second, before replacing it on the table cloth. "Perhaps the two are more comparable than they first appear. A police officer is judged on every case, a poet on every poem. Only in retrospect can we deliver a verdict on the whole career. It's difficult to say because I've never been a poet." He lifted his gaze from his plate and fixed his eyes on hers.

Ann found his intensity and willingness to cut to the chase more than she could handle and returned her attention to her food. "This is possibly the most delicious meal I've enjoyed since coming to Brazil. Mainly because I didn't cook it myself."

Maduro waited a beat before replying. "As I said, this is their signature dish and they hone it to perfection. I'm sure you sampled some exciting food while you were in Rio, no?"

She didn't react but continued to chew, swallow and take a swig of beer. The guy was good, an expert at probing under the guise of casual conversation. "I've had great food in many places, that's true, but here I should make a confession." She saw the flicker of interest in his eyes.

"I'm an appalling cook, always have been. Add to that a range of ingredients I've never seen before in my life and I think only the politest person in the world would describe my culinary efforts as exciting. This meal, I'm not joking, is like all my Christmases come at once."

He laughed, tilting his head in a kind of acknowledgement. She'd wriggled off the hook once again and this time he was prepared to let her go. But there was a leonine patience in his expression. Like any predator, he could wait.

"This is only the tip of the iceberg. If you know where to look, exceptional restaurants are everywhere on this island. I'd like to introduce you to some, if you're willing. But you said you had something to tell me. I assume it's relevant to the case we discussed?"

She was grateful for the deflection, and prepared to conjure an excuse why she would not want to have dinner with an erudite, knowledgeable and damned hot-looking man.

"Yes, I think it is." By the time she had finished explaining the incident on the beach, they had finished their meals and their beers. Maduro ordered two coffees and gazed out at the terrace once again, his expression thoughtful. In the silence, Ann waited, suppressing the urge to speak and add more reasons for her theory.

It took a long time for him to speak. "What you say makes sense. All the evidence indicates that our friend on the farm is making a name for himself. That injury you describe would be consistent with someone disciplining their foot soldiers. The problem here is that we are talking about two different crimes and my job is to investigate a murder. At the present moment, I'm absorbed with bringing the person or persons who killed Nelson Leal to justice. You'll understand I can share no details, but we're about to make an arrest. The individual in question has no association with the drug dealers, unless as a casual customer. Once this particular case goes to tribunal, I can take the Gonçalves situation to the Federal police. It's more complicated than it looks, I assure you, but I will fight both injustices with all my resources."

Ann studied his face, the jutting jaw, the unhappy set of his mouth and understood. He wasn't a superhero. He was a civil police officer, with all the bureaucracy and politics that goes with that role.

Her promise to Mike Ferguson triggered her to ask a question. "I wouldn't expect you to share any details. That would be unprofessional. The other evening, you mentioned a feeling you had about a well-known character but you were unable to do anything about it due to lack of evidence. My guess is you found something to incriminate that individual and proved yourself right." She scrunched her toes, painfully aware of how crass her flattery came across.

He lifted his gaze to study her and the light on the water carafe reflected in his eyes. "I used to go fishing as a boy. You cannot imagine the pride I felt when taking a bucket of catfish home to my mother. Then one day I hooked a *filhote*. Those beasts can grow to 200 kg. It dragged me off the boat and almost killed me. This situation is pretty similar. I've thrown a line and got a bite but the power behind this catch could take me under. Sorry, I have to leave you now. Too much work to do. I enjoyed our lunch. Have a good afternoon." He got up from the table, made a signing motion to the waitress and left the room.

Ann sat there for several minutes, disappointed by his sudden exit and worried she had probed too far. She left the hotel, still considering his words. How the hell was she supposed to put that in an email to Mike Ferguson?

Her bike was where she had chained it. She sent a prayer of gratitude to her guardian angel. The afternoon was sweltering and the journey home far from appealing. After the heavy lunch and two beers, Ann was ready for a nap in one of those clean, air-conditioned hotel rooms with its power shower and mini-bar. Instead she cycled to the supermarket, filled her backpack with essentials and began the ride home, still thinking about Gil Maduro.

16

On the road out of town, a horn tooted right behind her, making her wobble. She braked, placing her feet on the ground and looked over her shoulder to see a white pickup truck with a man waving through the windscreen. Her immediate instinct was to tell him where to stick his unwanted attention, until he got out of the cab.

"*Olá* Ann, *tudo bem*? You going home? I can give you a lift, save your legs. It's hot today, no? I'll put your bike in the back and you can sit in front with me. I have air con, you know."

Exactly what she needed. She smiled at Zé. "That's really kind of you, thanks. Yes, please. What took you to Soure today?"

He placed the bike on the flatbed beside a pile of boxes. "Those things. I'm Postman Zé again, collecting packages from the ferry. Stuff people ordered from Belém or the States or other places. You want to get in?"

Ann shoved her pack into the cab between herself and Zé. "No other passengers?"

"Not when I do the post run. I never know how much I have to pick up. Sometimes two tiny bags, other times massive cartons I have to tie down. Today was a mixture. There is a coffee machine I have to take to Praia do Céu, some agricultural stuff for Quinta dos Rios and there's a funny-shaped package for Tia Maria. God knows what's in there, I don't ask questions. What about you? Doing your groceries?"

The truck bumped along the track and Ann's post-lunch slump evaporated, her mind seizing an opportunity. "Groceries, yes. I had to buy some food for Nelson's dog. Did you say you're going to Praia do Céu? I've never been there. Could I come along for the ride?"

Zé changed gear and beamed. "Sure you can! Company for me and you won't find a better tour guide. I'll show you the sights. All three of them. Ha! Praia do Céu is pretty, I admit that, though Pesqueiro is the nicer village. They say the opposite, of course. It's the same with most of these places; we are rivals but best friends. Like siblings, always in competition but love each other dearly. You got any brothers or sisters?"

His casual enquiry caught her off guard and she almost blurted out her sister's name. "No, I'm an only child. What about you?" Ann only heard part of his answer, concentrating on remembering her role. Instead of turning to Pesqueiro, they drove past the airport and continued along the main road. Zé talked non-stop, switching subjects like a flea. It would have been faster to get from one village to another via the sea but due to the river tributaries Zé took a 15 kilometre detour. Ann asked questions about their destination, enquired about the region and cast the occasional hook and line, hoping to reel in some information.

"You mean there are two beaches? What's the other one called?"

"Praia do Cajuuna. Céu has a restaurant, but only the one. Both beaches are beautiful and natural. Now you have your bike, you could come up here and meet some other Americans or Brits. This time of year there are always plenty of tourists you could talk to. Nelson used to love hanging out with foreigners, speaking English. Viviane said he made more in tips than in wages. That kid had a lot of charm." Zé's face clouded for a moment. "I liked him. Everybody did."

Ann sighed. "I only met him a couple of times but he made a very good impression. It's a horrible shock for the village."

Zé nodded with emphasis as they approached a village by the beach. "For the whole area. We have deaths, like everywhere else, but not murder. This is not Belém or Manaus. We are a peaceful fishing village and tourist beach. It makes no sense."

"No sense at all. What about the other place you mentioned? Something Dos Rios? Is that another beach?" Her faux naiveté made her cringe.

"You mean Quinta Dos Rios? No, that's just an old farm. OK, this is the restaurant. Why don't you walk around the village while I get this installed? It'll take me around half an hour and then we'll drive the scenic route, drop the machines at Quinta dos Rios and head back to Pesqueiro. Maybe we can have a beer at the *padaria*?"

Ann noted the eager look on his face and chose to use it to her advantage. "Only if I'm buying. A thank you for the lift."

"Great! You don't need to carry your pack around, you can leave it in the car. I'll even lock the doors if you like?"

Ann opened the door to the heat of the afternoon and realised how the air conditioning had deceived her. "I'll keep it with me, thanks anyway. See you in half an hour."

She strolled down the dusty path, encountering a handful of beachgoers either heading for the beach or the restaurant. It was a spectacular location, a huge stretch of sand as far as she could see, the Atlantic Ocean rolling waves and palm trees leaning at an angle towards the ocean. A line of driftwood at the high tide mark looked like an exotic pattern from where Ann stood. She walked closer to the water, wrinkling her nose at the odd water bottle, cigarette packet or discarded flip-flop. To her left stood a series of palm-leaf umbrellas, casting patches of shade from the unforgiving sun. She decided to make use of one, leaning her backpack against the pole and sitting cross-legged to appreciate the view.

Why the view was different here she couldn't say, but travelling a few kilometres up the coast made her feel as if she was on holiday. A scream made her whip around to see a young couple fooling around in the shallows.

She watched as the girl ran after her boyfriend, failing to gain on him due to her laughter. He doubled back and pulled her by the waist into an embrace. The girl capitulated but in a neat move, curled her ankle behind his leg and pushed him over. Off-balance, he flailed and fell into the surf, only to sit up spluttering, with a huge grin on his face.

Ann smiled at their horseplay. Such freedom to spend the summer in a bikini, taking advantage of this glorious location while young and in love. It wasn't envy, exactly, just an awareness those two young people had no idea how lucky they were. She heaved up her backpack and walked along the beach towards the colourful houses on stilts, wondering if there was a bar where she might buy something to drink. As she clambered up the awkward path, Zé's truck came to a halt on the road ahead. He wound down the window.

"Finished! You ready to leave?"

Ann jumped into the cab, grateful for the air conditioning, for herself and the contents of her backpack. They drove along the coast to the next tiny hamlet and got out to admire the view across the river mouth.

"Do you get used to it, Zé? I mean, does all this beauty cease to affect you after the first year or so? Nobody else seems to walk around with their jaw on the floor like me."

Zé tucked his hands in his back pockets and leaned back against the truck. "The first few weeks after the rains, everybody is a tourist. We forget, year after year, how much we miss it: the sunshine, the beaches, the sea, the tourists, even our neighbours. It's like we're in hibernation and then life starts again. So no, you never get used to it. This is our springtime when we are excited about life. Let's go, I want to drop off the last packages before the boss comes home and then we're free to enjoy the sunset."

The track to Quinta Dos Rios was riddled with potholes and popular with water buffalo. Zé was forced to navigate a path between the obstacles, taking the pickup far too close to the edges of the washed-away road for Ann's comfort.

"I guess not too many vehicles visit the farm," she said, clutching her seat.

"Plenty, actually, which is why we're coming this way. This is the old road nobody uses since they made a tarmac version. I never use that if I can help it. I don't want to meet these people. I just drop off the stuff and go home."

"Right. Oh my God!" The tyres hit a rut and bounced downwards and up again. Ann's head hit the roof of the cab and her backpack jumped like it was on a trampoline.

"It's OK, Ann, I did this many times, even in rainy season." He switched to English. "Don't worry, be happy!"

She forced a grin. "You do the post run in the rainy season too? I hope they pay you a lot."

He grimaced and hit the brakes as a water buffalo changed course and blocked the road. They waited until the beast had lumbered into the other side, wading knee deep into floodwater.

"Most people do, but not this Gonçalves guy. I keep saying I'm gonna stop delivering to this farm. He never gives me a tip and always complains. That's why I want to drop his stuff and get out of here. This place," he shook his head with a frown and put the vehicle into first gear. "This place gives me bad vibes. You stay in the cab, out of sight."

Ann nodded but didn't reply. Finally the road broadened out to a rough turning circle, surrounded by a two-storey house and half a dozen outbuildings. It took her a moment to notice what was different. The house and barns were built on a concrete plinth, around the size of a football pitch. No stilts here. Whereas the villagers built their shacks high, allowing the floodwaters to flow beneath, this compound was the original immovable object. The waters were forced around it to find another route to the sea. The house itself had a pleasing aspect, with faded red shutters framing each window. The farm buildings, on the other hand, were grim and featureless, reminding Ann of a slaughterhouse.

Zé tooted the horn and yanked up the handbrake. "Stay down, Ann. We don't want them to see you. I'm serious." He slammed the door and began clattering around on the flatbed.

Ann slunk down in her seat so that only her eyes and top of the head were visible above the dashboard. Two men carried a sack from one building to another, each holding two corners. They glanced at the truck and called a greeting to Zé. Another man came from the house, heavier and bearded, wearing dungarees. He passed close by the cab and Ann slid lower but the man was already in conversation with Zé. The truck sank and rose and wobbled as the two men lugged the machinery off the flatbed and towards the farm buildings. Once they had gone through some double doors, Ann sat up and assessed her environment.

Tree cover around hundred metres behind the truck and her habitual outfit of green, grey and beige would enable her to blend into the jungle. All she needed to do was keep low to the ground. She eased open the passenger door and slipped onto her hands and knees. She knelt for several moments, assessing the risks. Due to the angle Zé had parked the truck, she couldn't be seen from the house. The people working in the outbuildings were not expecting anyone to peek through the window. Everyone seemed to be far too concerned with their own tasks to notice her. All she wanted was an idea of how this place functioned. There was another danger – leaving her rucksack in Zé's cab. If she was going to snoop, she'd better be quick.

She scuttled across the scrubby turning area and into the undergrowth. At each stage, she stopped, listened, surveyed and checked. The nearest farm building seemed the least active. No lights in the windows, no movement in or out. She flicked her glance to the double doors of the building where Zé had entered. Nothing. The angle of the sun threw a shadow to conceal her as she crept closer to the window.

Without warning, a door opened barely five metres ahead and a man strode out, his attention focused on Zé's truck. Ann dropped flat to the ground, barely breathing as she watched his snakeskin boots crunch away. If he turned, she was completely exposed. Thankfully, he did not, intent on reaching the shed where Zé had entered. He flung open the double doors and began shouting. She backed away fast, crablike in a reverse runner's lunge, until her progress was halted by a pair of sturdy legs.

She stifled a shriek of surprise and spun onto her backside, her hand reaching for her knife. The legs belonged to the heavyset male she'd seen assisting Zé. He gazed down at her, his expression dumbstruck. His mouth hung open, his bottom lip wet, his hands still in his pockets. Neither spoke.

The sound of doors slamming made them both turn. Mauricio Gonçalves powered across the yard, heading for the house. Before he went inside, he turned and pointed a finger at the truck.

"*A última vez!*" Another door slammed and he was gone.

The truck started up and made a slow revolution of the turning circle before inching its way down the road. Zé must be searching for her. She scrambled to her feet, bent low in a defensive pose, keeping her focus on the big man. The truck came to a halt and Zé leapt out of the cab.

"Ann! What are you doing? Are you crazy? Get in the truck! João, so sorry, this is a friend of mine. Nothing to worry about. I'll get her out of here."

He beckoned Ann, who moved in his direction, not once taking her eyes off the man in dungarees. He watched her go with all the curiosity of a child observing a beetle.

"Hurry!" hissed Zé, looking over his shoulder at the house.

Ann ran and jumped into the passenger seat, her sweaty palms slipping on the door handle. Zé took off immediately then braked with enough force to tip Ann's rucksack onto the floor. The bearded man stood in the road, blocking their escape. His impassive face stared at Ann.

Zé wound down the window. "João? What is it?"

João came to Ann's side of the truck and opened the door. She shrank away as his huge hand reached for her face, his touch as gentle as calloused hands could manage. He tilted her face towards him and whispered, his breath meaty and foul. "You are lucky it was me who found you. Don't come back." He patted her cheek, stood back and closed the door. "*Tchau, Zé. Bom fin de semana!*" He thumped the roof of the cab with enough force to dent the chassis.

Only when they reached the main road did Zé release his pent-up frustration. No matter how many times she apologised and made the urgent-call-of-nature excuse, he was not mollified. They drove into Praia do Pesqueiro in silence, his fury tangible. He stopped outside the bakery.

"Forget buying me a beer, I don't want one. Take your stuff and get out."

She dragged her bike off the truck and wheeled it to the driver's door. "Thank you for the ride. You're right to be angry with me and I'm truly sorry. Maybe we can have that beer some other time?"

He glared at her, his expression thunderous. "Angry with you? I was goddamned terrified for you! Sniffing around Quinta dos Rios is insanity. For a woman alone, it's like throwing yourself to the wolves. João was right. You were *very* lucky it was him who found you. God help us if he tells his brother, because then we're both in the shit. What did I say? Keep out of sight! Don't let them see you!" He shook his head and rubbed his forehead. His tone dropped from a hoarse shout to a barely controlled hiss. "I shouldn't have taken you with me. Well, it won't happen again. You're a stranger; of course you don't understand how dangerous it is. I'm going to tell you again, Ann, and this time you'd better listen. Stay away from that place. Even if you are invited, never go there on your own. In fact, never go there with anyone, no matter what the circumstances. You seen Serena recently? The surfer girl who knows no fear? No, neither have I. Why don't you ask her what happens to girls who accept an invitation to the farm? Go home, you stupid, stupid woman."

He drove off in the direction of the beach, leaving Ann in a cloud of dust and humiliation. She swallowed her embarrassment as half the patrons on the terrace were watching the drama and got on her bike. Her body weary and her head about to explode, she cycled in the direction of her shack. Tonight she needed peace, quiet and thinking time.

17

Blood on the sand. The instant her shack came into view, Ann could see something was wrong. Objects lay around the building as if they'd been thrown from the windows and curtains blew outwards in the wind. She quelled the impulse to dump the bike and run, instead approaching with maximum caution. The lumps in the sand took shape and she saw her kitchen chair, her cot and clothes, her cooking pans and two sacks of dried beans, torn and spilling their contents on the beach. Her breathing, already exerted by the ride, grew shallow. No white heron stood on the roof and Branca was nowhere to be seen.

Her practical side advised calm. Someone had broken in and trashed her hut, hurling her belongings outside and probably destroying the contents of her kitchen. All her security measures had failed and she had to start from scratch. That was not the end of the world. Most items she treasured were in her backpack, but in case she was ever mugged, she kept certain essentials in a hiding place behind the tiles. If the burglar had found that, she'd lost at least two of her insurance policies – the gun and the poison. Worse still, her real ID, cash in US dollars and her will.

Her emotional side drowned out commonsense, sounding the alarm. Where was the dog? What had they done to Branca? While her view of reality was clouded by tears, her subconscious mind recalled the graphic images from her nightmare. That dark stain on the white sand was blood.

She stopped at the end of her path, wiping sweat and tears from her face, elbowing aside her emotions and putting faith in her training. Laying her bike down, she slipped off her backpack and located her binoculars. She performed a slow, steady scan of the ocean, the end of the beach, her own house, the trail she had made on leaving the jungle, and the rest of the strand, reaching towards the village. Other than the destruction around her own shack, everything looked as it should be.

Once she had the big picture, she paid attention to the detail. The blood originated from a patch to the right of the house. There was a dip in the sand as if someone had sat or lain there. Most of the blood was concentrated around that area, with regular stains moving south-east, towards the seashore and in the direction of the village. She pieced together the evidence of her eyes and saw her early warning alarm system, the buried broken bottles, had taken effect. The intruder, or more likely one of the intruders, had fallen foul of her 'garden' and paid the price.

Flick knife in hand, she walked to the steps, leaving her domestic detritus scattered where it was. Her front door swung to and fro in the wind, a reassuring sound like a rocking chair on the porch. But there was nothing reassuring about the sight of her smashed-in portal. She stood at the base of the steps, absorbing the scene, attuned to the atmosphere. It was not the first time she had come across a destructive break-in. It had happened at her own home, more than once. But here there was no ugly graffiti, smeared faeces or symbolic sexual gesture, such as someone soiling her knickers. At least not yet. From where she stood, she could see the kitchen table broken into pieces, her shelves bare of foodstuff and crockery. On the veranda, there was nothing. Table, chair, tomato plant and Branca's water bowl all tossed into the sand near her feet.

She took her time ascending the steps, testing each one for damage before allowing it to bear her weight. With a huge breath, she flicked open her knife and entered the building. The destruction was complete. Every window broken, no piece of furniture left standing or undamaged, mosquito net completely removed and all her lotions, sun cream and toiletries had been squeezed into her tiny toilet. The cachaça emptied and the bottle smashed in the sink. She moved around the room with a professional eye, taking in the damage with no more emotion than a Sphinx.

When she had finally assessed the scale of what she would need to do, she returned and sat on the top step. Surely, some-where, they must be watching. No one leaves such wreckage without waiting to see the consequent grief. Today, they would be disappointed.

Her practical side was already rolling up its sleeves. Three things to be grateful for: whilst they had emptied her cold store, the generator was still running. Secondly, the tiles behind the sink still concealed her box of tricks. Lastly, and of the most profound relief to her fragile emotional state, there was no canine corpse in a macabre tableau. That dog was street smart and would flee at any threat. Ann willed that to be the truth.

Her dry mouth was becoming unbearable. She retrieved her backpack and picked up the tomato plant. She replaced it in its pot, withdrew her bottle and watered the little thing before slaking her own thirst. Time slipped past as the sweat cooled on her back and she considered emergency measures to protect herself as the sun slid towards the horizon.

Piece by piece, she collected any items of unbroken furniture and stacked them on the veranda. Then she swept the house, clearing it of broken glass, splintered wood and ruined food. She righted her cot and retrieved her mattress, pillow and bedcovers from outside. For tonight, security was a priority. While the glass had gone from every window, the shutters remained. The front door had been attacked with some sort of hatchet. Three locks were no match for an axe. Whoever wanted entry had forced their way in.

The idea of an axe made her examine the shack again. Her machete was missing. That hurt and for the first time, tears welled. She refused them. Instead of weeping, she gathered the trashed table, torn sacks and other flammables to make a bonfire on the beach tomorrow, taking them far enough away from the house not to cause a hazard. The irony of burning down your own house after they tried to destroy it was not even funny.

They. Who was she talking about? Up until today, the slightest threat or injury triggered the suspicion her past was hard on her heels. Now, she'd somehow gathered present enemies. But one thing was certain – these were amateurs. Vandals, smashing and destroying, fire-starters who ran from the scene.

She stopped in the act of filling a pan with water. Burning down the house. These flimsy beach structures were susceptible to fire. Before it got too dark she needed to check beneath the stilts to ensure there was no nasty surprise about to spark in the middle of the night.

In the doorway, she listened both with ears and instinct for any change in the atmosphere. Nothing as far as she could tell was out of the ordinary. She crouched to look beneath the house, scanning the shadows for anything other than sand. One shape shifted, transforming from indistinguishable greyish mound to skinny white dog.

"There you are!" Ann's relief was disproportionate. She crouched to stroke Branca's coat, wondering if she was imagining it. The dog seemed not just happy to see her, but overjoyed. Poor creature must have found the invaders terrifying. At least she'd had the good sense not to challenge the vandals and keep out of their way.

Branca accompanied her up the steps and into the house, tail still wagging and eyes eager. Having the dog in the house increased Ann's resolve to carry on regardless. She opened a can of sardines and mixed them with fresh tomatoes. The dry biscuits which had weighed her down on the ride home from Soure met with Branca's approval. They ate on the porch, which had suffered the least of the damage. One of the table legs was snapped, but by propping it against the railing, it was steady enough. The chair seemed none the worse for being hurled onto the sand.

Sleeping indoors was too risky. The only entrance she could not secure was the doorway. Ann made up her mind to spend the night on the porch, with the dog at her feet and the gun in her hand.

She took her firearm from its hiding place, loaded the chamber and locked the safety catch. How long since she'd handled a weapon? Who cared? It was the threat, and the sound, that mattered. One shot in the dark would be enough to scare one of the posturing surfers. If it was the posturing surfers. Supposing João reported to his brother after Zé's truck had rumbled down the road? More than enough time for Mauricio to send a warning via some of his men. She considered the evidence. Everything in her ice box had melted. The tray of ice cubes contained nothing more than warm water. That wouldn't happen in half an hour. This attack had happened shortly after she left for Soure, in broad daylight and in full view of the beach.

After one last slug of coffee, she switched off the lights and wrapped herself in a blanket. She reached out a hand to touch Branca's warm flank.

"You and me, girl, defenders of the homestead. Just let them try." She didn't even convince herself.

The night passed, eventually, after a succession of false alarms, most of them in Ann's mind. Only once did the dog raise her head to growl at something at the end of the beach. They stared into the blackness together, then Branca went back to sleep. Ann kept staring. When the sky eventually lightened, she was more exhausted than ever. Cat naps and sudden tension accompanied by worries crowding in from every angle left her physically worn out and mentally threadbare. Sunrise offered a sense of security and she closed her eyes, in desperate need of some rest.

"*O que é isto?*"

The angry demand slapped her awake at the same time as Branca began barking. Ricardo was standing at the end of the path to her shack, hands on his hips, glaring at the pile of broken furniture.

She shook herself awake, rubbing the sleep from her puffy eyes. Branca's bark was insistent and fraying her nerves. Guiding the dog by her bandana, she took her inside, closing the door as best she could. Ricardo, at the base of the steps, took one look at the damage and his outraged expression changed to one of concern.

"What happened?"

"A break-in. They smashed up the house." She slid the gun under her blanket while his attention was on the door.

"Who did this?"

"I don't know. I found it this way when I came home. I'll

ask Fátima if she saw anyone. Whoever it was cut themselves. There was blood on the sand." Her tiredness was such she was forgetting to make mistakes.

Ricardo gave her a sharp look. "Cut his hand?"

"Foot, I think." She pointed to the hollow in the sand where broken glass and dark stains were visible. "Why did you say hand?"

Ricardo went over to the hollow and prodded it with his foot. "You put these bottles here?"

"Yes. To deter intruders. Guess it didn't work."

"Was anything stolen? Did they take the computer?"

Ann covered a yawn. "No. I had it with me. Only my machete and my mosquito net have gone."

"What about your coffee?" He gave her a grin. "Make us a cup, I have news for you. Then let's get this place fixed up. I know people." He walked down the path to the pile of broken furniture and started picking out pieces of wood.

Ann yawned again and went inside to make coffee. After releasing Branca to roam the beach, she tucked the gun in its hiding place and replaced the tiles. The milk was sour but at least she could offer her visitor some hot, strong coffee with agave syrup instead of sugar.

On the veranda, Ricardo had upended the table and was winding string around the broken leg, rather like a bandage. "It will hold until we get it repaired. The stuff here needed replacing anyway. Dona Emilia hasn't changed a thing since she moved out in '98 and only bothers with maintenance when she has to. Coffee!" He righted the table and pressed a hand to the surface. It didn't even wobble. "Big news, Ann. That cop came this morning, early. They made an arrest last night. You won't believe who they think did it. Maybe you will, because you told me his name." He sipped his coffee. "Is there no sugar in this? Ah, they trashed that too? Little shits."

"Ricardo, who have they arrested?" She knew the answer but needed thinking time.

"Franck Fischer, the one we talked about. He's got history, you know. The cop says he was implicated in another death here in Brazil two years ago, but they couldn't make it stick. We're going to make it stick this time. You have to contact Mike Ferguson immediately. Cinthia Fischer can afford the best legal team and will get the kid off on a technicality unless we pay a good lawyer. We have no money, but Mike wants to help. You can tell him ..."

"Wait a minute. The police believe Franck Fischer killed Nelson? Why? What was his motive? You said Nelson never met him."

Ricardo's face clouded. "The cop didn't say. Maybe you should ask him. Or is that what caused all this?" He waved a hand at the battered shack.

Ann shrugged, her gaze on her coffee.

"Well, it's the lawyer's job to ask questions, not ours. Most important is for you to contact Mike this morning. Will you do that for me, Ann? It's urgent."

"Yes, all right, I'll do it as soon as I finish my coffee." Her tone came out as irritable and sharp. "Sorry, not much sleep. Of course I'll let Mike know. I planned to email him today anyway. Is Fischer in custody?"

It was Ricardo's turn to shrug. "It's not in the newspapers yet and the cop asked me not to tell anyone until it is." He pushed his empty coffee cup away and got to his feet. "Well, he said to keep it in the family. Mike is family. I'm going now, I have to go fishing upriver. But I'll be back later with some stuff. I'll fix the door so you can sleep in your bed tonight. Don't know about big knives or spare nets but the least I can do is bring you some sugar."

She smiled, caffeine, sunshine and a friendly face lifting her out a weary slump. "Thank you, Ricardo. By then, I should be able to report what Mike says. See you later."

"*Até logo*," he replied as he stomped down the steps. Then he stopped. "That blood on the sand. I saw Pedro Bandeiro had an accident. His hand was all bandaged up. Seems a coincidence."

She hesitated, careful not to incriminate anyone. "Pedro might have been one of the kids who did this. No one else other than the surfers has threatened me. But Pedro's injury happened the day before. I don't know what happened but he was hurt yesterday morning."

"Hmm," Ricardo grunted and continued up the beach.

She washed up and showered before making some griddled cassava pancakes. The only place to sit was on the porch, which served as outdoor living space and surveillance point. She booted up the laptop and got to work. She sent a brief email to Mike Ferguson, explaining as succinctly as she could the situation as it stood.

Her email icon flashed up only minutes later.

Dear Ann,

Thank you for your note. I wish I could say I was happy to hear this news but I guess a grim kind of relief is closer to the mark. Of course I'm ready to fund any kind of legal support to assist the prosecution. The question is, how long is a piece of string? What exactly am I funding and how does it help? If you or Ricardo can identify a lawyer and have him contact me, let's take it from there. Cases like this take months if not years to come to court, so we have time to plan. Of course, any kind of prosecution will need to come from the police. Do you have any updates from their side of things? I'm running blind here, Ann, so any sort of guidance you can provide is more than welcome. Please give my regards to Ricardo and Dulce.

Thank you once again, Mike

After half an hour's browsing law offices in Soure and

Salvaterra, Ann's eyes began to droop. She considered making more coffee but didn't have the energy to get up from her seat. She snapped the laptop shut, closed her eyes and rested her head on her arms. A fifteen-minute power nap and she would be back to full strength.

"Ann?"

A gentle voice woke her and she lifted her muzzy head. At the bottom of the steps stood Gil Maduro, carrying a motor-cycle helmet and a carrier bag.

"Sorry to disturb you. I heard you had some problems last night. Can I be of any assistance? Take a statement, secure the area, make you lunch?" His manner was delicate, as if expecting rejection.

She scowled at him, her face crusty and incredulous. "What are you doing here? The reason this place got trashed is because of you. They warned me about talking to the police but I didn't listen. In truth, you turning up here is the last thing I need."

He nodded once and turned to walk away.

Dual pincers of guilt squeezed her. "Inspector! Excuse me, I just woke up. I'm not a morning person, never have been. Please, come in to what's left of my house. Today's special is coffee with syrup, unless you prefer yours with sugar and broken glass."

She took the laptop inside to charge, patting her face to wake up her brain. Maduro turning up was exactly what she needed. Why attack the man? He was her one source of official information and she had to keep him sweet. His footsteps on the porch were hesitant.

"It's been a long night," she said, with an apologetic smile.

He stood on the threshold and surveyed the damage. His expression was clinical as he examined the door, the shards of glass between the floorboards and the slashed curtain demarcating sleeping and living areas. "You found this when you came home after our lunch?"

She chose not to mention her detour. "This is the sanitised version. My food, my toiletries and my furniture were smashed up, scattered around the floor or thrown out of the window. That's why it's dark in here. I closed the shutters last night and slept on the porch with the dog."

He placed his carrier bag on the floor and looked into her eyes. "But you're not hurt? How about your dog?"

A swell of emotion overcame her and she turned her back, taking a second to recover herself. "Fine. I'm absolutely fine. So do you want some coffee or not?"

For a moment, he didn't respond. Ann brushed away a couple of tears, maintaining a stiff spine.

"Coffee would be nice. So your generator still works. That's good news. I brought the ingredients to make *Arroz do marisco*. Nothing special, just rice, seafood and piri-piri. I'm not the greatest cook, I warn you, certainly not up to the standards of *Casa de Iemanjá*. May I?"

She stepped aside and gestured towards her basic hob, with its tiles hiding at least some of her secrets. "I've got almost nothing in terms of food. They wrecked the kitchen and threw the dry goods all over the floor. It was like a Moroccan spice market when I got home." Her throat swelled and she covered the catch in her voice with a cough. "The pans still work, I believe."

He came to stand beside her, surveying the work surface. "Then I have everything I need. We can eat straight from the pan with forks, if you have them. If not, fingers. You didn't answer my question." His gaze searched her face.

She gathered all her strength and raised her eyebrows. "Your question?"

"The dog. Did they harm the animal?"

Ann took a deep breath, shaken by the fact another person

understood her fears for that skinny white mutt. "No, she's safe. First sign of danger, she'll run for the jungle. She's a local and knows where to hide."

Gil unpacked his carrier bag, placing each ingredient on the work surface. "It's important we all know where to hide. What about you?"

His familiarity and concern caught Ann at a vulnerable moment. Her resistance was fragile and she needed some space. "Detective, it's kind of you to come and help me and make some food. If you don't mind, I'll have a swim to freshen up. Back in ten minutes." She unpegged the curtain dividing the living and sleeping quarters, and changed into her swimming-costume. At the same time, she ensured the laptop was out of sight. Even if he found it, the chances of him breaking her security code were negligible. She took a towel and flip-flops and went out the front door, confused about how comfortable it felt to have Detective Maduro in her kitchen.

Seawater did the trick, pounding and slapping her as if she was in a Turkish hammam. Skin, lungs, senses and instinct awoke. After fifteen minutes in the ocean, she was completely revived and conscious of a fierce hunger. Wrapped in her towel, she flip-flopped across the beach, up the path and into her battered little shack. En route, she coached herself into her role. Naïve newcomer, shaken by unexpected wreckage, thinking about moving on, just want to see justice for Nelson. Fragile, on a hair trigger and willing to share a limited amount, so long as it didn't incriminate her.

She showered off the seawater and pulled on a cotton kaftan, her hair wound into a towel. In the kitchen, Maduro had laid a blanket on the floor, found two bowls, two forks and an unbroken cup as substitute serving spoon.

"I can't help the fact that people saw me come here. But

eating together on the porch in full view of any onlookers might give the wrong impression. An indoor picnic might be better for your reputation. The food is almost ready."

Ann sat cross-legged on the blanket, receptive and hungry as hell. "That's very thoughtful. I'm sorry I was so rude earlier. It's hard to know what to do for the best." She watched as Maduro took the pot from the hob and placed it on a broken piece of wood between them. The scent of spices, tomatoes, fish and peppers overpowered her and increased her appetite to the level of savage.

"You have no idea how much I need this. Thank you." She gave him a grateful, embarrassed smile.

"I'm glad I can help. An intrusion into your home must be very upsetting. Eat. After a swim and some seafood, you will feel better. Then maybe we can talk."

Her curiosity as to the topic of their 'talk' made her pause, but only for a second. She picked up the bowl, inhaled the piquant fragrance and scooped up a forkful of rice. This was not the first time she'd eaten *Arroz do Marisco*. Yet in her current frame of mind, it was the most comforting meal she had ever consumed. She cleaned the bowl and accepted seconds. This time, she ate less like a starving stray dog and more like a human being.

"It's delicious. I feel stronger now. You're very kind to come here today as I know you must have a lot to do. How did you hear someone had broken into my shack?"

"If you don't know about the coastal grapevine by now, you're not listening. I wanted to visit because I have news regarding the death of Nelson Leal and when I heard what happened, I wanted to help. More bread?"

"Yes, please. What kind of news? Have you made an arrest?"

His face tightened and he put down his fork. "You know damn well we have arrested Franck Fischer because Ricardo rushed down here as soon as he heard. I came to share information with you personally, but not if you insist on playing the wide-eyed ingénue. I'm not stupid, Ann, so don't play me for a fool."

She flushed, considered the sleepless-night excuse and dismissed it. "Sorry. It's a bad habit; I never know who I can trust. Please, go on."

He gazed at her, his hands resting on his thighs. "Let's be honest with each other. Or at least as honest as you are prepared to be. You may see me as a country cop who rides a buffalo and is green as a coconut. Perhaps you're right. Maybe I see you as something quite different to a reclusive poet. I don't know your true story, but neither do I believe your cover. That's OK, we all have secrets. You're smart and have some kind of expertise, that much is obvious. Where you fall down is on local knowledge. You underestimate everyone you meet and think you know better. That's a mistake." He resumed eating, a new tension in his jaw line.

Moments ticked by as they ate in silence. Eventually, Ann had to speak.

"I don't underestimate you. The fact is, I know exactly how intelligent you are and that's why I need to keep my distance. For personal reasons. Let's stick to the subject at hand. Ricardo told me you have arrested Franck Fischer. He thinks the prosecution needs a strong lawyer as the Fischer family can afford the best. I'm trying to help."

Maduro mopped up the juices from the fish stew with hunk of bread. It took him a long time to reply. "The subject at hand, yes. Franck Fischer has not been arrested, but taken in for questioning. In the next few days, he will be charged with the murder of Nelson Leal. Under normal circumstances, we would work with international prosecutors and in a few months time, we would have a damning set of evidence to prove Franck Fischer operates on a right-wing vigilante agenda. As I said, under normal circumstances. However, Cinthia Fischer has connections in many areas of the civil service and in fact, the police. When we charge him, Franck Fischer's case is likely to come before a jury at the end of July."

Ann stared at the tines on her fork, her ears full of thunder. *We can't nail him, not yet. We need more.* More? How much, how many more?

"Ann?"

She swallowed and clenched her fists. "My concentration is shot today. Can we start from the beginning? Why do you believe Fischer killed Nelson Leal? If you can tell me as much as you permitted to share, I might be able to help. I mean, not me personally, but there's a possibility of financial assistance. You're right, we should be honest, while respecting each other's limits."

He studied her face, a hint of a smile playing on his lips. "Which means I tell you everything and you give me nothing at all?"

"Detective Maduro, I don't want to be in this situation. All I wanted ..."

"If you won't call me Gil, I'll have to get all formal and call you Ms Sheldon." A device in his pocket let off a beep. "Work. Listen, as I told you, Franck Fischer and his 'crew' have some twisted kind of court, where they try people and either acquit or condemn whichever poor bastards they choose. It's a far-fetched motive, I know that. We'll have to prepare to nail him on circumstantial evidence alone, considering the short time frame available. It will be touch and go. You want this as much as I do and the victim's family trust you above me. Could we work together, unofficially?"

She clasped her hands together, struggling to find a response.

"Ann, I have to go. Think about it. One thing I promise is

to respect your privacy. So long as you help me take Fischer down, I won't go digging. I swear. See you later."

He ran down the steps and around the shack. A minute later, his motorbike buzzed into life and sped away. She sat there staring at the leftover rice. *If you help me, I won't go digging.*

And if she didn't?

18

Around four o'clock that afternoon, a pickup truck rumbled down the beach. Branca watched until it stopped at the end of Ann's path, then slunk away to lie underneath the house. True to his word, Ricardo had returned with the cavalry. Along with Zé, Marco from the bakery, two fishermen and a bag of tools, he had brought a ragbag of furniture items and a sack of foodstuff. Amid much shouting and gesticulation, they set to work. Marco took the door off its hinges and started hammering planks of wood around the splintered section. Zé unloaded the ladders; the fishermen brought in the furniture and assembled some kind of metal shelving system in the kitchen. Ricardo handed Ann a packet with a smile and instructed her to re-hang her mosquito net. As she did so, she saw the peg tangled in the folds. This was not a replacement but the original.

She waited until Ricardo had stopped clanging and banging to ask where he had found it. He tapped the side of his nose.

"I put the word out. Some bastards wrecked Dona Emilia's hut, I said, the one where the *gringuinha* is staying. It's a pity and a shame, I told everyone. This village is in mourning for one of our own and the Englishwoman is on our side. It has to be strangers because no one in this village would do such a horrible thing. Decent people replace what is broken. Any donations to be left at the church. Anyone with information", he thumped his chest, "come to Ricardo Leal. Even if the kids' conscience won't make them act, their parents will."

Ann thought it over as she and Ricardo stacked bags of rice, manioc flour, dried beans, sugar and coffee in the metal cabinet he had constructed. While overwhelmed with gratitude at the villagers' generosity, she couldn't square the fact they knew who had done this. Were the perpetrators to get off with no retribution?

"I have to show my gratitude to those people," she said. "I'd like to do something. But how do I ... I mean ... which ones?"

Ricardo was selecting the right-sized nail to hammer into a table leg. "You're worried about thanking the people who smashed up this place, no? That's life. Nobody's going to confess or rat on their neighbours. You might live here but you're not one of us. Where do you want this table?"

By sundown, there was little evidence of the previous vandalism. The fishermen erected screens at the windows which would serve as a replacement until a glazier came from Soure. It meant Ann could keep the shutters open during the day to enjoy the light. Her cupboard was better stocked than it had been before. She had a table and two stools in the kitchen, an armchair and a rail for her clothes. It was impossible to retrieve her stash of cash with so many people in the hut. She thanked them in all sincerity and promised to return the favour, then waved them off as they headed up the beach towards the village. Tonight she could sleep in her bed, knowing the shack was as secure as it could be.

After a dinner of sweet potato and fried fish, she sat in her not-quite-new armchair and wrote to Mike Ferguson. She toned down the pessimism in Maduro's assessment of the case, but emphasised the urgency. They needed to act fast. It must be a frustrating position, so far away and unable to see what was happening on the ground. For a fleeting moment, she had some sympathy with her previous employers. She had always been on the inside, watching first-hand what the targets were up to. On many occasions, she would rather have been anywhere else in the world than up close and personal with those people. But how much worse to rely on someone else's eyes and ears? She caught herself dwelling on the past and switched thought tracks.

Since scarfing some leftovers and biscuits, Branca had fallen asleep across the threshold, as if she were a doormat. Ann closed up the shutters, called the dog inside and locked up for the night. It was only quarter past eight, but she was ready for a deep and hopefully dreamless sleep. She willed her subconscious to give her a break. Even as she did so, she knew it was futile.

No blood, no sand. This time it was ice. A wild exhilarating ride down a precipice, playing follow-my-leader. Until her leader was no longer visible. She curved an arc in the snow with her skis and came to a halt. Sun reflected off the white mountainside and she lifted her face to its warmth. Below, she saw him, in his red-and-white striped ski suit, waving a pole to attract her attention. She assessed the ground ahead, unsure of the safest route. He indicated left and with a sweep of his arm beckoned her to follow. With a giggle at his enthusiasm – Thanh hated skiing – she pushed her poles into the powder and prepared to descend.

The noise was elemental, as if the earth itself was waking up. What seemed to be a sheet of solid pack ice fractured and cracked, a crevasse appearing around two kilometres to her left. The mountain opened up like a clam shell, snow and ice and pine trees falling into the gap. Beneath her skis, she sensed a shifting. One word echoed around her mind like a klaxon in her Austrian ski-instructor's panicked voice: *Lawine! Lawine!* Avalanche! Avalanche!

The crevasse creaked apart, a lightning streak darting down the mountain at impossible speed. Thanh, smaller than a pine tree, saw the danger and pivoted to ski cross-country, using all his energy to flee the Alpine earthquake. Tonnes of snow roared like a thousand jets taking off, sliding down the mountain, smothering everything in its path. To escape such natural power would require something unnatural. She skied right, sobbing at the uselessness of the attempt, with a terrified glance over her shoulder. The avalanche knocked Thanh into the crevasse as if he were a piece of Lego. Ann howled, raging at the inevitable, until the snow silenced her screams, as final as a shroud.

She sat up, hugging her knees to her chest. Her skin was clammy, in spite of the warm night, and adrenalin pumped through her system like acid. On this occasion, the darkness reassured her. The blinding whiteness of the dream was yet to fade. Hands pressed together as if in prayer, she repeated her mantra, her affirmation, her Get-Out-Of-Jail card.

"I am Ann Sheldon. I'm a poet. I'm searching for peace and quiet and inspiration."

She wiped her face, lit a candle and went into the kitchen for something to drink. She wasn't thirsty but needed a reason to get out of bed. Branca woke and followed, always optimistic there might be something to eat. Coffee was a ridiculous idea if she expected to get any more sleep that night. Instead, she boiled some *jambú* leaves for slightly anaesthetic tea. Wind caused the shack to creak and bang, each sound jangling her nerves. The noise seemed to bother the dog too. She went to the front door and scratched, looking around to see if Ann would respond. She obliged, undoing all three locks and releasing the animal into the night. The wind rushed into the room, blowing out the candle. She didn't bother relighting it, but went onto the porch with her tea, closing the door behind her and peering for any signs of Branca in the blackness. The dog had vanished into the night. No surprise on a night as dark as this with no moon or stars. The sea boomed and roared, drowning out all sounds of the jungle, and powerful blusters turned her hut into a percussion instrument.

Traces of her dream floated across her consciousness and she made a concerted effort to remember the name of every capital city in Europe to distract herself. By the time she finished her tea, her eyes grew weary and a chill crept around her neck. She was considering whether to leave Branca to her own devices or fetch a blanket and sit outside a little longer, when a different sound added to the blustery night. Footsteps came up the path to her hut, sand crunching underfoot. She slipped onto the floor and froze in a crouch, with the realisation that her flick knife was beside her bed, the gun behind the kitchen tiles and her machete missing. In the dead of night, someone was paying her a visit and she was on the porch, defenceless as a baby rabbit.

Her body stilled, her breathing steady and silent while her mind readied itself for a fight. The only weapons at her disposal were her training and the element of surprise. Even the dog had deserted her. The visitor got to the bottom of the steps and stopped. Through the criss-cross slats, Ann could make out certain features. He was male and wearing a hooded jacket. Something about his demeanour told Ann he was young and frightened. She had a momentary interlude of calm until he ascended the steps and she saw the machete.

The sharp inhalation through her nostrils would have been a giveaway on a quieter night, but the battering gusts from the sea disguised every unusual sound. She thought the situation through. She wasn't close enough to be certain but somehow she knew that was her own machete. As he had her blade in his hand, she could safely assume he was one of the invaders. In which case, he knew which shutters led to her bedroom. He expected her to be inside, asleep. It was unlikely he would attempt to break down the door to cause her harm when the easier option of busting open the shutters and climbing through the window was available. That meant he would turn right, his back to her. Her options were to jump him just before he attacked or let him go through with it and catch him on the way out.

He reached the top step, his focus still on her bedroom shutters. Then, to her puzzlement, he laid the knife on the floor, blade pointing towards the sea and handle towards her front door. He crossed himself and began to retreat the way he came. The second he turned to the fierce winds, his hood blew off and Ann recognised his face. Her mind added all these elements into a coherent whole. Then she spoke.

"*Muito obrigada*, Rubem."

Her voice shocked him and he jumped several paces backwards, tripping over the machete he had just laid at her door. He swore in fear and she rose to her full height, taking one step forward to block his access to the steps. He could always jump from the veranda but he wouldn't; not now he understood the risks of her 'garden'.

"You scared the shit out of me." His voice was sharpened by fright.

"Likewise. But now I see you were only returning my machete. So I say again, thanks very much." She lifted it from the floor, its handle familiar.

He cast around him, evidently seeking a way out. "Ricardo said ... if we, you know, found anything ... we should return it. So ..."

"Ricardo also said that if you 'found anything', you should take it to the church. Which makes me wonder why you're creeping around here in the middle of the night?"

He didn't reply.

"Look, Rubem, I might be a foreigner but I wasn't born yesterday. I know it was you and your mates who damaged this place and I know on whose orders. What I don't know is why you took the knife and what made you bring it back."

"It doesn't matter now. I have to go." He took a step closer but Ann did not budge, still holding the machete.

"How's Pedro?"

His gaze flicked from the knife to her face, his eyes suspicious. "What you mean?"

"I was just wondering about his finger. My first aid was only rudimentary and he really should have gone to hospital."

"He *is* in hospital. Blood poisoning, they say, after the accident."

"Oh yeah, that was some accident. Tell me, what happened to Serena?"

This time she was close enough to hear his intake of breath. He stared at her, breathing heavily through his nose and although she couldn't see the tears, his rapid blinking gave him away.

"You shouldn't ask so many questions." His voice sounded younger and contained a tremble. "I don't mean, I'm not trying to threaten you. I'm serious. Asking questions gets you into trouble and you're already on his radar. Keep out of it, *senhora*."

"I was going to say the same to you. Listen to me. Xander, Pedro, Serena and you too, Rubem, you're all disposable. Mauricio Gonçalves is playing a dangerous game. When the big fish hear he's hunting on their patch, they'll come after him, tearing up everyone in their path. You're counting on his protection, aren't you? Well, don't. I guarantee he'll throw you to the sharks. Things could get very ugly. My advice is to walk away from this while you still can."

"It's too late for that. Things already got ugly. Sorry, I really have to go now."

Ann stood back and let him pass. He jogged down the steps and took off down the path at a run. She stood there, gripping her knife, the cold raising goosebumps on her skin. As she turned to go inside, a tiny light caught her attention. It came from the palm trees between her shack and Fátima's, which shielded her from the rest of the beach. It looked like the glow from a cigarette. She stared in that direction for a full five minutes but saw nothing but night.

19

How to tell the story? The background isn't significant to a man like Mauricio Gonçalves. He doesn't give a shit about Instagram or influencers and probably has no idea who Shelbee Spicer is. Serena can't put into words, not even for herself, why she wants to get up close to those people. She will never admit her obsessive stalking of this impossibly glamorous girl and her unattainable lifestyle, her craven need to see her icon in real life, the thrill of seeing such a celebrity on her own beach. Like all good storytellers, she tailors her tale. One story for her, one for him. He's watching her from the sofa, waiting for her to begin. She fiddles with the fabric of her armchair and looks around the room, taking in the leather sofa, the snakeskin boots, the Turkish carpet. Then she fills her lungs, desperate to get it out.

"That yacht drops anchor in the bay and the party people go jet-skiing or wakeboarding or surfing. Trying to surf, I should say. Then they come onto the beach with their picnic hampers and drink champagne. Sometimes they buy cocktails from the bars but not often. That day, I'm in the ocean. I see them leave and I know no one's aboard. I'm curious, OK? So shoot me. I leave my board on the jetty and swim out there for a better look. Up the ladder, onto deck and I've got the place to myself. Pretending to be a princess for half an hour, you know? I make myself a cocktail and lounge on the roof. It's fun but I'm not used to drinking and after a while, I doze off in the sun.

"Their voices wake me. I panic, ready to jump from the roof to the ocean. I'm not afraid of heights. I'm not afraid of anything. But the engine starts and the boat doesn't go in the direction I expect, down the coast. Instead, it turns around and sails towards the river. I figure that's no bad thing, so lie flat on the roof of the cabin, planning to dive off when they slow down.

"They're on the deck, shouting and laughing like idiots, and I hear a voice I recognise. Nelson Leal goes to my school, I'm friends with his sister and no way is he part of this crowd. He's not laughing, but pleading with them to let him off the boat. 'I want to go,' he says. 'I want to go home.' They're not listening, making caipirinhas and forcing him to drink and shouting over him, saying 'Arr' and 'A-hoi' and other words I don't understand.

"The boat sails up the river to a place I've never been. When it stops, I risk a look over the edge of the roof. Three boys and two girls are on deck. I know their names. Franck Fischer with his girlfriend, Shelbee Spicer, Junior Denis and a woman they called Coco. The other guy is Nelson. He's standing on the diving board, blindfolded. They're tormenting him, asking questions about his father, his mother, his hair, making him sing, throwing tennis balls at him if they don't like the answer. He can't see, so when each ball hits him, he recoils, almost losing his balance. They aim at his head.

"A tourist boat passes and everybody waves. Franck tells the others to wave back and laugh, as if we're playing a game. Nelson can't wave. His arms are tied. One of the tourists sees me on the top and points. I duck and wait to hear if the people on the deck below notice. I lie there like a beached starfish, ready to leap into the water. Only when I hear them talking again do I dare peek over the edge. The tour boat chugs out of sight. Franck takes off Nelson's blindfold. He says they found him guilty and he is sentenced to death.

"He begs them, in Portuguese and in English, but they're not listening. Franck starts the boat and turns it around, very slowly. The others watch Nelson, all laughing and saying 'Bye-bye'. Then Franck opens the throttle. The force throws me forwards and I grip the roof or I'll slide off the edge and onto their cocktail table. Nelson has no chance. The momentum topples him off the diving-board and he falls, screaming, into the river.

"My ears are pounding with my own blood and the sound of the engine. When the boat slows, I hear a sound I cannot believe. Four people just killed a guy and they're banging their hands together, whooping and yelling like chimpanzees. I'm not stupid. I know that if they find me, I'm next and it will be worse. I keep still, and wait for my moment.

"At the river mouth, the yacht slows, manoeuvring past the fishing boats heading out for the night catch. It's a crazy move I'd never usually attempt, but I gather my courage in one enormous breath and dive off the side. When I surface, *La Linda Lua* is accelerating out into the ocean and my hair is covered with oily slime. I swim to the jetty, collect my board and walk home."

The man in snakeskin boots hears none of this because Serena doesn't tell him. He smokes and smiles and waits for her to speak.

"Senhor Gonçalves, I witnessed Franck Fischer, son of

Cinthia, commit murder aboard his yacht. Fischer and his friends abducted and killed my schoolmate, Nelson Leal. Reporting this to the police is not an option. They will never go after people like the Fischers. Someone with power must make Franck pay for what he did. Which is why I come to you. Please can you help me avenge my friend?"

Gonçalves watches her through a veil of smoke. He waits a long time before replying. Cicadas chorus through the open windows and Serena's thirsty. She takes several swallows from her glass of guaraná.

"How old are you, Serena da Rocha?"

His voice startles her. "Fifteen."

"Is that right? So young and so brave. I admire courage. Yes, I think I can help. Unfortunately, you caught me on a day when I must leave for business, but only for a few days. We'll talk about this when I return. For now, you are our guest and my brother will make sure all your needs are met."

Serena scrambles to her feet. "No, I'm not staying, my mother expects me at home. Anyway, there's nothing to talk about. I told you what happened. Thank you for listening. It's time for me to leave."

From outside a car horn blasts, setting off an echo of screeches and squawks from the surrounding jungle. Mauricio stands up and holds out his hand. Manners override her discomfort. She places a stiff palm in his and withdraws it the second he applies pressure.

"I'll think about the Fischer situation while I'm away. We'll work something out. See you next week, Serena."

His boots make a crunchy sound on the wooden floor as he leaves. Sand gets everywhere, even somewhere as sophisticated as Quinta dos Rios. She drains her glass of guaraná and looks out of the window at Mauricio's white Porsche. She regrets not asking him for a lift. Eight kilometres on foot to Praia do

Pesqueiro in this heat is no fun. Hopefully when she gets to the main road someone will offer her a ride.

Outside, Mauricio is wagging a finger at the big guy in dungarees. They both turn to look at the window where she stands. She snatches up her bag and runs to the door. It's locked.

20

The search for a prosecution lawyer in Soure and Salvaterra proved fruitless. All day Ann and Ricardo went from office to office, pleading, promising and brandishing cash but no one wanted to take on the case. On the way home to Praia do Pesqueiro in Zé's borrowed pickup, neither said a word, both despondent and exhausted. Ricardo dropped Ann at the *padaria* and thanked her for her help. He drove away to return the vehicle and break the news to Dulce. Ann was equally keen to get to her own shack. Leaving the place unattended all day made her nervous. She ordered four bread rolls and told Viviane about their lack of success. The little woman was enraged. She packed up the bag of bread, cursing the legal profession to hell and back.

"Tomorrow, Marco can look after this place. It's not market day, so he can manage. I'm going to Salvaterra and talk to someone I know. If he can't help us, we'll have to look in Belém. Surely in a place that size we'll find a lawyer with a pair of balls. Here's your bread. How much time do we have?"

"I'm not sure. Around three weeks. How much do I owe you?"

"The *paezinhos* are on the house. Don't argue. Come here at eight tomorrow and we'll drive into Soure together. You talk to the police and I'll take the ferry to flirt with my ex-boyfriend. We need more information."

Ann agreed, with mixed emotions. She walked along the beach, preoccupied by how much influence the Fischers seemed to wield over the city of Soure. She found it hard to believe that Viviane would find it any different in Salvaterra, and Belém was probably even worse. Somewhere, there had to be a brief who would not be intimidated by Celebrity Cinthia's wealth.

She passed Fátima's shack and someone called her name. Nando was on the porch, smoking and drinking a beer. He raised the bottle and beckoned. She shook her head, pointing to her non-existent watch.

"*Tá bem. Amanha?*" he asked, his half-stoned expression guaranteeing he'd never remember issuing an invitation.

Tomorrow? Why not? She gave him the thumbs-up and a friendly wave, then proceeded past the palm trees towards home.

The shack seemed exactly as she had left it, bike locked on the veranda, heron on the roof and Branca waiting to greet her from under the steps. Reassured that all her markers were untouched, she opened a bottle of beer and unwrapped the bread rolls. Instead of the four she had requested, there were six and two *pasteis da natas*. She smiled at Viviane's generosity and tore into one of the cakes. While devouring the pastry, she gave some biscuits to the dog and pulled out her laptop. For the first time since arriving on Ilha do Marajó, she was acutely aware of what day it was. Tomorrow would be Friday and her last chance to get legal representation for Nelson's family before the weekend. Then and only then could she start digging for dirt on the Fischer family.

Her inbox delivered the first breakthrough of the day. A

response from one of the lawyers she'd emailed last night. He had worked with the police in Soure on several occasions and knew many state prosecutors well. Now based in Belém, he was a heavy hitter on the legal scene. Even as she sent her enquiry, she had known it was a long shot. Aim high, she told herself. And now it looked like she had hit the bull's-eye. Yes, he would be interested in taking the case, presuming they could afford the fees outlined in the attachment. Presuming the accused had already been charged, he would contact the prosecutor and the Soure police department. Although his schedule was tight, he and his team could start the moment she gave him the go-ahead. Her earliest response would be appreciated.

She let out a squeal of delight, causing Branca to lift her head from the dog biscuits for a second. Her immediate impulse was to grab the bike and cycle up the beach to share the good news with Ricardo and Dulce, until she realised they were not the ones paying the bill. She made a rough translation and forwarded the email to Mike Ferguson, emphasising the importance of replying by tomorrow morning. Elated by her success, she ate another cake and prepared a systematic search into Cinthia Fischer's finances and sphere of influence. She warned herself before she opened the first website that it would be a painstaking and laborious exercise due to download speeds and without the state-of-the-art technology she used to rely upon. Even so, she had the skills and the analytical ability to form a picture. Plan complete, she made two tomato and anchovy sandwiches, opened another beer and went on the attack.

The sun set, Branca went out for a meander, Ann switched on a lamp and closed the door against mosquitoes or other intruders. The night creatures of the jungle, so terrifying when she had first arrived, began their usual murderous shrieks. At ten o'clock, she finished researching and checked outside. Branca was asleep on the porch. Ann called her in, made a cup of tea and checked her emails. Mike Ferguson had replied. She had his permission to retain the lawyer for the next two months or until the case concluded. Finally, they were getting somewhere. She locked up the hut, switched off the light and lit a candle to drink her tea. Tomorrow, she would speak to Gil Maduro about how best to present the case. She knew as well as he did that knowledge was power. The question was, did they have enough?

Half an hour after the sun rose, Ann cycled down Praia do Pesqueiro's main road, heading for the Leal family house. Her mood buoyant after last night's discoveries and an almost nightmare-free night, she was eager to start the day. She parked her bike outside and was locking it when the front door opened and Dolores, Nelson's younger sister emerged in her waitress uniform.

She smiled at Ann and pointed to the bike. "How is it running?"

"It's exactly what I need, thank you. I have news for your parents. Are they awake?"

Dolores looked over her shoulder at the closed door. "My mother's sick. I don't know if she will ever recover from Nelson's death. Wait a moment, I'll call my father."

She returned a minute later. "He's coming. Please, Dona Ann, tell him the truth. My father puts his faith in the fact the police will punish my brother's killer. Everyone knows they won't. Except my father, the dreamer. Don't give him false hope. I'm late for work. Have a good day."

Ricardo looked dreadful as he leant on the door jamb, a cigarette dangling between his fingers. She relayed the good news and saw a spark in his exhausted expression.

"Thank you. Maybe it is possible to get a fair trial. Dulce has something to live for if she believes the murderer will go to jail. It's all we need, a tiny straw of hope to keep us going. Today, I have to go fishing; I can't afford another day off. Can I leave it to you to contact the lawyer, make arrangements with Mike and all of that police stuff? Thank you, Ann, you're a kind person."

She assured him she would do everything necessary and wished him a good day. As she cycled towards the main road, she considered father and daughter's differing opinions regarding hope. Better to be hopeless or hopeful? Despite herself, Ann identified with Ricardo.

Outside the *padaria*, Viviane was dressed in a sharp suit and carrying a handbag. She looked so different Ann almost rode straight past this strange, stylish woman.

"Where are you going, *inglesa*? Put your bike around the back and tell Marco I said to give you a coffee. Hurry yourself, we need to leave."

Five minutes later, Ann jumped into the passenger seat of a yellow Toyota, carrying her backpack and a sticky croissant Marco had pressed upon her. Between mouthfuls, she explained about the high-profile lawyer and her role as go-between. "So you really don't need to go to Salvaterra today. We have legal representation from someone who's friendly with state prosecutors and we can pay his bill. I sent him confirmation last night."

Viviane was concentrating on steering them out of Praia do Pesqueiro, wearing her habitual scowl. "Think this guy is any good? Of course he is. He's expensive and from Belém. That's the first news I've heard in a week that doesn't make me want to bite someone's head off. It gives us optimism. Still, nothing is certain till it happens. I am going to Salvaterra because we need as much ammunition as possible. Not only that, I'm curious to see my ex-boyfriend. I heard he's getting fat. What are you going to say to the police?"

Ann finished her croissant. She had been rehearsing her

speech for so long, she could have related it verbatim. She didn't. "Only as much as he needs to know. The main reason I'm there is to ask questions and get information."

"Good girl. You're smart, Ann. A lot smarter than you look."

Ann had a feeling that Gil Maduro would disagree.

Her excitement and enthusiasm lasted until she arrived at the police station. She waited an hour and fifteen minutes before Maduro had time to see her and the moment he closed the door on the little interview room, he punctured her bubble.

"My senior officers say we don't have enough to take this to a state prosecutor. I spent hours retrieving data on Fischer's previous accusations and have plenty of concrete evidence to try him for this crime. They don't want to hear it. Someone has leaned on them and yet again, that little bastard is going to get away with it. Given the speed events are moving, there's every chance I will be out of a job by the same time next week."

The outrageous corruption behind the decision robbed Ann of speech. Maduro was helpless and beaten by that knowledge. She understood.

"I came to tell you we've hired Milton de Souza to prosecute the case."

He looked at her under his brows. "Starting when?"

"He'd be ready to start on Monday, but I could ask him ..."

He shook his head. "Not even de Souza could get this to court. I'm sorry, but it doesn't help. This is how the real world works. Thanks for coming in."

She left the room, embarrassment flaming her cheeks, and walked to the river, where she sat and worked through her sense of injustice until the ferry returned from Salvaterra.

Viviane had a fierce temper, that much Ann knew, but she had never seen her quite as incandescent with rage. She ran through her substantial vocabulary of curses twice and drove the custard-coloured Toyota directly to the police station. A ninety-minute wait was out of the question. Ann stayed in the car but even at that distance she could hear Viviane roaring.

A door slammed and within seconds, the baker's slight frame was once again behind the wheel, still cursing. She hurled the Toyota out of the city and wrenched the wheel towards Praia do Pesqueiro, maintaining an unbroken diatribe against the police, the legal system and Inspector Maduro in particular. They approached the little shortcut through the jungle but Ann didn't dare interrupt and ask to get out. Instead, they bumped on to Praia do Pesqueiro and came to a sudden halt outside the *padaria*.

"I'm going to tell Ricardo. God knows what this will do to Dulce, she's already depressed. You make yourself useful. Get on your computer and see if the American can pull any strings. At least Maduro is willing to share what evidence he has with the legal guy. He knows him, apparently, and agreed to come with us to Belém on Monday. Arrogant bastard said it as if he was doing me a favour instead of the other way round!"

Ann sat up straight and stared at Viviane. "Umm, we're going to Belém?"

"Of course! The only way to do this if the slimy, self-serving cops won't proceed is to get the prosecutor to mount an investigation. We have to go, Ann, there's no way Ricardo can do this without you and me to support him. Small mercies but mercies all the same. We'll stay overnight and come back Tuesday. As if I don't have enough problems!" She slammed the door and stormed off towards the beach.

Ann retrieved her bike from behind the bakery, trying not to look at the river where she had found Nelson's corpse, just a few buildings away. She cycled along the tree-line, where it was a little cooler. How on earth Viviane expected Mike Ferguson to insist the police bring legal action against Franck Fischer from nearly 4,000 miles away she had no idea. But she had to try.

Belém. There was no way she could go with Ricardo and Viviane on Monday. It was too great a risk. A big city was not the place for her, and definitely not in such high-profile, gossip-worthy circumstances. Maybe she could fake an injury or contract a light dose of malaria. How was it possible she had got herself into a situation whereby she was involved in a murder case and trying to get an indictment from the Brazilian authorities? Did shitty luck just stick to some people?

Outside Fátima's shack, Nando was doing something to his motorcycle and simultaneously conducting an argument with the lady of the house through the window.

He grinned at Ann and rolled his eyes. As his girlfriend recited a long list of his failings, he said under his breath, "She's going out soon, thank God. Fancy a beer later?"

"Maybe. I have a few things to do tonight." Meeting Nando behind Fátima's back seemed inappropriate, if not downright dangerous.

"Lucky you." He raised his voice. "Yes, my darling, of course I'm listening. To be honest, I have no choice. The whole beach can hear you."

Ann laughed and cycled homeward, tension tightening her neck. She wondered how long it would take before she stopped holding her breath on the approach to her hut. The heron was missing. Ridiculous as it was, the idea the bird signified good luck had taken hold. Its absence cast a shadow over her already bleak mood.

Everything was in order, complete with a slightly less white dog under the steps. Once assured the house had not been breached, she knelt to check Branca's coat. She had two oily streaks along her spine, as if she'd brushed under an axle. The dog undulated and swayed, thrilled with the attention.

"You are a dirty mare," she said and heard the words in her sister's voice. The memory caused no more than a twinge, like stubbing a toe, so she ignored it and dug the laptop out of her backpack. She sent an email to Mike, apologising for even asking him for ideas, but detailing the latest brick wall she'd encountered.

Brick walls. She gazed out at the ocean, thinking of Quinta dos Rios and its concrete plinth. Most houses in the area worked around the waters, allowing geography to flow as it had always done. Money and influence put their interests above those of nature, changing the world to fit. Water would adapt and find a path to the sea. With imagination, Ann Sheldon would find a way to justice.

She ate some leftovers, fed the dog and settled down to do some digging in the darker corners of the web. One day, she promised herself, she would be free of these sewers and those who dwelt within.

The sun slid down an apricot sky and Ann logged off, a long-forgotten fizz bubbling in her stomach. She was onto something. A trail of electronic footprints connected Franck Fischer to some extremely disturbing ideologies. The signal here was not strong enough to play some of the videos or download the related material, so Ann had a swift change of mind. A trip to Belém meant access to a high-speed hotel Internet service. In a couple of days, she was convinced she could hoist Cinthia's son by his own petard. The law might not punish him for what he did to Nelson, but one way or another, she could make him pay for the reason why.

Branca let out a volley of barks, her oily hackles up as she stood on the threshold. Ann closed the machine and reached for her machete. By the time she got to the door, Branca's barks had stopped and her tail was sweeping back and forth. She trotted down the steps, ears softening to greet their visitor. Nando wandered up the path, carrying a six-pack of beers.

"*Olá, cachorrinha, tudo bem?*" He held out a hand for the dog to sniff. "Ann, hi! I brought some beers but forgot the nuts. Are you busy?"

Surprised by the dog's friendliness to a stranger, she didn't refuse. "No, I've just finished what I had to do. A beer would be nice. Come on up. I see you've met Branca."

"Yeah, sorry about the oil, by the way. She was hanging about while I fixed my bike and I gave her some buffalo milk. Whoa, what happened here?" He took in the less-than-subtle repairs to the door.

"I'm not really sure. I think this was a warning from the surf kids and their boss about talking to the cops."

He recoiled, his face losing all its easy-going humour. "What do you mean, talking to the cops? Are you some kind of snitch?"

She rounded on him, her temper flaring. "I found a dead body, Nando! The police want to know what happened and I told them. I'm not a snitch or a traitor or anything other than a woman who wants some peace and quiet. If you're going to get judgemental as well, you can take your beers and shove them where the sun don't shine!" She realised she was channelling Viviane. It wasn't the worst look.

Nando placed the beers on the table and raised his hands in surrender. "Easy, lady. You know what, your Portuguese gets better when you're angry. Same with me and singing. Can't hold a tune when I'm sober, but give me a couple of whiskies and I'm Billy Ray Cyrus. Got a bottle opener? If not, I can use my teeth."

Her steam evaporated. Nando's whole attitude was laid-back and non-confrontational. She had no idea what drew him and Fátima together.

"Your teeth? Don't you dare. Sit down." She went inside for the bottle-opener and a packet of chilli chips. "I don't have nuts but bought these in Soure today. How come you and Branca are such great mates?" She watched him from the interior, wondering about his motives.

He stretched his arms and laced his fingers behind his head. In a beige T-shirt and chino-style shorts, he could have blended into the beach had it not been for his thick black hair. "I like animals. They like me. Less complicated than people. You know what my favourite animal is?"

Ann emerged from the shack and sat opposite her guest. "I have no idea."

"A turtle. When the world gets too much, I retreat into my shell and listen to the ocean. You're the same." He cracked the tops off two beers and handed one to her. "Hiding away at the end of the beach, writing poems and pretending you're on a desert island. I'll bet 50 reais you have a guitar."

She drank, already wondering how to get rid of this affable sot. "I don't, but I'll bet a hundred you do."

He sat up, mock shocked. "How did you know?"

"Billy Ray Cyrus." She gave him a sideways glance. "Where's Fátima tonight?"

"Partying somewhere for somebody's birthday. Why don't you read me some of your poetry?"

"Why don't you sing me a country and western song?"

Her tone was snappy, but he laughed, throwing his mouth open to the sky. Branca responded by relocating from the steps to lie at his feet. *One bowl of milk and she's anybody's*, thought Ann, and opened the packet.

"Country and western, that's a good one." He cupped his hand to receive some chips and began eating. "Yeah, it's kind of similar. Poets and songwriters use words to manipulate our

emotions. It's a special kind of talent and I envy you that ability. What did you do with the chickens?" He took another slug
of beer.

His meandering conversation both entertained and irri-
tated Ann. "Chickens? Oh, you mean the ones Fátima brought.
I cooked them and ate them."

He laughed again, shaking his head. "I didn't expect you
to keep them as pets. That's classic foreigner. When someone
asks you what you did with the catfish or coconuts or
chicken, you are supposed to say I dipped it with cassava
flour and fried it with piri-piri and served it with mango
wrapped in a banana leaf. Not you. 'I cooked them and ate
them.' Brilliant!" He slapped his thigh. "You're quite the
comedian."

There was something about the man's relaxed approach to
life which soothed Ann's myriad worries. Why not watch the
sunset, drink a beer, eat some chips and talk crap? Not everything had to be analysed and dissected like a frog on a slab.

"True, I guess. I don't waste words on describing what I
eat, how I breathe or what happens in the toilet. Poetry is
making people feel what I feel when I look at something like
that." She indicated the sunset with a neck of her beer bottle.
"Poetry is about the essence of things. Anyone could sit here,
looking at that sunset, drinking this beer and eating these chips
and have a whole different experience. When I write a poem,
it's a prism, throwing reflections and colours and interpreta-
tions into the sky. If it's clean and unsoiled by my own fingerprints, everyone can see themselves in my words."

Nando crunched some crisps, then slapped a hand to his
neck to kill a mosquito. He drained his beer and let out a belch
before cracking open another bottle. He said nothing. If she
had made him uncomfortable with her speech, so much the
better. Perhaps he would go home and leave her in peace.

She lit a citronella candle and placed it in the centre of the table. "Bastards, aren't they? My mosquito net was the best buy I've ever made."

He reached down to stroke Branca's coat, but still said nothing. The silence was not intimidating or awkward after the first couple of minutes, just two people drinking a beer and watching the sun go down. She grew almost as relaxed as Branca, who let out a deep contented sigh from underneath Nando's chair.

His voice, soft and husky, startled her. "I asked you to read me some of your poetry. You refused. Now I understand why."

Relaxation tensed into caution while Ann tried to assess his mood and motive. Something in his speech had changed and one part of her brain was occupied in identifying what. Before she could formulate an appropriate response, he continued.

"Just by hearing you talk about your poetry, I can tell it must be beautiful. Isn't that something? People like you make a difference. Yeah, so do doctors and soldiers and teachers and farmers, but artists are special. Poems, songs, books, films and paintings don't just affect us now, but future generations. 'Everyone can see themselves in my words.' That speaks to me. That is art."

Ann took a moment to process a reaction to his words. She was flattered, surprised and also, damped down by a long history of smoke and mirrors; acknowledged a flicker of embarrassment.

"Thank you. Art is important, I agree. Then again, I have huge respect for people with practical skills. That takes a lot more than talent. Training, perseverance, resilience and clear thinking." She stopped; aware she had veered from her patronising assumption of the life of a ferry worker to her own past.

Night assumed control of the beach and Ann sensed the atmosphere had changed. They drank in silence while the jungle began its evening recital. Branca shifted and stretched her legs, then rested her head on Nando's foot.

He reached for the chips and grabbed a handful. "How's the bike working out?" His voice had returned to its normal pitch.

"Good. You were right. Other than a water buffalo, one of the best ways to get around."

"Yeah, unless you own a motorcycle. I swear that machine has given me everything. My job, my girlfriend, something to do when my girlfriend is pissed off and an endless obsession with making it better. You know why I bought a sidecar?"

The breeze from the beach blew out the candle. Ann went to switch on the lamp but Nando's hand rested on her arm. "Don't bother, it will only attract mosquitoes. Tell me, poet lady, why I bought a sidecar."

She sank back into her seat and removed her arm from his touch. There was nothing overtly threatening about the man but he made assumptions and that nearly always got awkward. "My guess? You bought it for your guitar, not your girlfriend."

That laugh again, his head thrown back and shoulders shaking. "Right first time. Open us another beer and then I'm going home. I'm on the early ferry tomorrow." He dragged a tatty rag from his pocket and blew his nose. "I gotta ask you, Ann, do you feel safe here? It's none of my business, but we're neighbours, sort of. We should take care of each other."

Ann popped open two more bottles, intending to drink no more than half. "That's nice of you. I wouldn't say I feel safe but I don't think the vandalism is likely to happen again. This village is a unique place with its own codes of loyalty I'm just beginning to understand."

"I know what you mean." His voice changed into the softer register and Ann decided to relight the candle. Something about talking to Nando in the dark seemed risky.

He finished his third bottle, the sound of his swallowing a counterpoint to Branca's snores. "Let me tell you something, Ann. Ever since I met Fátima, I'm a figure of suspicion." He gave a resigned laugh. "Circles of trust. This village, Céu, Cajauuna, Soure, Salvaterra are each contained communities and part of an island. I'm not local, but I'm more local than you, *estrangeira*. It's funny, I love poetry but I've never met a poet. Why do you think the surfers messed up your house? They are part of this village, and now, so are you."

She weighed up the pros and cons of talking to Nando about what happened. He was only interested in idle gossip and could offer neither reassurance nor insight. At the same time, talking to someone with no vested interest often clarified her thinking. Plus, he was a drinker and they usually had short memories.

"In a nutshell, I believe that a farmer not far from here is manufacturing Class A drugs and using local kids as distributors. The villagers are afraid of him and with good reason. Anyone who challenges his authority gets hurt. I found one of the surfers in the forest a few days ago. Someone cut off his forefinger and the kid is now in hospital with blood poisoning. This carries all the indications of drug dealing. The worst thing is that a new dealer in the region of Pará will come to the attention of established traders. The guy trying to break into the market has got all of the attitude but none of the nous. All I did was speak to a detective from Soure and Mr Heavy-Handed sent his minions to smash up my place. It will end in tears, I know that much. But sadly, he will drag the rest of the village into a violent and bloody confrontation which has nothing to do with them. Sorry, maybe I'm getting paranoid."

Nando let out a long whistle. He glugged more of his beer, smacked his lips and looked at her. "Paranoid is better than reckless. You know one of the surfer girls has gone missing? The blonde. No one's seen her all week." He shook his head sadly. "Like I said, keep out of it. If you're right, it's somebody else's problem. If you're wrong, even better. Don't try to save the village, Ann, because you can't. And I hear you have enough to worry about with the Leal case. Are you definitely going with them to Belém on Monday?"

She swivelled to face him. "How do you know ...?"

"I stopped in the *padaria* earlier. It's all Marco can talk about. Viviane leaving him at home while she goes to Belém with you and Ricardo to speak to a lawyer. I wasn't being nosy. To be honest, I'm not that interested. Just wondered which ferry you're taking."

Ann sighed. "I don't know whether I'm going or not. Probably. I feel a sense of duty."

He emptied his bottle and picked up the last remaining beer. "If you're on my shift, come say hello. You don't mind if I take this home with me?"

"All yours. As I told you, I don't drink much."

"Thanks for the chips and the company. Hey, if you're staying over in Belém, you want me to feed your dog?"

"That would be brilliant!" Her relief was genuine.

"No problem. *Tchau*, Ann, and stay out of trouble, yeah? *Boa noite.*"

He scratched Branca's rump, bumped Ann lightly on the shoulder with his fist and shuffled down the steps, humming a tune she didn't recognise.

The whine of a mosquito by her right ear provoked her to get up and go inside. Branca followed and Ann locked up. While cleaning her teeth she realised a chat and a beer had done her good. Small, uncomplicated pleasures were underestimated. Before getting into bed, she checked emails and found reply from Mike Ferguson. In answer to her question, 'Is anything you could do?', he'd replied 'You tell me.'

She was on her own.

21

Two ferries travelled back and forth to Belém each day. The first left from the port of Camará, a forty-minute bus ride from Soure. After the bone-jolting journey to the port, one boarded a double-decker vessel open to the elements and crowded with people on hard plastic seats. The boat took nearly three slow, sweaty hours to reach its destination. The second, an express service direct from Soure, departed horribly early, but had air conditioning, plush cinema-style seats with the added advantage of reaching Belém in two hours flat. Viviane and Ricardo opted for the former because it was half the price. Ann had no choice but to join them. She wondered how Maduro was making the trip.

Being in the presence of so many other human beings in a small space coupled with the concern about leaving her shack for two days made her panicky and claustrophobic. She yearned for the peace of her own porch, the cool breeze blowing in from the ocean and no one other than a snoring dog closer than a kilometre away. Thankfully, Viviane and Ricardo were too absorbed in their own problems to require lively conversation. The fact that not even wealthy Mike Ferguson could wield any influence had robbed the small party of any optimism. Among all the chattering passengers, excited children and dozing old ladies, the three of them sat in a dour silence, as if they were going to a funeral.

After an entire morning of staring out at the brown waters of the bay and very little else, Ann was profoundly grateful when the journey eventually came to its end. But it wasn't over yet. If the ferry seemed crowded after the village, the city of Belém was an assault on the senses. Hordes of people brushed and bumped into them, the stink of diesel and fried onions crept up their nostrils, and the sounds of horns, announcements and shouting voices presented an infernal aspect. Ricardo stood frozen in the slipstream of disembarking passengers, his posture mulish. Viviane linked her arm in his and jerked her head at Ann, who did the same.

They bundled him into a cab. With the doors closing out the chaos, some of the stiffness eased from his body. He sat between them, gazing at his hands while Viviane instructed the driver and Ann took in the kaleidoscope of signs and lights and advertisements. Ricardo was staying with a cousin, while Viviane planned to meet up with an old school friend. They were both apologetic there was no room for her, but she brushed off their concerns. She didn't say so, but the opportunity to stay in a four-star hotel was the only reason she had made the trip. It seemed as if a full day had passed already, but the real action was yet to start. At two o'clock, they had a meeting with Milton de Souza. Their last hope.

The taxi dropped Ann off first, outside a hostel where she wasn't staying. She agreed to meet the others outside the lawyer's offices at half past one and waved goodbye before lugging her backpack another three blocks to her true destination, Hotel Boavista.

Half past one. That gave Ann two hours in a fully appointed four-star hotel room. In days gone by, she would have considered this accommodation average. Standard-size double bed, ensuite bathroom, mini-bar, widescreen TV and high speed Internet access used to be the absolute basics. In Ann's opinion, after the privations of the last five months, it was the acme of luxury, including a jaw-dropping view from the balcony. She indulged herself in a long shower, using every item the hotel provided, including nail clippers, shampoos, conditioners and body creams. She ordered an extravagant room service lunch with a half bottle of wine and wrapped herself in a robe and hotel slippers. When the food arrived, she settled at the desk to eat her Club Sandwich with fries. Then she logged onto the web.

Her priority was to find evidence of Cinthia Fischer's influence over any governmental and legal bodies responsible for bringing this case to court. The connections were professional-looking and well disguised, rather like Cinthia herself, but Ann knew enough about lobbying and corporate favours to put together a web of her own. The only drawback was how long this kind of thing could take when working alone. At one o'clock, she had to stop, get dressed and walk a couple of blocks to the meeting.

Neither Viviane nor Ricardo had shown any interest in where she was staying but she wanted to maintain the image of the poor poet. Four-star hotels and overpriced food were not things she wanted to share. She walked the last street to find them already waiting, both dressed more formally than she had ever seen. Ricardo, chain-smoking, wore a grey suit and a black tie. He looked awkward and uncomfortable. Viviane wore something that looked like vintage Chanel, obviously borrowed from a much bigger woman. Ann's heart swelled in sympathy for a second until she checked herself. Whether or not this had been a deliberate choice, it was exactly the right look. Authentic. They trooped in single file through the lobby and took the lift to the fourth floor.

As they announced their names at the reception desk, Ann spotted Maduro in one of the offices. He was wearing a suit and tie, laughing and drinking coffee with another man Ann recognised from his online photograph. Milton de Souza was an imposing figure, a head taller than Maduro, with thick silvery hair and tanned skin. He gave the impression of being happy, healthy and rich, the kind of person you see on pension advertisements.

Maduro must have sensed her staring and his smile faded as he took in their awkward little group. De Souza followed his gaze and came out to greet them. His voice was deep and reassuring as he expressed his condolences to Ricardo. He shook hands with them all and gave Ann a brilliant smile.

"You must be Ms Sheldon, the enterprising young woman who wrote such an eloquent email. I'm very pleased to meet you. Come through to the boardroom and let's talk. Coffee?"

From Maduro, she got nothing more than a nod.

Viviane and Ricardo sat on the right of the table, their backs to the view of the street. Maduro sat on the left, with de Souza at the head. The logical place for Ann was beside Maduro but she felt curiously disloyal siding with the copper and sat the other side of Ricardo.

De Souza poured coffee and began to speak. "Time is money so I'll start proceedings by saying this is a preliminary meeting. From what I understand, Detective Maduro believes his superior officers will not take your case to the public prosecutor. If the prosecutor is not involved, there is no way of bringing this case to a state tribunal. However, if the evidence you have is sufficient, we can appeal to the prosecutor to mount his own investigation. This is the route we plan to take. Prosecutors, by and large, are invested in rooting out corruption and tackling those used to enjoying impunity. Yet their activity is overseen by a judge who may have no such compunction." He smiled at each of them. Ann was nodding whereas nothing but blank incomprehension registered on her neighbours' faces.

"Let me put it another way," said de Souza. "There are four steps to a judicial trial at state level. A civil police investigation is the first. If senior officers believe they have a strong enough case, they present their findings to the prosecutor. This is the tipping point. The wheels of justice are set in motion."

Viviane glared at Maduro. "So why don't you give what you know to the prosecutor?"

De Souza held up a hand. "The call is not up to Detective Maduro but the police chief, who could replace him on this investigation. By coming here today, he has shown remarkable determination to solve this case and, it's fair to say, jeopardised his own position. So, I think we can agree all of us in this room are on the same side."

Maduro did not look up but out of the corner of her eye, Ann saw Ricardo pat a heavy hand on Viviane's arm.

"But all is not lost. With Maduro's evidence and my connections, it's possible we can convince a public prosecutor to sue. If so, the case will go to tribunal. This meeting is for us to decide two things. One, do we proceed on the basis we can prove Franck Fischer orchestrated the death of Mr Leal's son, Nelson? Or do we take on the larger, more complex issue of Fischer's previous charges and demonstrate he has done this before, persecuting people of mixed race which results in their death? There are several factors to consider."

The clash of interests was clear. Ricardo and Viviane and the whole of Praia do Pesqueiro only wanted justice for their boy. Maduro wanted to land the biggest catch of all. With the hindsight of bitter experience, Ann thought the detective was on a hiding to nothing.

Evidently, he had other ideas. He took a deep breath and checked his notes. "Ricardo, Viviane, with your support, I can provide a prosecutor with circumstantial proof. I am sure

Franck Fischer, supported by his colleagues, abducted Nelson from the streets of Praia do Pesqueiro, took him to Fischer's boat, sailed up the river, tried him for his parentage and condemned him to death. I'm sorry to say this, but pathology reports show us Nelson suffered other injuries in addition to being tied at the wrists and ankles and thrown into the river to drown. Witness statements from a passing tourist boat and forensic evidence confirm Nelson was on *La Linda Lua* the day he died. What I don't have, because no one will talk to the police, are any local witnesses. It's not possible that not a single person saw Nelson forced into a vehicle. Someone must have seen him boarding the yacht. Dozens of people saw the boat travelling upriver with Nelson on deck. But not a single person will talk. I need a reliable witness, ideally two or three, but one believable voice can change a prosecutor's mind."

No one spoke.

"That's very good, thank you," said de Souza. "I will work with Detective Maduro this afternoon and arrange a meeting with a prosecutor tomorrow morning. Does anyone have anything you would like to add?"

Ann looked at Ricardo and Viviane, whose expressions had frozen.

"Well, think about it overnight. I'll send Ms Sheldon a message when I know what time we gain our audience. I appreciate your trust and will see you tomorrow."

He stood up to escort them out. Ann lifted her backpack onto her shoulders and found herself face-to-face with Maduro.

"Where are you staying?" he asked, without preamble.

She glanced at reception, where de Souza was shaking hands with Ricardo and Viviane. "Hotel Boavista. Two blocks away."

"Their chef has quite a reputation. Have dinner with me tonight."

She snatched the opportunity. "I'll book a table for eight."

"No, order Room Service. Our conversation must be private. I'll have a steak and salad."

"Steak and salad. My room is 409."

Viviane and Ricardo were waiting for her by the lift. They said nothing until they had left the building.

"Do you think it will work?" asked Viviane, peering past Ricardo at Ann.

"I honestly don't know. De Souza knows what he's doing, so I'm hopeful. What I'm curious about is the question of witnesses. If someone saw Nelson taken, surely they would have spoken up by now?"

"No," said Ricardo, as they approached the taxi rank. "If someone saw him taken, or saw him on that boat, they did nothing to help. Maybe because they were intimidated, maybe they didn't realise how serious it was, but now Nelson is dead, they can't admit it. I don't think we'll persuade anyone to talk. But we have to try. Ann, you want to share a cab with us?"

"I can walk from here, thanks. I'll call you as soon as I know what time we're meeting. Have a good evening."

"What did the cop want?" asked Viviane.

"He asked me to dinner tonight."

Viviane nodded. "Mm-hmm. I thought he had a look in his eye. You be careful."

On an impulse, Ann took a detour to the commercial district, snatching the opportunity to browse the kinds of shops she hadn't seen for months. The temptation to splurge on new underwear, face creams and a swimming costume were soon suppressed. Simply looking had scratched an itch. With a few mental calculations, she decided a new bra and some all-over moisturiser were not extravagances. Her fund was intended to keep her for the rest of her life, if she was careful. Maybe just a pair of earrings as a treat. She could wear them to dinner tonight.

En route to the hotel, she paused to listen to a samba band playing on a street corner. Music was another luxury she missed. She stood there for twenty minutes, swaying, bouncing and filling her reservoirs with some free joy.

At five past eight, wearing clean linen trousers and a white shirt, new silver earrings and her hair loose, Ann opened her door. Maduro stood in the corridor, also wearing a white shirt. He took in her appearance with an approving smile.

"I've never seen you with your hair down. You look pretty."

Awkward at the compliment, Ann fidgeted with her earring. "Thank you. Come in, the food is here and I'm hungry."

Her balcony overlooked the pool. Something about the reflections of water soothed Ann's nerves. Each dish already on the table under a cloche, the evening air heavy with the scent of exotic blossoms and a sense of privacy set the scene for ... whatever was going to happen.

"Steak with salad, I think you said?" She lifted the silver domes to reveal two identical platters and poured them each a glass of Bairrada. "Medium rare, I assumed. Selfishly, I ordered a plate of fries because I've no idea when I'll eat like this again." She was babbling and she knew it.

"Good choice. I've been looking forward to this all day." He cut into the meat and savoured the first mouthful. "The chef deserves her reputation."

Ann waited, allowing him to steer the conversation. She didn't have to wait long.

"When I was in police training, I made a friend. His name doesn't matter but his integrity does. Our motivations for joining the police were the same and if you don't know what that means after today, there's no point in this conversation. We graduated and found ourselves at opposite ends of the island. Him in a remote town up the Amazon, me in Soure. The only crimes on his patch were the logging companies and he couldn't stop them because they're protected by the government. He became disillusioned, a law-enforcement officer who cannot enforce the law.

"Then he was called to an 'accident'. A girl hanging from a tree in the forest. He did the legwork, interviewed witnesses, took photographs and compiled enough evidence to show Fischer had abducted a teenager, subjected her to a kangaroo court and hanged her. My friend was relentless when everyone else thought him crazy. That includes me. Powers-that-be called in favours, throwing obstacles in his path but he would not stop. He had proof Franck Fischer and his friends executed this girl for no other reason than her mixed-race heritage. He dodged, confronted and pushed back against every dead-end, and believe me, there were many. After months of work, he brought charges.

"Rookie cop against influential Mommy's boy. We all know how that ends. The prosecution's case was thrown out and Fischer walked free. My friend was demoted to a park ranger. He didn't fall into a depression or turn to drink, just kept doing the job."

Ann stopped chewing. "What job?"

"Investigating. He never gave up. Information about the fraternity case was only available in English, so he learned the language specifically to communicate with American detectives. He shared everything about the girl's murder in return. When he heard about Nelson Leal, he made the connection and travelled downriver to give me everything he knows. Ann, we're dealing with a serial killer who kills people like some kind of vigilante."

In the distance, a mature female voice sang *fado*, a sound to rend Ann's soul. "Thank you for sharing that with me. I thought it was personal and now I understand. How's your steak?"

"Good. Argentinean beef. I still prefer buffalo, though. A true son of Soure."

He grinned and she couldn't help but return the gesture. The white shirt suited him. So did that smile.

They lapsed into a thoughtful silence until she realised Maduro was watching her.

"What?"

"I tell you everything, putting all my cards on the table. You hide behind your cover and share nothing. A poet, who speaks fluent Portuguese, can spot all the signs of drug dealing and understands public prosecution. You're an anomaly I can't work out. I'm curious."

"Curiosity isn't always healthy. Anyway, some people don't want to be worked out. Have you known Milton de Souza long?"

"Six years, maybe more. All right, if you won't talk about yourself, tell me one thing. Why do you care so much about getting justice for Nelson Leal?" His eyes searched her face.

"I care about justice." She placed her knife and fork beside her plate. "It drives me mad to see immoral behaviour go unpunished. And it's hard to take the bad guys down when the system favours the wealthy. Even when you get as far as the court, it's still not fair and always subject to prejudice. Of course it is, because courts are made up of people, who are unfair and prejudiced."

"Are you talking about Brazil or where you come from?"

She decided against having another glass of wine and continued eating. Maduro was clever enough to pounce if she let down her guard. "I'm talking about generally and not necessarily about the legal system. These days, everybody believes they can be judge and jury. Fortunately, very few take it as far as Franck Fischer and play the executioner."

He caressed his glass, swirling the liquid so it caught the light. "So you do believe me. Thank you. Sometimes I feel I'm fooling myself, only just keeping cynicism at bay. I have to believe that in the majority, people are good and justice will prevail. This case is going to test my faith to its limits."

She gazed at him, noting the lines around his mouth. He met her eyes and something passed between them she could not explain. Her stomach fizzed and it had nothing to do with wine or fries. If she had any sense, she'd stay as far away from Gil Maduro as possible. She poured them both another glass of wine.

"A nightcap to help you sleep," she said, dismissing her earlier promise.

He studied her face. "Thank you. I enjoyed having dinner with you somewhere nicer than the floor of your shack. Can I ask another question?"

"You're fond of questions, aren't you?" she said, breaking eye contact. "Sure, you can ask but just remember I'm not under oath to tell you the truth, the whole truth and nothing but the truth."

A hint of a smile crossed his face. "Is Ann Sheldon your real name?"

She lifted her chin and looked directly at him. "It is now. Goodnight, Inspector."

Two hours later, hunched over her laptop, she found her real name. On an obscure website, the kind of place where you could tender a contract for less conventional services. She had to admit, she was an attractive proposition. Whoever provided them with accurate information regarding her whereabouts stood to earn themselves a small fortune. The specifics were very clear. This was not a hit. They wanted her alive.

22

The prosecutor, Simon Pinto, was a tiny, balding man and seriously good at his job. He listened to Maduro's evidence, heard de Souza's plan of attack and allowed Ricardo to deliver a testimonial to his son. He expressed his sympathies with warmth and sincerity to the bereaved father, then brought out his big guns, taking aim at both detective and lawyer.

Viviane was horrified and Ricardo confused, but Ann reassured them it was the only way to test the hypothesis. He was playing devil's advocate, finding any weak links and examining the facts. Because if he didn't, his opponents would.

This was a witch hunt. Fischer had been acquitted of two crimes and the justice department held a grudge. Persecution. Paranoia. Police obsession. Resentment of outsiders. Ann actually snorted with laughter at that one and turned it into mangled sneeze. Franck Fischer was an upstanding young man, destined to follow in his mother's footsteps, making the state of Pará proud of raising such a high achiever. Allowing his comet-like career to be extinguished by the pettiness of some small-town cops, resentful of his success would be farcical. Franck

Fischer was destined for great things and a trumped-up charge such as this was a disgrace.

Maduro was on the back foot but de Souza had seen this before and was enjoying himself. If the public prosecutor could not appreciate how one young man with a cruel agenda operated with impunity, how could anyone have faith in the law? Did lobbying, bribery and corruption reach into the very fabric of Brazilian institutions? No wonder the man on the street distrusted those in authority. It would take a man of extraordinary courage to reject both reward and threat, his clear eyes on the truth, regardless of the accused's celebrity status.

Posturing and declarative speeches over, Pinto stood and walked over to the window. De Souza and Maduro exchanged a glance.

"Milton, the rule of law is such that the accused should be tried on the evidence available to this case and this case only. The evidence is insufficient to sue and I am forced to agree with Detective Maduro's superior officer. It does not help that the officer leading this investigation seems to be driven by personal retribution. Fischer was found not guilty by two official tribunals. Your refusal to accept this leaves a bitter aftertaste. Any prosecution, unless you can provide more witnesses or tangible proof, is doomed to fail. Senhor Leal, I am profoundly sorry for the loss of your son, and do not wish to add to your sorrow by pursuing a case which will bring no satisfaction and may well bankrupt you."

Ann only just managed to contain a groan at this disappointing but accurate assessment of the situation, but she had her emotions under control after years of practice. Viviane did not. Her shriek of fury made everyone in the room jump. On her feet, Viviane threw her coffee cup at the prosecutor's head, missing by millimetres, while screaming a tirade of abuse and insults at him, the lawyer and Gil Maduro.

Nelson was a brilliant kid, a shining light in their community, but what do city sleazeballs know of the communities, the villages, the island of Marajó? Nothing apart from a summer playground where imbeciles like that piece of shit roar in at the weekend, make a lot of noise, leave a lot of trash and treat the locals like servants. This system is an embarrassment and everyone knows it. In thrall to the dollar sign, each of them is a shame on the whole country. Apart from Ricardo, not a man in this room has a full pair of testicles. She would be surprised if a single one of them has a functioning penis.

Her language grew still more vibrant and personal as Ricardo bundled her out of the room. The three men seemed shocked into silence. Ann was about to excuse herself when Maduro stood up.

"I will get your evidence, Senhor Pinto. You're right at this point in time, but this is not over. Milton, thank you for trying. If it takes a federal investigation to take Franck Fischer down, I will make that happen. Goodbye, Ann."

He was out the door before she could react. She stayed to thank the prosecutor, settled the lawyer's invoice and went out into the street. To her surprise, Ricardo and Viviane were not waiting for her. Neither was Gil Maduro.

What the hell to do now? The answer came loud and clear. *Use your skills and do what you came to do. And when you've done it, move on. Forget going back to Praia do Pesqueiro.*

Her sense of being misunderstood and unjustly treated was as familiar as a pair of uncomfortable shoes, painful and blistering. She didn't have to force her feet or her emotions through this again. What did it matter if two men she would never see again thought she had failed them? Three, if you counted Mike Ferguson.

Let it go. San Fairy Ann.

For once, she welcomed the return of a memory. *San Fairy Ann*, her father invariably said whenever she encountered a disappointment. Hot tears on discovering she was the only one of her friends not to be invited to a birthday party. The shame and heartbreak of not making the hockey team. A full set of rejections to her university applications. *San Fairy Ann, there's more than one way to skin a cat.*

Her own voice echoed over the years, sniffing and gulping after getting dumped by her first love. 'Why do you call me that, Dad?'

Concentration on his face as he poured the tea. 'Call you what, love?'

'San Fairy Ann. Whenever I'm upset or angry or I've made another stupid decision, you call me that name.'

He took a second to process her question and broke into a broad smile. 'I don't call you anything, sweetheart. It's French, something your mother used to say.' He spoke slowly, enunciating each word. '*Ça ne fait rien.* That means it doesn't matter or it makes no difference. You thought it was a nickname? You'll never stop surprising me, my girl.'

In an instant, the smile dropped from her face. *That much is true, Dad. You never expected my last surprise.*

One of the shops up ahead had rails of clothes outside and a neon-coloured sign screaming SALE - 50%!!! Most of the items were shades of violet and Ann slowed. A farewell gift for Fátima would perhaps encourage her to take care of Branca. She browsed the leggings, guessing her neighbour's size as medium. An awareness of another presence stilled her and she raised her eyes to the window. A middle-aged woman stood on the opposite side of the street, her phone raised as if taking a selfie. Ann noted two things. First, the phone was at arm's length, but aimed straight ahead. Any woman worth her salt knew one should lift the device and look up. Far more flattering. Also, the backdrop was a mobile phone shop. Why would anyone want a selfie against that? She grabbed two pairs of leggings at random and went inside the boutique.

The interior was loud and brightly lit, but the sun was shining on the other side of the street, enabling her to remain in shadow. She watched the woman, who appeared to be studying her phone, but lifted her head every few seconds to glance at the door of the shop. After a minute, she crossed the street at a diagonal, disappearing from sight. Ann assured a shop assistant she was just browsing and squatted to look at a display of shoes. It took three more minutes before the same woman – mousy hair, T-shirt, jeans, unremarkable handbag – walked by the shop in the other direction, stopping to examine a denim jacket on the rail outside.

Ann's racing pulse slowed with the conviction she was being followed. All the time she'd been in doubt, her breath was short and her adrenalin pressured her into fight or flight. Now she was sure, panic was her worst enemy. She took several calming breaths until the woman moved on and applied logic. There could be any number of reasons a deliberately nondescript woman, if indeed she was a female, was following her and trying to get a photograph. A journalist who'd seen her with Ricardo, perhaps, looking for some background on the drowned boy story. Or she was a bounty hunter and all she'd need was photographic proof of Ann's identity and location. Last night, Ann had stumbled across evidence that certain people wanted her alive. Presumably so they could administer their own form of punishment. The third option was a hit. Other people just wanted her dead.

She dawdled around the shop for another twenty minutes, finally emerging with a bagful of purple, pink and far-too revealing clothing. After two more stops and frequent switches of direction, Ann was ready. Her tail was good, still with her and camouflaged by the crowd, but nowhere near as smart as she believed. Although if she was an assassin, it was a good choice. Women tended to have greater instinctive trust in their own gender. In this situation, trust could be lethal.

At the hotel, she stopped to ask a random question of the receptionist, just to give her pursuer ample time to catch up. Then she ascended to her room and got to work.

She laid out all her purchases on the bed, shaking her head at the expense. *This had better be worth it.* Other than a pair of yoga pants, clean underwear, a baseball cap and a grey varsity sweatshirt, she packed everything in her rucksack, essential items uppermost. She showered, slathered herself in fake tan and scoured the room for anything she'd forgotten. Then she changed, laced up her trainers, heaved her pack onto her shoulders and walked down the stairs to check out. At reception, she adopted an American accent when ordering a taxi – loud and unmistakeable.

"Can I get a cab to the airport? My flight to Miami leaves at eight."

She paid her bill and left, her peripheral vision scanning the lobby for any observers. The middle-aged lady with the phone was not immediately obvious. Ann was shoving her backpack onto the back seat of the taxi when the doors opened and her tail emerged, now wearing a blazer with loafers. Ann smiled. *Chameleon? That makes two of us.*

She thanked the taxi driver for his patience. "To the airport, please."

The whole journey, she was a pain in the arse. "Could you slow down, please? I'm very nervous in traffic. Thank you."

"My flight's not till eight, so what's the hurry?"

"Driver, I'm feeling a little sick. Maybe you could pull over for a minute."

"Thanks, I feel better now. Let's get to the airport, but slow and steady, if you don't mind."

If her tail had lost her after all that, the woman was an amateur.

She took out her backpack and paid the driver, counting notes from her purse. She added a decent tip, as if she was made of money. "Have a good evening!"

He grunted and drove away.

Now timing was everything.

The second she entered the terminal, she took off at a run. People were always in a hurry at airports, so she attracted little attention. She ran away from Departures, in the direction of Arrivals, her eyes scanning signs for a bathroom. The crowd at the barrier, waiting to meet their loved ones, was a welcome sight. Yanking off her cap, she weaved a path between the throng, now carrying her backpack in her right hand. The toilets were behind the café. Only one woman was inside, reapplying her lipstick while chatting on her phone. Ann made for the last stall without a backward glance.

She stripped off her clothes and balled them into a plastic bag. Next, she unfolded the silver duffel-bag with wheels and put everything inside. Baggage disguised, she began on herself. Underwear first, including padded bra, followed by pink tiger-print leggings, a silvery lace-up top and a purple fringed jacket. Pink wedges with ankle straps on her feet. Heels would be more convincing, but there was always a chance she'd have to run. The brunette wig slipped over her tight bun with ease and double-sided tape secured it to her scalp. Quality make-up required a large mirror and more products than she had at her disposal. No matter. Ann had managed enough back-of-a-van-and-you'll-do jobs to approximate the look she wanted. The false eyelashes were the tricky part, when the only reflective surface she could find was a stainless steel bin for disposing of sanitary towels.

She flushed the toilet and emerged into an empty bathroom. In the mirror, a clown stared back. Ignoring the impulse to laugh, she tossed some curls over her shoulder and gave herself a sultry stare. Now the final touch. She traced the outline of her lips just a bit larger than their natural line and filled in the rest with Bruised Blackberry gloss. She looked ridiculous and unrecognisable. Which was exactly the point. Earphones in and microphone lifted to her mouth, she wheeled her bag behind her and opened the door.

Sashaying across the concourse, she made straight for the exit, laughing and carrying on an imaginary conversation. Taxi drivers with admiring looks tried to attract her attention, but she stalked past, heading for the Val do Cães airport hotel. As she wheeled her bag up the path, the sky closed in and it began to rain. She sped up, with a glance behind her. The airport was at least a kilometre away and no one was in sight. She'd lost her. Time to check in.

23

The first thing she did once in her rather less swanky hotel room on the fifteenth floor was to wash off the make-up. The eyelashes and trashy garments she kept, just in case. Dressed in her own clothes, she drew the curtains against the hammering rain, logged onto the Internet and got to work.

Step one: create a fake identity. Cuca_vai_pegar would do nicely. Firstly it was a Portuguese name and only a Brazilian would understand the reference. *The witch will catch you.* Secondly, she was using her own kind of magic. This particular witch was a mysterious journalist who never frequented the sites she used with her other aliases. Her interests were quite specific.

She started with Fischer's university and some of the groups to which he belonged. Naturally, the ones that interested her most required either a recommendation by an existing member or an application approval by administrators. She didn't have time for either. Instead, she tried hacking into an existing member's identity. Belém was four hours ahead of Seattle's time zone, so she could roam the message boards in relative confidence, as the vast majority of activity took place in the evenings. If whichever member she hacked happened to log on at the same time, the worst that could happen would be the admin in charge cancelling the account. She browsed the member list for a quarter of an hour, looking for an easy way in. One profile caught her eye – that of Junior Denis, a name Maduro let slip. In his bio, Denis mentioned his nationality, his coaching profession and his men's retreats. Curious, Ann followed the link and discovered that SRY Play Hard Weekends were about a little more than tennis.

Participants could enjoy various forms of recreation, including archery, shooting, survival training and combat sports. In addition to such activities, there was an educational program including lectures, films and support groups to discuss rediscovering masculinity in the modern world. While it was obviously misogynistic in tone, Ann could find no link to racial attitudes, other than the fact every man in the photographs was white. She navigated to the About section and found something which made her eyes widen. Franck Fischer was on the board of the company. The email address was simply inquiries@ sry.com but the chairman, Junior, could be contacted at j. denis@sry.com. Ann located the host platform and typed in f. fischer@sry.com, which instantly asked for a password. She grinned. One more step and she'd be in. What would Franck Fischer use as his password?

For a company all about exploring maleness, it seemed unlikely he'd use his girlfriend's name, if indeed she had been his girlfriend when he set it up. It would do no harm to Google her anyway. Shelbee. Ann groaned when she saw the endless pouting pictures next to perfumes, cosmetics and ugly jewellery.

When creating passwords, people tended to use dates of birth, pets, middle names and love objects – personal, mean-ingful and memorable. Apart from himself, Franck Fischer loved the trappings of status, that much was obvious. So when choosing a password for his role as manliness facilitator, he would opt for his car, his watch or something else with a name, such as his boat. She checked her notes for the name and make of the yacht, VQ48 and made an educated guess.

She typed his email again and when the password box popped up she entered ALindaLua48. Incorrect log-in details. He was an American. How would he say it? She tried again without the article: LindaLua48. The portal opened and she had access. Ann rubbed her hands together, grinning with glee.

A flash of lightning lit the room and although she was expecting it, the subsequent crack of thunder made her jump. Wired and hungry, she needed to concentrate. Food first. She ordered a burger and fries from room service and dived into Franck Fischer's emails. Prepared for a long night, she began sifting through all the tedious business discussions. One particular exchange between Franck and Junior made her jaw drop. *Jackpot already? Too good to be true.*

It wasn't so much the tone, which was pretty bad in itself, but the fact Franck had copied in his personal email. The exchange was about how to deal with a disgruntled participant who wanted a refund. A guy called Jefferson Rogers objected to the excessive use of violence during a paintball game and claimed he'd sustained severe injuries as a result. Junior and Franck were dismissive and insulting.

'Excessive violence?!? It's called paintball battle, not paintball picnic. Tell him to go screw himself, JD. He's not getting one cent from us. If we give that dickless pussy a refund, we leave ourselves wide open for legal action. No way.'

'I'm with you, Franck, my man. No apologies, no refunds and we stonewall the whiner. If he can't handle the heat, he should take his pansy ass out of the kitchen. Or maybe into it. Guys like him are better suited to a pastry-making class with a bunch of Karens and Beckys. Who does he think he is? Those severe injuries? Poor ickle Jefferson broke a tooth and sprained his wrist. Loser.'

'Major loser. He'll write a couple more times, we'll ignore him and he'll threaten to sue us. That's when we tell him to go ahead. He doesn't have the balls. Imma show this to our attorney, just to confirm, OK?'

Ann clasped her hands together and tapped her chin. The email exchange was relatively recent so she assumed Jefferson Rogers was still involved in the dispute. Even if he wasn't, this attitude from company directors could prove useful. She saved it as evidence.

But the real payload was Franck Fischer's personal email. With his address, she was on the way to accessing his inbox. The security was bound to be greater than for a men's retreat, she was prepared for that, but she had one of the keys.

The bell rang and she checked the peep hole. Her lunch had arrived. She asked the guy to leave it outside. She'd reward herself with food the second she cracked Fischer's personal email. Because therein lay her pot of gold.

Forty minutes later, she was still facing a blank screen. Fischer had set up two-step-verification. The neat little piece of software she had downloaded could get his password in a matter of minutes, depending on its strength. However, when she entered it correctly, he would receive an alert on his telephone asking him to approve access to his account. She couldn't find a way around it and accepted defeat. For now.

Time to refuel. She looked through the peephole at the bland, empty corridor and opened the door to retrieve her dinner. The second she stuck her head out, someone grabbed her, pressed a knife to her throat and shoved her inside.

She reacted on instinct. Pivoting on her left foot, she twisted and hit her assailant in the jaw with her elbow while tearing the hand holding the blade from her throat. The woman let out a grunt of pain and stumbled. Ann bent to grab her leg, toppling her over to crash against the wardrobe. Her attacker recovered fast, twisting onto her hands and knees but Ann was faster. In a second she leapt on the woman, kneed her between the shoulder-blades, forcing her to the ground. Wind escaped her lungs, and before she could draw breath, Ann grabbed her head with both hands, twisting it sharply to the right. The sound was nauseating. The body went limp and Ann scrambled to her feet, her breath short shaky gasps. For the first time, she registered pain at her throat where the knife had caught her skin. Her hand came away from her neck bloodied.

The incident had taken fewer than five seconds without a word uttered. The months of training, the simulations and assurances she'd never need to use such techniques had seemed a waste of energy at the time. Even so, she always applied herself as if intruders lurked around every corner. Now muscle memory had taken over and there was a dead body in the room. She pressed a hand to her throat and took three calming breaths, studying the woman at her feet. It was the same person who had followed her to the hotel. Her hair had changed, now shoulder-length, highlighted and glossy. Loafers and blazer gone, she wore a beige jacket, a turtleneck sweater, black trousers and white Adidas trainers. Ann slipped a foot beneath her shoulder intending to turn the body over, but changed her mind. She didn't want to see her face.

Her DNA would be all over the body after such a fight. Adding blood was not the best idea. The clock was ticking, but she took the time to wash her hands and wrap an entire roll of toilet paper around her neck. She switched off the lights and focused. *Make a decision and act fast.* Her mind raced over her options. After searching the woman's pockets, Ann found no ID, only a mobile phone, presumably containing photographs of herself on the streets of Belém. She removed the SIM card and put it into her pocket, praying the device hadn't any auto-mated cloud backup enabled. It would disappear in one of the huge rubbish containers on her way out of the city. Then she opened the balcony door to the elements. Violent gusts of wind blew the curtains inside. Ann's face was immediately soaked with rain as she surveyed the scene below. Her room was at the back of the hotel, overlooking a car park. She waited a couple of minutes, looking to either side and above for observers. Walls separated her balcony from her neighbours and no one was likely to sit outside while a storm lashed the building.

Trying to heave the corpse up and into a fireman's lift, she almost collapsed under the weight. She staggered a few steps and put it down. That was not going to work. Panting, she assessed the distance from body to railing and noticed the woman's hair had slipped to one side. She caught a hank in her right hand and pulled. The wig came off with the sound of a plaster being removed, revealing fuzzy dark hair with a bald patch. Ann rolled the body over and studied the face. Younger than she'd assumed, this man was around thirty, squat and muscular, with a strong jawline. She knew with absolute clarity she'd never seen him before.

Whoever he was, rigor mortis would soon set in. She lugged him under the armpits across the carpet and managed to drape his top half over the balcony railing. Crouching out of sight, she pushed the legs upwards until they were horizontal. Gravity did the rest.

The body fell in silence, hitting the cars below with a dull crunch. Ann stayed out of sight, listening for any sounds other than creaks and moans from the twenty-storey hotel battered by the weather. It might take until the morning until someone spotted the broken body. Ann hoped so. But she was taking no chances.

She closed the balcony door, locked it and removed the key, which she tucked into her wallet with the SIM card. After that, she put the plug in the bath and turned on the taps, emptying both complimentary shampoo and shower gel bottles into the water. In the mirror, she examined her neck wound which was a little deeper than a graze. Antiseptic wipes and a plaster took care of it and she flushed the bloodied toilet paper away. Wrapped in a robe with her hair in a towel, she hid the hotel hairdryer under her pillow and reapplied the Jessica Rabbit eyelashes and make-up. Finally, she went into the corridor to look at the hotel cameras, under the guise of remembering her dinner. Even at this distance, she could see the cameras at either end of the corridor had been covered with black tape. Her would-be assassin was a pro.

She wheeled the trolley inside and tossed the plate like a frisbee. The bun fell apart, fries scattered everywhere and little bits of lettuce stuck to the full-length mirror. She called Room Service and apologised. She'd had a little accident. Could they send a cleaning team? And maybe another burger with fries? With a beer this time.

When the two members of staff arrived, the scene was set.

"Hi, there! Oh, thank you so much! So sorry I made such a mess. I tripped and dropped everything! What am I like? Could you just clear that up? Maybe vacuum the carpet a little. Thank so much. Is that my replacement meal? Great, I'm starving. Put it on the table, please, I don't wanna screw up again, right? While you're here, could you do me a favour? I can't find the hairdryer but maybe I'm looking in the wrong place. Not there? Hey, you know what, forget it. Tonight, I'll let it dry naturally. No, that's all, thank you. Please, take this for your trouble. You're welcome. Oh, one other thing! I can't figure out how to open the balcony. I'm wild about storms, but can't open the door. A key? I wondered about that, but there was nothing in the lock. No, don't worry about bringing up another, I'm leaving early. Thanks anyhow. Have a great evening."

After they'd gone and she double-locked the door, she kept her disguise on. Just in case. In spite of recent events, her appetite was as keen as ever. She wolfed down her food, cracked open the beer and just before she knuckled down to finish the job, she closed the balcony curtains.

The sun was rising on a beautiful day over the city of Belém. Ann checked and double checked everything she had prepared but no longer trusted her own judgement. After working through the night, she was tired and crusty and nervous. Not just about the effectiveness of her all-out assault on Franck Fischer's character, but the risk of leaving any fingerprints, whether digital or physical. She had to ensure no trace of the perpetrator remained. She stood on a chair by the window, peering down at the car park. No sign of activity yet. Time to leave before the shit hit the fan. She packed everything but the laptop and headed into the shower. When she was ready to leave, she would re-read each draft and press SEND. Or not.

She washed away the night, questioning her motives and as a result, her moral imperative. Last night, she'd killed a man. A man who fully intended to kill her, so it was a clear-cut choice. Him or her. Or her and her as she'd believed in the moment.

Now she planned to destroy another man's life on little more than supposition. But her gut instinct told her to strike the match.

No smoke without fire. As an adage, it held a grain of truth. The problem was that a grain of truth could be twisted to serve a lie. With enough time, resources and support, Ann could have taken down a hundred Franck Fischers. If only.

One thing she did know was how the Fischers of this world play their advantages. Gil Maduro knew the odds were stacked against him, but even so he pursued it, drawing attention to the smoke. It wasn't enough. Ann understood the frustration and disappointment he was suffering right now. To wreak justice on Franck Fischer, someone had to light the fire. Even so, the money wielded by Cinthia Fischer would act as an effective extinguisher. Rather than one conflagration, Ann had set up a series of sparks, destined to catch light, connect and spread.

Ann dried herself, dressed her neck wound and twisted a scarf around her throat. In the mirror, she judged it passable. Sophisticated, even. It was time. She sat in front of her screen and asked herself aloud, "Is this the right thing to do?"

The answer came in her father's voice. *There's more than one way to skin a cat.* Ann rubbed her hands together, generating some friction and opened her box of matches.

Strike One. As Cuca_vai_pegar, she emailed six slightly different dossiers of evidence to investigative journalists in Washington, Seattle, New York, São Paulo, Belém and Rio de Janeiro. Each concerned the ideologies of Franck Fischer. Some connected the dots between his tweets, posts and likes on social media. Some shed new light on the crimes of which he had been accused and acquitted. Others included links to blogs where he had exposed his theories on racial identity or gender politics. One thing each dossier shared was the video. She allowed herself a wry smile, recalling Maduro's wretched face.

'Do you have video evidence?'

Why yes, detective, it just so happens I do.

When she had burrowed into the archives of an organisation called SRY NOT SORRY, she hadn't immediately joined the dots. The only reason she had checked it out was due to a series of comments Fischer had made on Twitter, referring to an event he attended. Once again gaining access via a member's account, she waded through photographs and speeches until she struck gold. The smartphone recording was shoddy quality but the speaker was recognisable and other than the parts drowned out by hooting and hollering from the audience, every word Franck Fischer said was audible. Better still, it was dated eighteen months ago. Six months after he was acquitted of hanging a teenage girl.

SRY. The male sex determination gene. *Come on, Ann, I know you're tired but not spotting that? Seriously. Srsly?* She took a moment to watch it again, shaking her head at his vocabulary. Purity. Usurped. Rightful place. Blood. His speech, cheered and applauded by the audience of around forty young people, was indisputable. Franck Fischer was a white supremacist.

Match number two. One touch paper dividing into three. When the video surfaced, as Ann would ensure it did, Cinthia Fischer's PR organisation, her law firm and business would all scramble to whitewash, litigate or make a sizeable donation to the university. Fischer Jr. had a small army working to protect his interests. If each of those institutions realised the damage to their own reputations, weighted by the fact their wealthy benefactor was liable to lose it all, his defences looked rather more flimsy. Cuca_vai_pegar simply offered them a friendly warning.

Which led her to match number three. Damon Wright was CEO of one of the ten biggest tech companies in the world and a champion, at least on paper, of equality and diversity. He was also Cinthia Fischer's fiancé. Publicly accessible accounts showed that various sister companies owned by Wright had loaned Cinthia's empire amounts in the excess of $20 million. Her business was like a house of cards. Take one of the basic structures away and the entire thing would collapse. So what would happen if you set fire to its foundations? Nothing left but smoke and ashes. A concerned email to some of Wright's biggest shareholders regarding ethical associations should ignite trouble.

One last spark and this one a slow burner. The email discussing Jefferson Rogers could be reused several ways. First, she redacted Fischer's contributions and sent it to Rogers from Fischer's own account. It wouldn't take them long to work out the sabotage, but the shouting match resulting from Fischer throwing his buddy Junior under the bus in the middle of a reputational implosion would add some decorative fireworks.

Second, she scheduled another email from Fischer's account 24 hours later, containing the full content. Third, and this was purely out of mischief, she collated hundreds of abusive terms Franck and Junior had used to refer to their clients, frequently by name, and sent a newsletter to their entire database.

The moment she finished lighting fuses on all her sticks of dynamite, she slipped the laptop into her backpack and left the room. She used the electronic check-out and walked the kilometre to the airport. Only as she entered the terminal did she realise she had no idea of her next destination.

24

The Departures board offered so many possibilities. When word got out about the body in the car park and its identity, smart people would put two and two together. The hit man had missed. Meaning she was still on the run. Anyone hunting this bounty expected her to flee Brazil and go underground. That was always an option. Flights to the States were affordable and imminent. Or she could stick around. Maybe disappear into the crowds of Recife or São Paulo?

Her first thought was to get out of this city and fast. Her second thought was for her stomach. That cheeseburger seemed a very long time ago. She opted to eat and make a plan. *Think it through then double think it, because they're pretty good at second guessing.*

On the first floor, she found a café-bar with a news channel playing. It had only just opened but the yawning waitress served her a *tosta mista*, coffee and with undisguised amazement, a glass of champagne. Even as Ann ordered, she knew it was too early for something to celebrate. She ate the melted cheese and ham while listening to the television news. The first story was not the one she expected.

DRUGS WAR CLAIMS THREE LIVES

The sleepy beachside village of Praia do Pesqueiro was rocked yesterday afternoon by an outbreak of bloody violence attributed to drug dealing gangs. Witness reports told of two SUVs speeding through the village and onto the beach, scattering locals and terrifying tourists. Outside a beach bar, four masked men emerged from the vehicles carrying guns and opened fire. Immediately after the attack, the vehicles drove away.

Two people were pronounced dead at the scene and a third died in hospital. The names of the victims have not yet been released. A police spokesman said the investigation was focused on a turf war between rival drug gangs. We'll keep you updated on that story as more information arrives.

She stared at the footage, both familiar and strange. Her beach, filled with emergency vehicles and flashing lights. The bar with its yellow and green sign, riddled with bullet holes. The camera zoomed in to an overturned table and a bloodstain on the wooden floor. She shook her head in disbelief. Three dead? It was inconceivable. The news programme moved on to a fire in an industrial zone and Ann tuned out. She paid the bill and made directly for the taxi rank.

"Can you take me to the port? Go as fast as you like. I have to catch the express ferry to Soure."

Quite a different journey to the slow chug in the opposite direction, the express ferry was enclosed and air-conditioned with TV screens showing a movie. Ann dozed most of the way, her waking mind a constant loop of worry. Her positive side chanted the plus points. The storm must have washed away any traces of DNA on her assailant. The carpet had been cleaned by Room Service, who might even provide an alibi. Her disguise was convincing, as least on CCTV. Meanwhile, her guts churned over the minuses. *Someone found you. He won't be the last. You killed a man and you will have to pay. Why the hell are you going back to Ilha do Marajó?*

The Fischer story broke near the end of her journey. She was idly watching the credits roll at the screen when the programme switched to regional news. This time, they led with the explosion on the industrial estate, but the second story made her sit upright. Engine noise and general chatter made the story impossible to hear, but she read the subtitles.

Fischer family embroiled in more scandal. Revelations rock the son of Cinthia Fischer, Franck, recently arrested and released on a murder charge. Footage emerges of Franck Fischer addressing right-wing rally. Family depart Brazil for the US.

The images showed a media scrum outside an elegant villa as a door opened and Franck Fischer, flanked by security guards, was hurried into a waiting vehicle. The journalists clamoured for a comment. The picture then showed an extract from the incriminating video, with several of the offensive terms bleeped out. The report ended with a shot of a private aircraft departing Belém airport.

We were in the same airport at the same time, Ann thought with a sardonic laugh. *We could have shared breakfast.* She itched to take out her laptop and peruse the news sites, but worried anyone sitting beside or behind her could observe her screen. She would just have to wait it out. She watched the rest of the news, hoping for an update on the shootings in Praia do Pesqueiro, but the only other piece before the weather was a bus crash in Belém. What a change in fortunes for young Mr Fischer. Last night, he would have been celebrating the lack of evidence against him, released without charge, congratulating himself on not getting burnt. But the embers remained.

Ann had fanned the flames. She allowed herself a smug smile. *You can run, Franck, but you cannot hide. Take it from someone who knows.*

. . .

On arrival in Soure, she stepped onto the gangway, dropping a tissue containing the last quarter of the SIM card into the muddy brown water. The other three were in litter bins at the airport, the ferry terminal and wedged into a piece of chewing gum on the ferry itself. The key to her hotel balcony was taking a tour of Belém in the back of a cab, although the view wasn't great from the ashtray.

Once on land, she made straight for the police station. The heat of the afternoon made her a little lightheaded. Instead of the usual laid-back atmosphere at the police compound, the place was buzzing. A small crowd of people filled the yard outside and police vehicles were parked both sides of the street. Ann waited on the opposite pavement, trying to assess the situation. It seemed the majority of the crowd were journalists, carrying cameras and microphones, playing the waiting game. The others were harder to define. Some weeping, some smoking and two enterprising kids selling bottles of water. There was no way she could walk in there and ask for Detective Maduro without drawing attention to herself.

Instead, she beckoned one of the water sellers. He offered her a bottle, assessed her with sharp eyes, taking in her ruck-sack and asked for three reais. She pulled down her lower lid, gave him a hard stare and handed him one.

"What's going on here?"

The kid took the money without argument and placed his water bottles on the ground, settling in for a chat. "Assassins," he said, with a knowledgeable air. "They shot up a beach bar in Praia do Pesqueiro. Killed three teenagers. The police think it's drugs."

"Drugs? Here? I find that hard to believe."

"You can believe what you like. Why else send two cars and

four men with guns to shoot up a beach bar? It's a bad sign. Violence and drugs put the tourists off."

"Have they released the names of the victims yet?"

"Not yet. That's what everyone's waiting for."

"So how do you know they were teenagers?"

"My cousin's girlfriend was at the beach. She saw the bodies. She told him there was blood and … *ai*! I gotta go, there's the detective."

He snatched up his water bottles and ran across the street. In the scrubby yard in front of the police station, everyone rushed to the veranda, where Detective Maduro stood at the top of the steps. He gave a short statement, which was impossible to hear at that distance. Immediately besieged by questions, he gave brief answers to one or two and then held up a hand. His sergeants came out of the building and began herding the crowd into the street. Maduro watched proceedings from the top of the steps and his eyes locked onto Ann.

She lifted a hand in greeting but he continued to stare, his expression stony. Her arm wilted to her side as he re-entered the building. There was nothing for it but to walk back to her shack and find out what she could from the villagers.

Things are going to get ugly. Her exact words to Rubem. And his response? *Things already got ugly.* Teenagers, that water seller kid had said. Not that he could be trusted, having gained his rumours from conjecture and guesswork and gossip. First Nelson and then these three young people, executed by professionals. Despite the heat, the insects, the dust thrown up by passing vehicles and her own weariness, Ann focused on the facts.

An afternoon shooting on a public beach was either a reprisal or a serious threat, by people who feared no punishment. Until she found out who had died, it was only supposition to attach this brutality to the Gonçalves operation. Whereas Nelson, as far as she knew, had nothing to do with

Gonçalves, drugs or the surfers. Perhaps that was his crime? If he refused to cooperate with the drug peddlers and Franck Fischer was a customer ...

Her concentration was distracted by two federal police vehicles thundering past. She knew where they were heading and why. This was the endgame. She'd have done anything to be a part of it.

A car came to a halt by her side. Instantly, she snapped around, her right hand on her back pocket for her flick knife. It was a police Jeep and Maduro was driving.

"Get in. I want to talk to you."

She shrugged off her rucksack and did as she was told. He drove away and she kept a lid on her bubbling questions, waiting for him to speak first.

"Do you happen to know anything about *Cuca vai pegar*?" he asked, his jaw jutting and eyes on the road.

She waited a second before replying. "The kids' cartoon? I'm pretty sure I saw it while I was in Rio. Something to do with crocodiles and naughty children, right?" She changed her breezy tone. "Gil, who did they shoot at the beach?"

The Jeep sped up. Ann assumed he was trying to catch up with the others. They drove past the little blue marker indicating her shortcut and past the turn-off to Praia do Pesqueiro.

Finally, he spoke. "Pedro Bandeiro and Xander Fortes were killed on the spot. The owner of the bar suffered fatal chest wounds and died in hospital. Aged 18, 19 and 25 years old. Several other associates of the dead teenagers have gone missing and a federal organised-crime unit is en route to Quinta dos Rios. Civil police are back-up, directing traffic to turn around."

She had no answer to that, sensing his indignation and an odd note of humility. She watched the jungle ripple by, suppressing simultaneous urges. One, to leap out of the cab and run in the direction of her shack. Two, to ask him for a professional assessment of the situation. She did neither.

He spoke again. "When did you return from Belém? Have you seen the news?"

"About the shooting, you mean?"

"You know what I mean. Franck Fischer landed in Miami this afternoon and was immediately taken in for questioning regarding hate speech. An online campaign has exposed him and his ideologies. Whoever orchestrated that did a great job. I just hope that this *cuca* has not exposed herself. Because she just made some powerful enemies."

"Fischer? I hardly had time to read the news this morning. Well, his past was bound to catch up with him sometime. I think the turning to the farm is up here on the left. Yes, I was right, there it is. What the hell is that?"

Maduro hit the brakes as they saw a blazing vehicle lying on its side, blocking the road to the farm. The Jeep engine idled from a safe distance as they stared at the stricken Ford.

Ann took a deep breath. "So the two police vans which passed me earlier …"

"Just drove right into an ambush. I'm guessing traps are set on the road to the farm, maybe even explosive devices. We're too late. They've already let off the fireworks." A rattle of gunfire echoed through the forest, sending monkeys and parrots into shrieks. A nerve pulsed his temple.

"Call for back-up." Her voice was tight.

"We *are* the back-up." He snatched up his radio and notified headquarters of the situation.

Ann strained to understand the police acronyms but learned more from his face.

He ended the call and stared at her. "They're sending the military. God knows how long that will take. I think I already know the answer to this, but can you handle a gun?"

Ann dropped all pretences. "Like a pro. Drive on and take

a left in about half a kilometre. There's a delivery lane used by suppliers. It's another access route to the farm."

"Yes, I know that. How the hell do you?" He rammed the Jeep into first and drove past the burning Ford and along the dusty road.

She didn't answer, her eyes fixed on the road. She'd only seen this track once before, coming from the other direction, and seeing as she could hardly find her own shortcut through the jungle on foot, she feared he would miss it. She nearly did. Only a few scraps of broken branches distinguished the turning from any other stretch of road.

He swung left before she could speak and slowed to a crawl. Buffaloes believed the track belonged to them and although Ann would not have thought it possible, the road had deteriorated since her last visit. Another factor accelerated her heartbeat. If anyone fled from Quinta dos Rios, this was the obvious route. There was every chance a vehicle would round the next corner, all guns blazing.

Maduro crept along the track in second gear. Precious little sunshine penetrated the leafy coverage and their route grew treacherous. While he devoted his attention to the uneven terrain, she scanned both sides of the jungle for any signs of a threat.

A rapid series of gunshots and a sudden explosion made her start and him brake. The sounds came from directly ahead. Maduro clenched the steering wheel and glanced at Ann.

"You shouldn't be here."

She yanked her binoculars from her backpack. "Just give me the gun. I can obey orders."

He opened the glove compartment and handed her a pistol. "This is a last resort. We are here to save lives."

She took it and examined the weapon to make sure she could use it at speed. When she looked up, Ann realised the darkening sky was not due to dusk but a huge plume of smoke, emanating from Quinta Dos Rios.

"Drive!"

Maduro put the Jeep into gear, set his jaw and drove into the fray.

25

Around 50 metres before the track opened onto the courtyard, Maduro slowed to a halt, turned off the ignition and got out. Ann did likewise, closing the Jeep door silently. Smoke was thick and acrid in her throat and the first thing she noticed was the deathly silence from the jungle. As if every living thing was shocked into silence.

Gil went first, motioning for her to follow in his wake. Just behind the tree line, he stopped, assessing the situation. Ann let out a long, low breath and counted the bodies. Crumpled against the outbuildings lay eight corpses. With a chill, Ann saw the blood splatters on the wall above them, each at head height. Hallmarks of an execution. On the steps of the house, a man wearing a balaclava was spread out like a starfish, blood pooling down the steps in a macabre facsimile of bridal train. The house was ablaze, belching smoke into the air.

Three vehicles were parked a good distance from the buildings. Ann crouched and raised her binoculars to her eyes. The two armoured SUVs had tinted windows meaning she could see nothing of the occupants, if there were any. The third vehicle was a white Porsche Carrera punctured by bullet holes along the chassis. Ann traced a line downwards from the driver's door and saw a leg, wearing a snakeskin boot.

"They're still here," she whispered. "Shot the workers, set fire to the house and now…?"

"Destroying the equipment," whispered Maduro, his eyes on the outbuildings. "The only reason to burn the house is because someone's still in there. Cover me. I'm going round the back. If I'm not here when they return to the vehicles, get out of the way and do nothing to stop them. Let them go but note everything. Only use that gun in self defence."

She slipped the safety catch off the gun. "Understood. Destroying the equipment means a permanent solution. Gil, they may have explosives. Be careful."

He nodded but said nothing and crept away through the jungle towards the concrete buildings. Flies were already descending on the corpses and the house fire had reached the second floor. Mauricio dead or fatally injured should have been enough. Why were these people still here and who else did they want to punish? She recalled the older brother, João, and his puzzled expression on finding her in the undergrowth. He'd scared her to death, but somehow she knew he shouldn't be part of this bullshit.

She watched Maduro creep along the shadows behind the nearest outbuilding. Ears alert for any sound, she shifted her position to get a better view. Smoke billowed across the compound making visibility unreliable. A movement between the two armoured vehicles caught her attention. A masked figure slid sideways, his attention on Maduro. He raised his weapon in the direction of the detective's back.

Ann couldn't yell a warning; it was too dangerous for Maduro and for her.

'Only use that gun in self defence,' he'd said. That was open to interpretation. She took aim at the masked man's shoulder and pulled the trigger. With a cry, he recoiled, bouncing off the vehicle and crumpling to the ground.

She ducked and rolled to one side, face pressed to the ground. No retaliatory fire followed so she assumed the man was a lone lookout. She counted to twenty before lifting her head from the dirt. Maduro had vanished. The man she'd shot lay still beside the SUV. Her lungs wanted to cough, but fear repressed that urge.

She was easing herself into a crouch, ready to move behind the Jeep, when a sound behind her made her stiffen. Before she could turn her head, the barrel of a gun pressed against her neck.

"Put down your weapon and raise your hands."

She obeyed.

"Where's Maduro?"

She pointed at the outbuilding. "Behind there. He's going into the house."

"Shit." The man spoke into a radio, his gun still pressing into her neck. "Hold fire. Officer on site. Wait for my order."

Ann frowned in concentration. His voice was familiar.

The weight of the gun barrel lifted. "Ann, listen to me. Get into the Jeep and turn it sideways so it's blocking the track. It won't stop them, but it might slow them down. As for you, run and hide."

Hands still in the air, she turned to see who was addressing her by name. Her mouth opened in astonishment. "Nando?"

"Agent Fernando Alvares of the Federal Police, actually. Take the gun, you might need it. Move the Jeep and … shit. Looks like we're too late. Get down."

A group of men ran from the outbuildings in the direction of the armoured trucks. Through the smoke, it was impossible to be sure but Ann thought she counted seven. Nando gave an order into the radio. Immediately gunfire strafed the compound. Several of the running men raised semi-automatic weapons and began shooting into the jungle. Nando took aim and hit one man in the leg. Ann dodged away to the side of the track as bullets flew in their direction. In a crablike scuttle, she took a wide circle through the undergrowth and came out at the rear of the house.

Two corpses lay on the ground and smoke poured from an open door. At that moment, Maduro emerged, carrying a body over his shoulder, his blue shirt tied around his face and eyes streaming.

He saw Ann. "Help me move them! This place is going to blow up. Get them as far away as possible! There's another one inside." He laid his load on the ground and Ann realised these were not dead bodies but living people, bound and gagged. Maduro ran back into the building.

Ann flicked on the safety catch, shoved the gun in the waistband of her jeans and pulled out her flick knife. They had to run for themselves because there was no way she could drag them all to safety. She recognised Rubem's tearful, terrified face as she cut the plastic ties binding his wrists and ankles.

"Run!" she told him. "Go that way!"

She set to work freeing a guy wearing the uniform of a domestic servant. Once untied, the white-faced man fled like a gazelle. She'd just started on the last when an explosion from inside the house knocked her sideways. The man she was freeing made a muffled sound and she scrambled to release him.

"Run into the jungle!" she yelled.

The man got to his feet, towering over her, just like the last time. João, Mauricio's brother, shook his head. Instead of dashing away like the others, he turned towards the building.

"It's too dangerous!" she shouted, but he paid her no heed and walked through the burning doorway. She tried to pull him back but the heat and choking black smoke repelled her. Eyes watering, she scanned the building to see if there was another way she could get in. A coughing, spluttering sound came from inside and João emerged, dragging Maduro with one hand and carrying another person under his arm. His cough seemed to shake his whole huge frame as he placed the limp body on the floor. Ann recognised the girl's sun-bleached hair.

"Serena!" She cut the girl's ties and tore the tape from her mouth. She was unconscious, so for the second time in twenty-four hours, Ann dragged a deadweight by the armpits. João did the same with Maduro and led the way into the jungle.

They staggered around 100 metres before João collapsed to his knees. They hadn't come far enough to escape another explosion but João could go no further. He gasped for breath as he put Maduro on the ground. The girl Ann was dragging seemed impossibly heavy, so she did the same and checked for a pulse. Serena was alive. She put her in the recovery position and attended to Maduro. His breathing was ragged but his eyes were open.

"Are you injured?" He looked uncomprehending for a moment, then lifted his arm. The skin on the right side of his torso was red, blistered and even blackened in patches. At that moment, three explosions came, one after another, throwing debris high into the sky. She curled her body over the unconscious girl, protecting Serena's head and her own.

When the rain of objects ended, she lifted her face to see Nando coming through the jungle towards them, his gun cocked.

His eyes took in the party and he addressed Maduro. "You got them all out. Well done."

Maduro attempted to speak but simply pointed a finger at João.

"I know." With no hesitation, he raised his gun to the big man's forehead.

Ann's anguished scream melded with Maduro's. When

their voices faded, João crumpled to the ground in prayer, still coughing.

Nando holstered his weapon. "I'm not going to kill you, Gonçalves. We've seen enough bloodshed for one day. It's over. Let's go."

Soure didn't have enough ambulances to cope with the numbers of injured and dead. Ann was pressed into driving the Jeep to transport three of the less-seriously injured to hospital. They included Rubem, Serena and the servant from the house. The journey was silent, each face pale with shock or pain. After delivering them safely, she returned the Jeep to the police station. The compound was swarming with police, journalists and local people demanding answers. Ann threaded her way through to the reception desk, intending just to leave the keys, but someone placed a hand on her shoulder.

"Give those to me. Come, I'll take you home." Nando guided her through the crowd and into the fresh air.

Of all the people Ann wanted to speak to at that moment, Gil Maduro was in pole position. But until he'd been treated for his burns, she'd have to wait. Second in line was the man she believed was a ferry worker, part-time drunk and harmless neighbour. A thousand questions buzzed around her brain as the Jeep rumbled out of the city towards the jungle, but she couldn't find a way to begin.

Once they left the city lights behind them, he cleared his throat. "Branca's foot is healing. She had a skin inflammation and I treated it with the same stuff you use on a baby's bum." Even his voice was different. The lazy, slow, half-sozzled delivery had gone and this man was a clipped professional.

"Thank you for taking care of her." She attempted to organise her thoughts. "Nando ..."

"Agent Alvares, if you don't mind. Ask me no questions and I'll do you the same favour."

She said nothing as they drove through the mangroves, still processing her confusion. He drew to a halt at some random point and turned to her with a half smile. "Through the jungle or would you prefer the beach tonight?"

"The beach, please. The jungle is a bit too scary in the dark."

"Scarier than what you saw today? I doubt it. They trained you well."

"Thank you." She said no more, her heart sinking.

Nando stopped at the turning to Praia do Pesqueiro. "I'll take you no farther, for both our sakes. Goodbye, Ann. You won't see me again, that much I guarantee. People like you and I can keep secrets. But you need to up your game."

Her pulse fluttered. "What do you mean? In what way?"

"Water your damned plants. That tomato was shrivelled as hell when I got there. *Boa noite.*"

She watched him do a three-point turn and waved as the red tail-lights disappeared into the dark.

26

The horrors of that afternoon would reverberate through the whole of Ilha do Marajó but nowhere more than Praia do Pesqueiro. Ann intended to avoid the place entirely, planning her escape the soonest she could get out. From the moment Nando let her out of the Jeep at the turnoff, she limped down the beach, dragging her backpack, with one thought. Sleep. If her shack was damaged, she'd simply curl up under the stilts like Branca. Her knife was still tucked in her jeans so anyone attempting to do her harm was going to get one hell of a shock.

Night had fallen when she grew close to the hut. Shutters closed, it appeared untouched. The heron was absent, presumably gone to roost for the night. She stepped onto the path, noticing a glint from the porch. In a second, she grabbed her knife and tiptoed nearer. It was only moonlight reflecting from a bowl of water. A movement under the stilts brought a wave of emotion to cloud Ann's exhausted eyes.

"Branca? Good girl! I'm so happy to see you!" The dog licked her hand, bunting her nose into Ann's palm. A squawk and clatter made them both tense until Ann saw the white arcs of a heron's wings fly out to sea.

The door to the shack seemed unchanged and the interior was as she'd left it. Almost. The tiles behind the kitchen sink had an azulejo pattern, symmetrical squares of blue and white. You could put them vertically or horizontally and the design would be the same. Except one tile had a tiny chip on the bottom right-hand corner. Ann always replaced it exactly the same way. Now, in the light of the lamp, the chip was at the top right.

Someone had been in here and found her hiding-place. She removed the tiles and checked the contents. Everything was as it should be. Gun, bullets, documents, poison and Thanh's bracelet. The person who had entered without leaving a trace and removed the tiles now knew the truth about her. The only saving grace? She knew the truth about him.

Considering what she'd witnessed the previous day, Ann enjoyed a peaceful sleep. The nightmares would come, she knew that, but one night's rest was exactly what she needed. When she woke, she showered, made coffee and sat on the porch, planning her departure. Branca drank some water and trotted off down the path to do only she knew what. Ann wondered if Fátima would be prepared to take care of the dog after she left. If not, maybe Ricardo? The last thing she wanted to do was go to the village and meet grieving parents, gossipy locals or answer any questions. However, she could not prevent the village coming to her.

It was no surprise that before she had finished her second cup, Fátima came striding up the path, brandishing a letter. She began speaking long before she was within earshot.

"… because what would he know about it? Of course I thought he was lying. He lies all the time. The only decent-sized thing about him is his imagination. So I went to the *padaria* this morning and turns out it's true. He was there at Quinta dos Rios, overseeing the operation! All this time, he was an undercover cop! He was using me as a way of getting close to the surfers. *Ai, ai, ai,* I don't know what to think. Is there any coffee?"

Ann feigned a yawn. "Good morning, Fátima. I only got back yesterday, so I'm not sure what's going on. Let me make some coffee and you can tell me all about it."

"I don't know if I can tell you all about it because I don't understand it myself and I'm not sure anybody else does. As I just told you, Nando hasn't been home for two days. No word, no explanation, nothing. This morning, I wake up to find a letter on the table. The whole working-on-the-ferries thing was a lie. He's never worked on the ferries and now I think about it, I had my suspicions about that story. Every single time I or any of my friends went to Belém, he was missing. Nando, an actual undercover cop! Can you believe it? See, that is sexy. I would have fancied him a lot more if he told me. Why the hell didn't he tell me?"

Ann rubbed her eyes. "Kind of defeats the undercover part, I guess. Had you two been together long? Here, coffee, and before you ask, I don't have any whisky."

"That's OK, I brought my own bottle. We've been together for ages! I can't believe he deceived me for so long. Let's see, we met in November." She counted on her fingers. "So that's over six months. It's not fair, is it, to make me fall in love with him and believe we had a future together, when all he wanted was information on Gonçalves and his drugs operation. I should sue the police. And now," she smacked the letter with the back of her hand, "he says I'll never see him again. Apologies and pretty words and a few nice compliments, but now he's got what he wanted, he's gone. I feel such a fool." She poured a slug of Scotch into her coffee and was about to do the same for Ann, who placed her hand over her cup.

"If I have any hope of understanding what went on, I'm not drinking whisky for breakfast. I'm not sure you should either."

"Shut up. That's what he said. You know it was him marking the bottles? Checking how much I was drinking! What a bastard!"

It made sense. No one had been marking Ann's alcohol, only Fátima's. But she knew in her bones Nando had been into her hut. She changed the subject. "When I arrived in Soure yesterday, I heard something about a showdown at the Gonçalves farm. Do you know what happened?"

Fátima launched into long and lurid description of events which bore a tangential relationship to what had really happened. The only factual element she delivered that Ann did not already know was the number of bodies.

"So if you add those nine to the three at the bar, that makes ...who's that?" She squinted down the beach at an approaching figure. "Oh hell, it's Ricardo Leal. Listen, I'm going because he'll only drone on about that lawyer in Belém and I've already heard it three times from Viviane. We'll talk about this later."

She chugged her coffee in one and headed off down the path, stopping to exchange the time of day with Ricardo. Ann made more coffee.

"*Bom dia*, Ann! I have very good news! Ah, coffee, just what I need. Thank you. Everyone is talking about what happened at the Gonçalves place, but I'm not interested. Seattle is the centre of my attention. I need to you send a message to Mike Ferguson on that machine. You won't believe this, but Franck Fischer has been arrested and charged with something or other about racism. I know, I know, we've been there before. The difference is the media this time. It's all over the news! Ferguson probably knows but send a message anyway. Tell him what happened in Belém and explain how Nelson died. He won't like it but he ought to know. And you? You deserve our thanks. You tried your best to help my family and we appreciate it. None of this was your business but you are a good friend to Dulce and me. I brought you some fish. This is fresh, caught three hours ago. Cut the meat finely and soak it in lime juice. Add some vegetables and fruit and you have yourself ceviche. I have to go. How's that dog working out?"

Ann stood to say goodbye. "She's been a great companion. Ricardo, listen, I'm leaving soon. Will you look after her?"

Ricardo took a step backwards, his face agape. "Leaving? Why? The beach is not normally like this, I promise you. Now that shitty Gonçalves is dead, we can sleep safely in our beds. Don't go, Ann, please don't go. This is a nice place and you're a nice lady."

She smiled but couldn't reply, her throat choked.

"OK, I understand. If you have to leave us, yes, I will take care of the dog. Just make sure you come and say goodbye."

He took her by the shoulders, kissed her on both cheeks and was down the steps in three paces. "Lime juice and keep it cool. No cooking! *Tchau!*"

She waved goodbye and went inside, more than a little shaken by the first physical touch of affection in many months. Part of her recoiled and wanted to scream. Another part, silent for a long time, wanted to rest her face against his stubbly cheek and let him hold her.

Following Ricardo's instructions, she cleaned the fish and let the citric acid do its work. Then she sat down to write to Mike Ferguson, only to find he'd beaten her to it.

Hi Ann

I'm watching developments in the Fischer case avidly. Looks like our best efforts failed and under the circumstances, I'm not surprised. The chances were always slim. I was pretty hacked off when hearing the result of your meeting, I admit. Let me say now that I don't blame you in the slightest. You did your best and I'm grateful. Even though the case won't get to court, Fischer is undergoing a whole other kind of judgement. I'm not sure how much news you have heard, but I can tell you Franck Fischer has been 'cancelled'. Some guy published details online of his affiliations, including a very nasty speech. If you can find it, have a look. It's enlightening. Even more significantly, his mother has cut ties. She made a statement condemning his language and behaviour. I guess she won't be funding his future defence team.

Thank you for your help and please keep the laptop and phone with my compliments. On a personal note, I don't think Praia do Pesqueiro is any place for a woman on her own. Wherever you go next, I wish you every success.

With warmest regards, Mike Ferguson.

The feeling of invisibility wasn't new. Ann wrote a reply, bland and indifferent, celebrating Fischer's downfall at the hand of a stranger and promising to think hard about whether to leave her beach hut. Ironically, his well-meaning caution impelled her to stay.

Her head was muddled and over-caffeinated. A swim would help her think more clearly. She spent half an hour in the sea, powering through a crawl, relaxing with a backstroke and then turning around to repeat the pattern. It worked. Seawater, physical exercise and fresh oxygen grounded her in reality. She wrapped herself in a towel, aware of some appetite signals and returned to her shack, ready to make ceviche. Only when she'd eaten would she make a final decision.

While the vegetables and fruit marinated, she dried and dressed herself, half wishing she had a bottle of white wine to accompany her lunch. *That was what two days in Belém had done*, she thought. *Turned me into a spoilt brat.* Even so, clean sheets, fluffy towels and reliable Internet access couldn't hold a candle to this view, this air. She leaned against the door jamb, gazing out at the ocean, absorbing its beauty and peace. As she stood there, a figure appeared at the side of her house. Inspector Maduro moved with all the caution of a cat. He must have come through the jungle and crept along the tree line before approaching her hut. He didn't want to be seen, which was probably for her benefit. His imbalanced gait indicated his injury and he carried a paper bag.

Ann watched him, still as a statue. When he got to the bottom of the path, she straightened up and came to the top of the steps.

"Hello, Gil. I didn't expect to see you today. How's the burn?"

He stopped and looked up at her. "You're still here." His voice was raspy and hoarse, as if he'd been shouting.

"For the moment. I was about to have lunch. Will you join me?"

"Does it go with white wine?" He lifted the paper bag.

She laughed. "Ceviche and white wine? A match made in heaven. Come in."

They ate on the porch, saying little, other than praising the food and the wine. Maduro was still in pain, that much was clear, but he seemed comfortable in her company. Neither of them mentioned Quinta dos Rios. She wondered if he knew she'd saved his life and realised it didn't matter.

"Where's your dog?" he asked. The hoarseness in his throat made her wince.

Ann shrugged. "She goes out every morning and returns at night. I have no idea what she does during the day. I never intended to look after an animal, but she followed me home."

"So did Agent Fernando Alvares, apparently."

She put down her fork and met his eyes. "I thought he was my neighbour's boyfriend. He came round one evening with beer and talked about poetry. Did you know who he was?"

Maduro shook his head. "The undercover operation was at federal level. I know you warned me about Gonçalves but drugs are out of the civil police's jurisdiction. Anyway, I was too focused on trying to take down Fischer. Meanwhile, Alvares was gathering info on the drugs operation. We only found out how much intelligence he had two days ago. That guy's good at what he does."

Ann couldn't argue. "Yeah, he is. He had me fooled."

"Even you." His stare burned into hers. "You don't have to tell me anything, but I'm not an idiot."

She averted her gaze, unwilling to react.

His voice dropped to a whisper. "You're leaving, aren't you?"

She hesitated, unsure of the truth herself.

"Does he know who you really are? Is that why you're going to disappear?"

"Tell me something, Gil. Did you ever enter this shack when I wasn't here? You have the skills, I know that much."

His brow creased. "No. Never. I swear. The only time I was here without you was when you went for a swim."

She assessed his face. "In that case, yes, he does know who I am. That's why I need to run."

"I wish you'd stay." He reached for her hand, his knuckles scratched and scuffed.

The injuries he'd sustained rescuing the people in the farm-house made her well up with emotion. She couldn't afford to get attached, not to a dog and certainly not to a detective.

She shoved back her chair and reached for his plate. "Have you finished? The fish was a present from Ricardo Leal for trying to help Nelson's case so it's only right we should share it." She took the empty plates into the kitchen, calling over her shoulder. "I can't offer you a dessert, but how about a coffee before you go?"

He didn't answer and for a panicky moment she thought he'd left, affronted by her rudeness. Then she felt his presence behind her, his hands on her shoulders, turning her to face him.

His expression was tender as he pulled her closer to his left side. She knew the gesture was driven by self-preservation, protecting his burn, but it seemed gallant and cinematic. When his lips met hers, she wanted to swoon. His touch awoke a hunger in her, an insatiable need. Lust, but only partially. Her body craved his touch. She wanted to be held, to be kissed, to feel safe in someone's arms. She wanted to be vulnerable.

He broke the clinch and looked into her face. "Please stay."

Her fingers traced his face and he closed his eyes. "Gil, if you have any feelings for me, you'll wish me luck with vanishing off the face of the earth."

His eyes opened. "I have many feelings for you. The last thing I want is for you to vanish. Ann, I know you're not ..."

"Don't! Just don't."

He released her, unable to hide the pain in his eyes, and took a step backwards.

She took a deep breath, struggling to compose herself. "People are looking for me. Some good, some bad. If the bad guys succeed, what happened yesterday will look like a teddy bears' picnic. I'm sorry. I have to go."

"When?"

"Soon."

"Will I see you again?"

She kissed him again, this time gently, and shook her head. "But my imagination will always wonder. In my head, there'll be a hundred happy endings."

He didn't return her smile. "Goodbye, Ann. Good luck." He was out of the door and down the path before she could answer. Her throat swelled and she dug her nails into her palms to prevent the tears.

27

A ll the way through packing her belongings, she muttered to herself. *It would never have worked. Intimacy means revealing secrets. Dating a police officer? You're out of your mind for even considering it. The village hates cops. An inspector's job is to dig out information. He'd never rest until he knew your identity and then his power over you would be absolute. Like sticking your head in a noose. Forget it. San Fairy Ann.*

Anyway, the decision was made. She was leaving from Soure Airport tomorrow morning for Brasilia and would decide her final destination when she got to the capital. Rucksack ready and case zipped, she sat on the balcony to finish Gil's bottle of wine. It was warm in the afternoon sun, so she emptied the remaining ice cubes from the cold box into a jug and shoved in the bottle. Not quite a champagne bucket, but it would do.

She'd killed two people, rejected an attractive, intelligent man and could be certain her cover was blown. Rather than racing for the next bolthole, she was sitting by the beach, drinking lukewarm wine. How had her brilliant plan come so badly unstuck? *Because of people, that's how.*

The sun sank along with the level of the wine bottle. Branca returned, tail wagging. Ann checked her foot and as Nando had said, the raw patch was calm. The dog submitted to the examination, scoffed a plate of biscuits and drank from the water bowl until satisfied. Then she curled at Ann's feet and fell asleep. The evening was perfect, exactly the dream she had envisaged when running from ... all that.

She lit the lamp, stroking the dog's warm flank. "Where do you go, Branca? How do you spend your days? Don't answer that, it's none of my business. You deserve your secrets as much as anyone else. A woman of mystery, just like me. Ha! Except I'm not." She tipped the rest of the bottle into her glass and accepted the fact she was less than sober. Some people sing and become overly affectionate when alcohol loosens the tongue. Not Ann. She always grew maudlin, dwelling on regrets. Now another regret was about to join an already extensive list. Leaving Praia do Pesqueiro was a wrench. The shack, the dog, the village and apart from a bloody drug-related shoot-out and racially-provoked murder, the peace. Then there was Gil Maduro. The expression on his face when saying goodbye hurt her chest. *Stop feeling sorry for yourself, you indulgent mare. Moving on is the only way to survive.*

A tear escaped and she brushed it away with the heel of her hand.

A low growl rumbled in Branca's throat and Ann noticed a figure standing at the end of her path. The white-blonde hair in the moonlight was almost ghostly. She placed a calming hand on the dog's bandana.

"Serena? Is that you?"

"Hello, Dona Ann. I came to say thank you."

"How are you feeling? Come on up. Branca won't hurt you."

The girl approached. "I know. We're old friends." She bent to let the dog sniff her hand. Branca wagged her tail and wound herself around Serena's legs. "I'm better now and I brought you a present." She held out a little package of tissue paper.

Ann unwrapped it. Colourful glass beads threaded onto a length of black leather cord made a pretty homemade necklace. Of all the gifts people had given her – dead chickens, watermelons, a laptop, fresh fish, a bottle of wine – this was the most personal.

"It's beautiful! Thank you, Serena, I'm touched."

"It's not enough to thank you for saving me." The girl sat on the top step, stroking Branca.

"I didn't. Inspector Maduro saved the others and went back in for you. There was an explosion and João Gonçalves dragged you both out. All I did was get you away from the house and take you to hospital. You should be thanking Gonçalves and Maduro. But this necklace wouldn't suit either of them, so I'd better keep it."

She smiled. "Yes, you keep it. I am going to thank João. He looked after me, you know." She gazed out at the ocean, nodding as if she approved. "He wouldn't let me go because of Mauricio's orders, but he did look after me."

Ann opened her mouth to say something about Stockholm syndrome, but changed her mind. "Can I offer you a tea or something?"

"No, thank you."

Ann watched the girl, puzzled by why she wanted to stay after delivering her gift. "By the way, it's dangerous to come wandering down this end of the beach alone in the dark."

"I'm not alone. Rubem came with me. He's a nice guy. He went to Fátima's for a drink and he's going to walk me home when I've finished."

"When you've finished what?"

Serena swivelled to face her. "Dona Ann?" She inhaled and released a deep sigh. "I have something to tell you."

. . .

Long after Serena had gone, Ann sat on the porch, mulling over her story and admiring the girl's courage. Her choice to confide in Mauricio was foolhardy in the extreme but it must have taken real guts to go to the farm alone. When it came to the police, however, she still couldn't bring herself to talk to an officer of the law. No matter how much Ann assured her of Maduro's credibility, Serena wanted a go-between. Something Ann could not, would not do.

They reached an impasse until something the girl said offered a pressure point – her gratitude. Using João as a starting point, Ann led her to draw her own conclusions. What would matter most to João Gonçalves? He had almost died and lost his brother when the rival gang shot up the farm, but he would still have to face trial for his role in the drug business. With most of the other employees dead, who was going to testify that João was only following orders?

Her shot hit its target and Serena stopped her nervous chewing on her thumb. Ann redoubled her efforts. By giving the whole story to Maduro, who had risked his job to stop Franck Fischer and risked his life to rescue her, she would express her thanks not only to him but to the man who had cared for her while a hostage. Two birds with one stone and no necklaces required.

Serena tucked her hands into her armpits. "But I can't do it on my own."

Incredible as it was to Ann, the girl was more fearful of the police than that brutal bastard in snakeskin boots. The answer emerged out of the darkness.

"I'll go with you." Rubem stood at the end of the path, hands in his pockets.

Serena stared at him for a long time. "OK, Rubem." She nodded and looked up at Ann. "OK. We'll go tomorrow. On the way back, I'll come by and tell you what happened. Thank you, Dona Ann."

They said their goodbyes and the two young people walked up the beach to the village. Ann didn't tell them she wouldn't be there tomorrow.

The moon's reflection shimmered on the sea and banshee wails came from the jungle. She drained her wine glass, gazed down at the dog and whispered, "I'm going to miss you, you grubby little girl. Goodbye, my little corner of beach. So long and good luck, Praia do Pesqueiro. *Tchau*, Gil Maduro. At least you'll get one thing you wanted."

Over-emotional and weary to her bones, Ann knew it was time for bed. She picked up the jug and empty bottle. The ice cubes had long since melted, so she used the jug to refill Branca's water bowl. In a sentimental move, she poured the dregs into the tomato plant. As she did so, she noticed a plastic bag beneath the pot. She slid it out and saw it contained an envelope addressed to her. Inside there was a single sheet of A4; a handwritten poem written in English.

The White Heron

He chases shoals across the waves
On ocean and up creeks
A hunter till the end of days
To net the haul he seeks

He salutes the mermaid every day
As she swims beyond the beach
The only one who got away
And shall be left in peace

F.A. (31 years old)

Ann read it three times and folded it again, pressing it to her chest and processing the implications. She examined the tomato plant and noticed a tiny green fruit. Thrown in the sand, neglected and dry, the plant was still thriving.

I don't think Praia do Pesqueiro is any place for a woman on her own.

"But we're not on our own, are we, Branca? You know what? I might just stick around a while."

Thank you for reading *White Heron*. I hope you love Ann and the exotic setting as much as I do. Will she be able to stay, and can she keep her demons of the past at bay? Learn more about old dangers and new threats in her next thrilling novel.

Turn the page for an extract from BLACK RIVER.

EXCERPT FROM BLACK RIVER

Monday and Tuesday were the quietest nights of the week. Obviously you'd expect Friday and Saturday to be crazy busy, but often it was Sunday too. The good thing about Sundays was they wanted to be tender. Only when the men went back to work on Monday did the girls find a few days peace.

The plane flew in every Wednesday and that could go any number of ways. Sometimes they were homesick and missing their wives; maybe they had something to celebrate; or they brought her presents. Hard to tell what kind of a mood they'd be in.

If Alexandra had any hope of succeeding, it had to be Tuesday. It had to be tonight. She lay on her bunk, visualising every stage of her plan, trying to convince herself she could pull this off. Her pulse sounded like a gong in her ears and she stroked her hands over her stomach in a reassuring caress. The camp lights went out at midnight. It would take another hour before the last stragglers had left the bar, returned to their bunkhouses and the camp was asleep.

Just before one o'clock in the morning, Alexandra slid out

of her bunk and onto the wooden floor. She waited several minutes for any change in the breathing patterns of her three roommates, then lifted her bag from beneath the bed. The weight simultaneously comforted and concerned her. She had everything she needed. Her clothes, a few gifts from her regulars, her toiletries and a blanket to protect her until dawn. But it was so heavy. How could she run carrying such a burden? She steeled herself. She had no choice.

With nimble fingers, she lifted the latch and bore the weight of the door with her arm. She'd practised the move a hundred times but never in the dead of night. As expected, it swung open with no more than whisper. Alexandra slithered through the gap like a ghost and closed the door behind her.

Night air came as a relief after the stuffy room filled with the breath and perfumed bodies of four young women. She waited a moment until her eyes adjusted to the starry but moonless sky, breathing in the smell of sawdust, chopped timber and diesel fumes. Nothing moved other than the jungle trees swaying in the warm winds. Everyone was asleep, dreaming of what the plane might bring tomorrow. Alexandra was dreaming of what the plane might take away.

With another last look behind her, she crept away from her sleeping co-workers. When they awoke, her roommates would assume she'd gone out early with her best friend. She wouldn't be missed until five o'clock, when expected to turn up for work. By the time they came looking, she would be far away where no one could touch her. Despite her qualms, Alexandra sensed a bubble of triumph.

Her planned route longer than necessary to avoid Dona Candida's sleeping quarters. Why that *bruxa* needed sleeping quarters, Alexandra had no idea. If Dona Candida slept, she did it with her eyes and ears open. The slightest sound of conflict or fear in any of the rooms or huts and she arrived as fast as her broomstick could carry her. Usually to punish the girls.

The long way round involved passing another girls' bunkhouse, circling the medical tent and tiptoeing past the brothel to the priest's place. Wandering around in the half-dark, Alexandra knew one false move could prove fatal. The camp was littered with life-threatening objects and machinery. Vigilance was a hard-learned lesson; she had the scars to prove it. One cautious step at a time. After all, she had all night.

The Rio Negro camp was roughly divided into four uneven sections. Logging work took place at the westernmost point. Chainsaws screamed, earthmovers rumbled and trees crashed with such force into the undergrowth, you could feel the vibrations beneath your feet. North was where the loggers lived, in portable bunkhouses like the one Alexandra had just escaped. That quadrant, the other side of the solitary road, also housed the canteen-church-cinema building, occasionally used as a meeting-room when the management made their rare announcements.

East lay the cargo area, where pyramids of felled timber awaited the river boats or long-haul trucks. Huge yellow machines with grab hooks and caterpillar tyres sat under a tightly stretched tarpaulin when not in noisy use. Beyond that ugly mess of torn-up earth sat the landing strip, the only way in or out, unless you were dead wood. The weekly plane delivered provisions, letters, or sometimes people. It represented a distant promise of escape. Because everyone wanted to escape this hellish confusion of mud and metal and relentless show of force against the natural world.

Alexandra and her colleagues were quartered in the south, on a scrappy section of barely-cleared jungle. Southside, as the inhabitants called it, was what passed for infrastructure in this far-flung corner of the Amazon. Three rows of three buildings provided all the camp could desire. Row one contained a shop and two bars. The bars were differentiated by entertainment: one had a TV, the other a jukebox. Behind them lay three buildings: the doctor's clinic to the left, the priest's surgery to the right and in the middle, Alexandra's own workplace, the brothel. The rest was four basic bunkhouses. Three for the girls and one for their hateful shrieking boss.

Never show weakness! You may not get sick, have a period or contract anything which renders you unable to work. Nothing can interrupt our business. Three months working these camps and you'll have more money than you can ever imagine.

If Alexandra was honest, she could imagine a whole lot more cash than the bundle of notes wrapped tightly inside her bra. Another week's pay was owed but Dona Candida could stuff it. She suppressed her own aggressive thought as if that evil witch could hear her. Fewer than fifty metres from where Alexandra stood, her boss was laying awake, ears cocked for any hint of an escapee.

If everything worked out, this would be the first time one of Dona Candida's girls succeeded in getting away. It *would* work out. The alternative was unbearable. Alexandra paced behind the bunkhouse, testing each step before putting any weight on her foot, along to the second hut where Juliana was sleeping. The thought of leaving her friend behind constricted her throat, but she pressed on. One girl would have a chance. Two? Forget it. Juliana only had four weeks to go and they would be reunited at the beach. *Please God.* She missed the sea almost as much as she missed her family.

Not a single light shone from any of the buildings. Alexandra took a wide detour, closer to the bars and the shop, aiming for the priest's hut. Her intention was to hide, wide awake, beneath his place until morning. When the plane landed, she would wait until the pilot had unloaded his cargo and gone to the canteen for some food. His routine was so predictable, Alexandra even knew exactly what he'd eat. While the men filled their bellies, she would run like the wind, cross the landing strip and bury herself somewhere in the cargo hold. The pilot would finish his meal, load whatever needed taking to Manaus or the coast and by sunset, Alexandra would be home.

Or as close as she could get. Assuming she didn't get caught, she could walk from Soure Airport to Praia do Pesqueiro. What happened after that was anyone's guess.

Juliana's voice echoed in her head. *Don't waste the present worrying about the future.*

Her own voice responded. *But it's not just my future any more, is it?*

She edged around the final corner and judged the priest's hut around 10 metres ahead. Almost there. Before she took her next step into the shadows, a repetitive noise made her stop. Beneath the wheels of the hut where she planned to hide, a silhouette of spiky ridges and steady scraping indicated an iguana had got there first. Generally, she wasn't afraid of iguanas or any other reptile, but had no intention of sharing two square metres with a huge lizard. She squatted on her heels, reassessing her plan. Patience.

A watery sound preceded an unpleasant smell. Piss. Strong beery urine with an overtone of black tobacco assaulted her nose. The association rang alarm bells before he lit the match. The sulphuric glow illuminated his face as he took a drag of his cigarette and gave her a lop-sided leer.

Alexandra didn't hesitate. She whirled around and ran straight back the way she came. No more guarded paces but a blind bolt from danger. When she passed the final bunkhouse, rather than turning left to her own cabin, she ran into the jungle. No matter what predatory creatures lay in wait, she'd take her chances. Anything was better than Bruno.

.   .   .

Her breath short, she stumbled her way along the path, her arms raised and crossed in front of her face for protection. The ground was dangerously uneven so she slowed and controlled her panicky panting, balancing hazards ahead and behind. Bruno's crunching boots had slowed to a halt. The stupid lump knew better than to approach the girls' cabins or he'd be banned for another month. Drunk and unimaginative, he would never think she had run into the jungle. In ordinary circumstances, she would never attempt such a crazy move, but what was the alternative?

Alert to every sound and ready to leap from harm, she moved along the path like a cat. A snort escaped her nostrils. Some cat. No nocturnal panther or jaguar prowling its domain but a terrified teenager in total darkness with all the jungle savvy of a domestic kitten. Alexandra took several deep breaths, calming herself. Stress was not good.

If she could find it, the pool would be the good place to hide until daylight. Their pool. Even the thought of it soothed her nerves. Juliana, always the braver of the two, had gone exploring and found a little body of limpid water, just a short way into the jungle. A minuscule beach between two huge rocks hid them from everyone and everything. Nothing more than a collection of pebbles and silt, really, but they named it Copacabana and called it their own. The two of them sneaked off there as often as they could, sure no one would follow. Two silly girls swimming, sunbathing and talking about the future. Such plans! Such dreams! Four more weeks and if she was lucky, those wild imaginings might come true for Juliana. For Alexandra, it was too late. It was already beginning to show.

On bright sunny days, it took the two girls around ten minutes to walk to the pool. How long it would take at night, Alexandra had no idea. Mosquitoes pierced the skin of her neck and the damp dripping of condensation from the trees began to penetrate her clothes. She stopped, wondering if it might be wiser to turn around. Her plan was still achievable; she had to believe that.

A sound up ahead caused her to freeze. It wasn't a voice, more like a sigh, but it didn't sound human. Something freakish was coming along the path, soft-footed and making a gentle hum. She dropped to a squat, her eyes wide. What kind of animal hums?

Alexandra clutched her belly, frozen in a petrified crouch. Her stomach began to cramp. She peered ahead, searching for the yellow eyes of a jaguar, demon or *cuca*. The spasms got worse, all caused by fear. She had to relax or lose the life she was carrying. After hiding her condition for so many weeks and risking this insane escape to keep her child, it would break her heart. The baby was the only thing that belonged to her. The hum grew louder. Frigid with fear, she took long steady breaths on all fours, her head swivelling to make out any kind of shape in the darkness. The tone, alien as it was, reassured Alexandra. It sounded like a lullaby.

A dim glow, no bigger than a firefly, floated towards her. She was crying now so didn't trust her vision. Two human figures approached, carrying a ball of light. Their faces, in shadow, looked like Mexican sugar skulls.

Alexandra scuttled backwards until something sharp and painful stabbed her knee. Her observers didn't move, simply watching as she whimpered and keeled over.

ACKNOWLEDGMENTS

Thank you: Florian Bielmann, Jane Dixon-Smith, CS Wilde, Katharine D'Souza, JD Lewis and my fantastic ARC team.

ALSO BY JJ MARSH

Other titles in the Run and Hide series

BLACK RIVER

My Beatrice Stubbs series, European crime dramas

BEHIND CLOSED DOORS

RAW MATERIAL

TREAD SOFTLY

COLD PRESSED

HUMAN RITES

BAD APPLES

SNOW ANGEL

HONEY TRAP

BLACK WIDOW

WHITE NIGHT

THE WOMAN IN THE FRAME

ALL SOULS' DAY

~

My standalone novels

AN EMPTY VESSEL

ODD NUMBERS

WOLF TONES

And a short-story collection
APPEARANCES GREETING A POINT OF VIEW

For occasional updates, news, deals and a FREE exclusive novella, subscribe to my newsletter on www.jjmarshauthor.com

If you would recommend this book to a friend, please do so by writing a review. Your tip helps other readers discover their next favourite read. Your review can be short and only takes a minute.

Thank you.

Printed by Amazon Italia Logistica S.r.l.
Torrazza Piemonte (TO), Italy

30579360R00162